The Seed of Change

To Barbara,

With best wishes.

[signature]

5/11/2010.

The Seed of Change

Richard Paul Winston

Matador
5 Weir Road
Kibworth Beauchamp
Leicester LE8 0LQ, UK
Tel: (+44) 116 279 2299
Fax: (+44) 116 279 2277
Email: books@troubador.co.uk
Web: www.troubador.co.uk/matador

ISBN 978 1848 764 699

British Library Cataloguing in Publication Data.
A catalogue record for this book is available from the British Library.

Typeset in 11pt Garamond by Troubador Publishing Ltd, Leicester, UK

Matador is an imprint of Troubador Publishing Ltd

Printed in Great Britain by the MPG Books Group, Bodmin and King's Lynn

With much love and appreciation to my wife Denise and my son Sam for their help and encouragement.

Chapter One

A cold morning for early spring. An easterly wind still chilled the faint rays of the sun. 7am. The electronic bleep sounded shrill against the quiet of morning. The drawn curtains allowed a single shaft of milky light to penetrate the room. Groping sightlessly for the button which would close off the intrusion of noise, Frances found it, pressed lazily and the piercing bleep ceased.

Dust particles danced and swam in the thin beam of light, as they do in a darkened cinema. Frances opened her eyes and blinked several times against the beam, against the twilight zone of half sleep. Her hands clenched into small fists, found her eyes and screwed into them. She blinked again and repeated the ritual. This morning, consciousness was slow to come. She lay there in the warm cocoon of her bed, trying to think. That in itself was not normal. The routine of a weekday morning usually replaced real thought, allowing her to do all that was necessary to get her from bed to office in proper shape. She stared at the dancing dust before her eyes and followed the beam back towards the curtains. The crack was wider and grew as she stared and now filled one whole side of the room and the shapes were no longer shapes but people, slowly taking on substance and colour. They were laughing and talking loudly, and there was music from a stereo machine, loud music, so loud that they now had to shout to be heard. Frances could not quite hear what they were saying but she could feel their laughter. It came in waves over her. She tried to close her eyes against it but this only served to exaggerate the noise. She felt through the scramble of sound, the thump-thump of the bass guitar through the stereo's overpowered speakers. The body heat generated by the dancing crowd sank through the blankets of her bed and her cotton nightdress felt sticky against her own perspiring body.

Frances felt sick. She was hot and now fully awake. The screen and the people and the noise had gone, but her head ached and her heart was thumping and the nausea in her stomach threatened to do more than make her late for work. She pulled the bedclothes aside and was only half surprised to see the dark patches of sweat which caused her nightdress to cling to her thighs and breasts. She had little time to reflect on this however. Barefoot, she rushed into her small bathroom, relying on sense rather than sight to find the toilet bowl.

It was now 7.45 and Frances was still in her nightdress, supplemented against the cold of the morning by a flannelette dressing gown. She sat at the kitchen table sipping hot, weak tea. The nausea had gone, but the headache was still there and she now felt cold. Two aspirins were all the breakfast she would take today. Soon she would have to phone the office. She could not possibly go into work. Her boss would understand. After all, she was not in the habit of taking time off, although today would be the second time this month.

* * *

The shrill double ring of the phone repeated in Frances' ear.

The morning seemed full of such noises; mechanical, electronic, less than human. Noises to annoy. She waited impatiently for someone to answer and she was glad of the certainty that it would be a some one rather than the soul-less machine that greeted her phone call to the office.

"Good morning! Doctor Taylor's surgery. Can I help you?"

Frances made an appointment for the afternoon, 2.45. She hated the doctor's surgery, the waiting room with its ragged pile of magazines on the occasional table, the smell of iodine or disinfectant, the mothers and their scruffy children. She hated the waiting and could never understand why an appointment at 2.45 in the afternoon in fact meant being seen by the doctor at 3.20. But the truth was that this morning's little trauma was not the first, or even the second such event to occur these past few weeks. Three or four times recently Frances had woken feeling sick. The nausea had soon passed and she had felt well enough to go to work. But two days off within a couple of weeks…

* * *

By mid-morning Frances was feeling better. She had taken a long, hot bath, soaking in the tub for almost half an hour, letting the silky water smooth out the final folds of ache in her head. She lay motionless, staring at the white frosted globe on the ceiling, feeling the soap suds lap against her tingling nipples. She was hungry and considered the wisdom of eating before going to the surgery. Deciding that it was only when going to the dentist that such questions arose, she towelled herself down, pausing momentarily to note her reflection in the bathroom mirror. Her blond hair, already streaked with grey, usually neat and trim, but now wet from her bath, hung in ragged kiss curls around her neck.

* * *

To her surprise Doctor Taylor's surgery was empty when Frances arrived. The magazines and the smell were still there but no mums with noisy children. She was called into the consulting room at precisely 2.45. Doctor Taylor, young for a doctor Frances thought, greeted her with a 'good afternoon' and the standard 'now then, what seems to be the trouble?' This invariable opening line was another reason for her dislike of the surgery. She always hoped for something more original. Frances explained her recent history of nausea and of generally feeling unwell in the mornings. The doctor seemed to pay her scant attention as he jotted apparently absent-mindedly on a note pad in front of him. Beside the pad Frances could see the manila envelope which contained her medical records.

The doctor looked up from his scribbling and smiled reassuringly at Frances, and, as if about to answer some nagging question about her medical history, he picked up the manila envelope and scanned its front cover. Frances felt her cheeks flush as the doctor removed a sheet from inside.

"I see that you'll be 41 next birthday, Miss O'Donnell."

Frances nodded an affirmation to what she felt was a somewhat impertinent observation by the young man.

"Can you describe any other symptoms you've experienced during these past, what, 7 weeks?" the doctor continued.

The question was answered only by a deepening of colour in her cheeks. Frances considered her reply carefully. She was not a fool and she knew exactly where the doctor's question was leading. She also knew that a truthful answer would go a long way to confirming his suspicions. The doctor, young though he was, took her silence in his stride and gently prompted:

"Has there been any swelling or tingling of the breasts, have you put on any weight unexpectedly in the last couple of weeks? Have you missed a period Miss O'Donnell?"

Frances could stall no more…

* * *

The nurse took the baby and wrapped it in clean white towels which smelt of disinfectant. She placed it carefully in the bowl of the weighing machine and watched the hand move swiftly up to quiver around the seven pound mark.

"7 pounds 3 ounces," she called out and another nurse wrote this down on a clip-boarded form. The baby, still sticky and wrinkled, scant blond hair platted to its scalp, gave a hearty yell in apparent satisfaction at this news. Its mother, as sticky as her child, mouse brown hair wringing with the effort of childbirth, smiled with fatigue and contentment. Her smile broadened into a grin as the baby, now clean and sparkling, was laid by her side. She looked at the cheaply framed photograph of the uniformed soldier and took it from the bed-side table. She held it in one hand and caressed the tiny child's forehead with the other.

"This is your daddy, Frances. Doesn't he look handsome in his uniform. He'll be home soon and won't he be proud of you."

She replaced the picture and lay back, exhausted but happy, on the layer-cake of pillows behind her neck. She listened to the baby's rapid breathing and felt the hard press of milk in her swollen breasts. Soon the child, her child would be taking this life from her. She reached out a hand to search absent-mindedly for the glass of water on the table and as she found it the framed photograph of her soldier husband was dislodged from its precarious perch. It fell with a clatter onto the hard floor, thin slivers of glass splaying outwards to look for impossible hiding places beneath the bed. The baby woke with a hungry scream.

* * *

In the porters' lodge the radio crackled. George put down his mug and leaned across the table to turn the dial. The Harry Roy band was playing one of his favourite tunes; a welcome change from all that stuff about Poland and what Mr. Chamberlain had said to Mr. Hitler and what Mr. Hitler had promised to do or not do. George's elbow caught the mug as he leaned back across the table. The tea spilled out onto the cloth, darkening the checkered pattern as it spread outwards. The porter swore as hot liquid reached the edge of the table and splattered onto his blue overall trousers. He leaped up and grabbed a dishcloth.

The music stopped abruptly and a stiff-voiced announcer cut in:

"We interrupt this programme to bring you a special announcement from the Prime Minister, Mr. Neville Chamberlain."

***

Frances could not remember the ten minute walk from the surgery. She could remember handing over the bottle containing the urine sample and how embarrassed, maybe even ashamed, she felt. Her quickness to blush, even in middle-age, providing the world and its nurse with a window on her innermost feelings. The nurse had told her that the results would be back from the lab the day after tomorrow and that she could phone the surgery then.

"And now it's time for Play School."

She could not remember switching on the television either, but she must have, of course. The machine gun discord of the 6 o'clock news which normally greeted her homecoming was missing, replaced by a gentler music and a presenter in full view.

"Now children," he began brightly, but faded into a small dot in the middle of the screen.

Frances regained the settee, now fully aware of where she was. The TV screen continued to fluoresce dully. She stared into it as if staring into the fading embers of a fire and thought deeply. She thought about her morning dream but now she was not dreaming and the images and people in it came back to her in blurred and disjointed snapshots of memory.

* * *

"Alec! Alec Samuels, you old sod. How are you? Long time no see, hey." Frances never could get used to the gutter language Adrian, her boss, insisted on using at public gatherings. She liked him well enough but why must he be so coarse? The well dressed, slightly greying man at whom the salutation was aimed did not seem to mind at all. Glass of whiskey in one hand and cocktail sausage on a stick in the other, he joined Frances and Adrian.

The party was in farewell to a colleague of Adrian's, a junior partner who had been tempted to join one of the big boys by promises of wealth and riches. Frances was sorry the young man was leaving. He had always treated her with great respect and courtesy. A rare attribute among the young these days, she thought.

Alec had little need to answer Adrian's opening question. He was obviously very well, at least financially. The suit was no off the peg job and the tie, Frances was pretty sure, was pure silk. He spoke with an ease and assurance of one who has indeed done well and has returned to the testing ground of his youth. Like the young man whose parting was now being feted, Alec, Frances was told during the triangular conversation, had also left the small company for the promise of richer pastures and he had clearly not been disappointed.

Frances found herself enjoying the party. She had gone because Michael, the young man who was leaving, had made a particular point of inviting her. She would normally have made some excuse, preferring to spend her time in her own company. But now she was glad that she had been persuaded, that a ready excuse did not materialise, and she was glad that Alec was still talking to her long after Adrian had found another long lost friend, this time an 'old bastard', and had left them.

By midnight the party had reached an Everest of decibels, distorting the notes at each extreme of the scale. To one more used to the gentler strains of Schubert or Brahms, this cacophony could no longer be tolerated and Frances decided that it was time to go. The throbbing beat of the bass guitar, and perhaps the three or four glasses of white wine she had casually downed, had given her a slight headache, and conversation with Alec was now impossible. Much to her surprise he offered to drive her home. He too had found the music not to his liking and would be glad to escape the somewhat frenzied atmosphere of the party. Frances declined the offer. It was much too far to expect him to drive her home, she would be quite happy to call a taxi. But Alec insisted and they left together, not bothering to make their farewells to Adrian or the guest of honour.

The car, a Jaguar, pulled into the short driveway fronting the small block of flats. Little had been said during the 15 minute drive from the party. Alec had turned on the car radio, tuning to a light music station. Such a relief from the noise of the party, Frances thought, leaning back into the luxury of the leather seat.

The music stopped as Alec switched off the car engine. He stepped out, moving to the passenger side to open the door for Frances.

"Yes, I'd love to," Alec replied to Frances' offer of a nightcap.

* * *

The phone rang. The noise cut through the remembering and the snapshot disappeared. Frances picked up the receiver. It was Adrian:

"How are you old girl? Hope it's nothing serious. Remember we've got that new contract to sort out tomorrow. You be able to make it in?"

Frances reassured him that she would almost certainly be at work tomorrow and that there was nothing to worry about. She thanked him for his call but made a mental note that the concern was more for the business than for her health. She said goodbye and put the phone down then went into the kitchen and filled the electric kettle. She watched it slowly come to the boil, the steam eventually gushing from the stubby spout, forming clouds on the low ceiling and for the first time since the night of the party she tried to make some sense of what had happened, of what was now happening. But the clouds kept getting in the way, obscuring the whole picture, refusing to let her see clearly the sequence of events which left her, Frances Mary O'Donnell, unmarried and 40 years old, carrying a child.

She made tea, pouring the brew into a delicate china cup that had belonged to her mother. She thought of her mother, of the times a cup of tea, the 'universal panacea' someone had called it, would be conjured up in times of crisis. It would take more than tea to cure this problem, her rueful smile acknowledged as she sipped the brown liquid.

* * *

Her mother's face was ashen. Deep lines furrowed her forehead and she gazed, unseeing, into the cup. She had been able to drink only a sip and the tea was beginning to lose its warmth.

"Try to drink a little more, Mary, will you not now?" The soft Irish brogue of Mrs O'Driscoll was heard only by Frances. Her mother did not react to the neighbour's kind words and Frances could not understand why the postman's letter had caused such sadness. Usually, at least once a month, the letters would make her mother really happy. But today was very different and the letter lay open on the kitchen table and it looked different from the normal letters. Frances looked from her mother to the writing on the short, dull-coloured piece of paper and she wished that she could read all the big words. She secretly promised herself that she would spend more time with her reading books trying to understand the words and less time just looking at the pictures. She could make out some big letters written at the top of the paper. 'OHMS'. She tried to say the word but it made no sense and she gave up and looked back at her mother.

Mrs. O'Driscoll sat down and spoke softly again:

"And wasn't it the same with my Michael? Mary Mother of Jesus, what a day to get news like this."

* * *

She had apparently gone to bed with Alec Samuels. She had been a little tipsy, a little lonely and off her guard and she must have slept with the man. She knew very little about him, except that she did not say no to his advances. Who was he? In retrospect she was not sure that she could even remember what he looked like. Their conversation at the party had in fact revealed little about him. What had they talked about for so long? She could no longer remember. There were no more speech bubbles in her snapshots of memory. She could remember the name "Alec Samuels" and saying it over to herself now, clutching at this solitary straw while all the rest seemed to have been blown away, the name itself began to lose shape and meaning.

She had known she was pregnant for some time. Not just suspected, but known. The phone call to the surgery would be superfluous, she knew the test would be positive. But until now she had tried to blank the idea from her mind. Only subconsciously the notion would not go away. Dreams of the party and the night with the man: it would not take Sigmund Freud to explain that these were the mind's way of bringing her face to face with reality.

No panacea, but enough of a stimulant to force an appraisal of the situation, Frances downed the last drops of tea.

Chapter Two

"Bless me father for I have sinned. My last confession was a week ago."

Frances heard her voice echo slightly as it seemed to find an impossible way out of the confessional and up into the vaulted roof of the church. The sound of it hung there, seeking cracks and crevices in the ancient stonework in which to linger, soaking into the walls, covering the interior with an indelible truth… 'for I have sinned'. It echoed again in Frances' head and she began to cry.

"Now what sin can you have committed that should make you cry like that, young lady?" the voice on the other side of the grill enquired softly.

"Take out your handkerchief and dry your eyes," it continued. The gentle tone reassured Frances and she recognised the voice as belonging to Father Lennon. Her sobbing stopped and in truth there were few tears to wipe. Crying at confession had become almost a ritual, a necessary accompaniment. She did not exactly do it on purpose, but it just seemed right, as if the gentle scolding of the priest was not enough to purge the guilt.

She liked Father Lennon. He did not smell like the other priests who took confession. Perhaps it was because he was younger than the rest, although Frances was not very good at judging the age of anyone who was over 25. But she knew that the other priests were old. They smelt old, of moth-balls and stale whiskey.

Frances made her confession and the priest listened patiently as he must have listened to the confessions of hundreds of girls. She told him of the library book that was overdue and of the homework that she had forgotten. Then she began to cry again, and this time the salty tang at the side of her mouth suggested that these tears were of deeper origin. She tried wiping her eyes, but the handkerchief was no match for the flood and was soon wet through.

Father Lennon's insistence that such sins, although regrettable, were not so great that the Lord could not find it in his heart to forgive, failed to stem the tide.

"Is there something else you're not telling me, girl? Come now, what's brought this on?"

But Frances was not able to tell. Her secret was too dreadful to share with anyone, especially a priest, and although she liked Father Lennon, he was still a man. Through her sobbing she heard the door opening on the other side of the screen. She stood up, shaking, the tears filling her red-rimmed eyes. Her own door opened abruptly and soft light filtering though the stained glass of the chapel touched her face.

"Come out girl, come into my office and we'll have a little chat about this. Frances isn't it? Frances O'Donnell?"

* * *

The room smelt of polish, accompanying the shine on the wood panelling that covered the bottom half of the walls. The chair was not uncomfortable, but Frances felt ill at ease. She had been left alone for a few minutes, giving her time to reflect on what she would say. Whether the priest had given her this time deliberately or not she could not say. She had, of course, thought about this meeting for some time, and it was not *what* she would say but how which gave purpose to her reflections. She decided that the priest's 'excuse me for a moment, will you Miss O'Donnell' could not be a ploy. After all, how could he know the reason for her urgent wish to speak to him? She believed in God of course, and that priests, particularly catholic ones, were frequently in communication with Him, but she doubted that with all the other problems the world seemed to give Him, God would have made a particular point of informing His man that she was pregnant. Her own prayer had not carried the news either.

The priest came back. Frances watched him as he crossed the few steps to sit opposite her. Funny how the 'old' priests of the convent school now seemed so much younger and their peculiar smells no longer there. She had known Father Donne for some time, since taking her present job with Adrian and moving into the area. He had made a point of welcoming her to the parish after Sunday mass the third or fourth time she had gone to the church. She had appreciated that and, although not quite attaining the status of friend, the priest figured among the few acquaintances in Frances' world.

"What seems to be the trouble, Frances? You sounded a little distraught on the phone."

Priests and doctors, Frances thought, always that same opening line. 'What seems to be the trouble?' As if the whole thing were inside her head, just a stupid dream, not real at all. But it was real. She had the report from the laboratory to prove it. Now she was about to let someone else in on her secret. She was not, of course, able to tell anyone at work. Certainly not Adrian. Those few days in the office since her return phone call to the surgery had been strange, almost surreal. Polite questions about how she was. Answers which appeared to satisfy. Thankfully no-one was really interested enough to delve very deeply. The possibility that she could be pregnant had crossed nobody's mind. Outside, the morning threat of rain was being realised. Heavy drops splattered noisily against the tall windows of the panelled room, running in rivulets down the leaded panes. The priest's question hung in the heavy atmosphere and Frances thought of pregnant pauses and felt like laughing and crying at the same time. She did neither and the Father prompted again.

"Are you unwell, Frances?" A natural assumption, Frances thought. Is pregnancy an illness? She had never before considered the question. Her diffidence was broken only by a frown and a shake of the head.

"Come now, Frances, whatever it is, you know you can tell me. I'm here to help you, and through me we can call on God's help. You have nothing to fear from letting God into your mind as well as your heart."

"I'm going to have a child, Father." Frances heard herself saying and she attempted a smile, as if to cushion the shock that she imagined the priest must be feeling. She added nothing, letting the words sink in. He removed his glasses and held them in both hands, seeming to examine the lenses closely, but in fact not seeing at all. The rain stung the windows more fiercely, shrouding the room in white noise. Frances watched the priest as he toyed with the curving arms of the glasses. She did not know what to expect from him or what she wanted him to say. Her inability to confide in any other living soul and her desperate need to do so, had led her to this meeting. She had tried to think of it as just another confession, but the petty sins of daily life which in her childhood consciousness had loomed so large, now served only to give substance to the routine of the confessional. But this was not routine and the word 'sin' invaded her thoughts and clung to them like poison ivy. She felt guilty and she was sure that in the priest's eyes, in the eyes of the Church, she was guilty. She remembered the nuns at school and their warnings of eternal damnation, of burning in hell, should she or her classmates ever dare to smear their mouths with lipstick, or wear their skirts so much as an inch above the regulation length. And what of the consequences of 'associating' with a member of the opposite sex? Too dire to even contemplate.

Well, she had 'associated' with a man, with... what was his name? Frances could not remember. It was strange how the detail of that night had slowly and imperceptibly been stripped from memory, gradually covered by the poison ivy until nothing else remained. That and the word 'sin', repeated constantly, like tiny, malignant fruits of the ivy itself.

Father Donne began to speak. Frances was sure she could see his lips moving, but she heard nothing. She fought to break out from under the carpet of green that was dulling her senses. The priest's lips moved again, concern showing ever more deeply on his face. He rose from his seat and Frances followed his movements. They seemed slow and awkward, as if the poor man was also struggling to free himself of the clinging vine. As he moved away from his chair Frances could see the rain continuing its steady fall, but the drops were large, too large and they fell in the unreality of slow-motion. The deepening drone of the rainfall added to the sensory deprivation that prevented the now shouted words of the priest from reaching her mind. Her eyes fixed on the water cascading from gutters unable to cope with the torrent, crashing down on the deep, stone sill of the high leaded window before her. The olive green leather of the priest's empty chair glistened; everything she could see in her blinkered stare glistened. The whole room filled with water and Frances felt the wetness around her and she tried to push upwards, away from the rising tide, but could not. The ivy, tight now around her legs, held her firm in the chair. She felt the water reach her stomach and wondered if the child growing there would drown before she did. She wondered whether she cared.

* * *

Frances' lips trembled slightly as the hot liquid touched them. She swallowed the tea before it had time to cool and she felt the pain inside her. She had stopped crying but her eyes were still red and the pain of the hot tea flowing through her body was mixed with a tightness around her chest. She held the cup in both hands, not daring to trust herself with its slender handle. She had thanked the nurse for the hot drink and Frances now watched her make her way back to the ward, her stiff blue skirt swishing tunelessly against the dark stockings. The even darker seams held a fascination for Frances and she followed them until the nurse turned a corner and disappeared from view. She looked at her own stockings and felt envy and shame. She saw the ugliness of the thick grey wool which so completely hid the shape and curve of her legs. Her inspection continued down to her shoes. They too were ugly; functional, stubby black clods with hardly any heel at all. She glared at her feet for several minutes, taking occasional sips of the cooling tea still held in both hands out in front of her. She was alone and the corridor was silent apart from the soft click of the wall clock. She raised her head and leaned back against the green-painted brick wall and felt its coldness even through her woollen school duffel. She watched the second hand of the clock as it made its stuttering way around the dial. The minute hand moved on to 12 and Frances waited for the hour, now 2am, to chime, like the big wooden cased clock in school. But of course it did not. Chiming clocks and hospitals were not made for each other. A more insistent click made her turn her head to one side. She recognised the blond woman she had seen earlier talking in whispers to the white-coated doctor. Frances noted the stiletto heels and thought jealously and irrationally how inconsiderate it was for the woman to wear such noisy shoes so late in a hospital. She then felt even more ashamed and her face reddened and more tears welled up in her eyes. The blond woman appeared to be thanking the doctor, although from where she was Frances was unable to hear their conversation. The doctor smiled at the woman; they shook hands and she clicked noisily out through the big swing doors at the end of the corridor.

The nurse reappeared and stretched on tip-toes to whisper into the tall doctor's ear. The stretching movement enhanced the seam line on the young woman's legs and Frances stared again. The doctor looked in Frances' direction, his face a reflection of the grave news he had just received. The couple approached the seated girl. Frances made a movement to stand up, but the doctor put a hand on her shoulder and sat down beside her.

"I'm sorry, Frances," the doctor began in cathedral tones, his face pale, the eyes flitting from Frances to the nurse standing by his side.

The doctor continued and Frances tried vainly to sort through the jumble of whispered words and shattered emotions. Her eyes were wet again as the message began to make sense, except that it made no sense at all.

* * *

The train from Bristol had been late, something to do with ice on the tracks, but her mother was still there of course, waiting at the station. Frances had been sent home from school shortly before the end of term and under something of a cloud, after Sister Bernadette had discovered a 'love letter' which the girl had apparently written. The fact that the letter was never sent or that nobody, least of all Frances herself, had any idea who the potential recipient might be, made no difference.

"Why did you write that stupid letter?" her mother asked as they turned out of the station, freezing rain and yellow light from the street lamps splashing onto the black surface of the road. Frances had pulled the hood of her duffel coat over her head and was looking down at the shining pavement in protection from the rain and perhaps from her mother's anger. Her mother struggled against the wind to open an umbrella.

"I really can't see what all the fuss was about. Why was it so wrong?" Frances countered, feeling guilty but prepared to defend herself. She felt a curious freedom at her own questioning of the convent school's apparent harshness. She did not understand why a letter, even if it was supposed to contain some doubtful prose, should cause a 15 year old girl to be sent home from school with a severe warning about her future behaviour.

Perhaps her mother did not hear her daughter's question;

quite possibly she was ignoring it deliberately. Frances was about to ask the question again, to attempt to open up an area of discussion which had always been taboo at school and at best deflected at home. The wind tugged at her mother's now open umbrella, turning it inside out and pulling the frail woman in its wake.

"Why, mother?" The question was lost in a gust of wind and driven rain and the screech of a car turning a corner at speed. The screech turned into a skid as the tyres failed to hold the icy tarmac. Frances caught the yellow glare of the headlamps looming large, growing until they filled her frozen view. She covered her eyes and instinctively pulled away from the brightness. She did not see the black car climb the kerb; she did not see the shiny, wet chrome of the bumper tear into the wire ribs of the umbrella, cutting the flimsy shield to shreds. She did not see the horror on the hapless driver's face as the car hit the woman still holding onto the curved handle of the umbrella.

* * *

The water in her eyes splashed onto her hands and she gasped audibly as air rushed into her lungs, stinging them as much as the slap had stung her face. Father Donne was standing over her, holding her by the shoulders and gently shaking her. She could see his eyes and the little red mark on the bridge of his nose where his glasses usually sat. She could also hear the anxious pleading of his questioning.

"Miss O'Donnell, Frances, can you hear me? Tell me if you can hear me, do you hear what I'm saying?"

"I'm being punished, Father," Frances said, looking straight into the priest's eyes. Father Donne stopped shaking her and stepped back. She repeated herself with such an air of certainty that the priest took a further step back and stumbled into his desk. He sat on the edge of the desk, put his glasses on again and folded his arms, studying the face of the woman in front of him.

"Now who do you imagine is punishing you Frances? Is it God you think is doing this to you? And why Frances, what have you done to deserve such special attention? You're not the first girl that's come to me carrying a child outside of marriage. Although, of course, you'll forgive me for saying this Frances, they're usually a little younger. Come now, I understand that at your age this is something of a shock. But why should you feel that you're being punished?"

Frances remained silently staring into the priest's bespectacled eyes, seeing the judgement of the Church through them despite his words. Clearly she was guilty and must be punished. She knew that. God knew that. Why was this man being so stupid. Maybe he was just trying to be kind. But it wasn't helping. She wanted to tell, she wanted the truth squeezed from her, not by kindness, not by forgiveness. Her sins had always been forgiven, or so she had thought. But now, this child inside her that she did not want, this was her punishment. Where had the child come from? Why was she pregnant? She didn't understand. She only knew that she was guilty and it was right for her to be punished. The priest spoke again:

"You must tell me Frances. I can't help you, the Church can't help you unless you let us into your heart. Why did you come to see me if you're not going to share the problem with me? God forgive you Frances if it's an abortion you're thinking of."

The word shocked Frances and she blinked, a residue of

tear running down her cheek. An abortion? The thought had never even crossed her mind. Why was this priest, this man of God using such words, suggesting such things? No, of course she was not thinking of an abortion. She shook her head.

"Look, Frances, the Catholic Church is not in the market for martyrs. Haven't we enough of those already in Ireland at the moment. Neither is the Church looking for souls like you to punish. What you have done is, in the eyes of the Church, a sin, yes. But it's done, Frances. It would be a far greater sin to think of destroying the life that's now developing in your body. The Church understands that. And so must you."

"Father, I'm not even considering an abortion," Frances answered, swallowing hard as if the last word had left a nasty taste in her mouth.

"Then in heaven's name, why do you imagine that this pregnancy is a punishment?"

She looked up at the priest again and saw her mother's face in nun's habit, still holding the tattered remains of an umbrella which had given no protection at all. She heard Sister Bernadette accusing her of writing filth, telling her that she would burn in hell if she ever so much as thought such terrible things again. She saw the blond woman at the hospital and remembered how, on that terrible night so long ago, instead of thinking about her dying mother, she had been jealous of the woman's fashionable shoes, had envied the nurse with the black seamed stockings, had been ashamed of her own lack of sexuality. She remembered the rain that night and she was there again, waiting in the green painted hospital corridor until the doctor told her he was sorry. *He* was sorry! She heard her mother's question again. The last thing she had heard her mother say. 'Why did you write that stupid letter?' She could not remember why. There was no boyfriend, no reason to write what she did, at least no reason that had made any sense at the time. But the time was now and it was still raining and she still had no explanation. She only knew that she was carrying a child and that somehow this was a punishment.

Father Donne took her hands.

"Let me explain something to you, Frances. I've said to you that the Church can take care of you, of the child. You must not see this as a punishment. The birth of a child is one of God's greatest gifts, even when it happens outside the sanctity of marriage. You must also consider the wishes and feelings of the father. You've said nothing about him so far."

He stopped, waiting no doubt for Frances to take up his cue. How could she tell him that the man no longer had a name or even a face, that she was beginning to lose even the memory of the night of conception. Her only reply was a barely perceptible shake of the head. The priest did not press.

"That is your business, of course, Frances, and I don't want to appear to be prying. But the child is our responsibility, yours and mine and the Church's. You must continue with this pregnancy, you must have the child and, if it's what you want, I can make arrangements for it to be cared for, to be adopted. How would you feel about the possibility of adoption?"

Adoption? Frances considered the word and then the idea. She did not want to keep the child. Of that she was certain. What would she do, at her age, with an infant, a babe in arms, waking her up in the middle of the night, screaming for food, for comfort, for the love of the mother Frances thought she would never be? Maybe the priest's suggestion was an eventual way out. But in the meantime she would go through with the pregnancy. That would be her punishment.

She looked up into the priest's blue eyes, enlarged by the thick lenses perched on his nose. She felt a strange relief and, perhaps for the first time, an acceptance of her situation, now that there was some plan, a road ahead which might lead to a solution.

"Yes, Father."

She said no more than this, but slipped off the chair onto her knees before Father Donne. She took his hands and pressed them to her lips. He withdrew a hand from the supplicant grip and signalled a blessing over her inclined head, while outside the sky still hung its grey curtain over the church and the rain beat a softer tattoo on the tall windows of the wood panelled room.

Chapter Three

The weekend crop of messages on the answer machine contained little of much interest. Apart from this mechanical babble, the office was quiet and Frances would normally enjoy the peace that this time of the day gave her, allowing a few moments to tidy up the odds and ends of the previous week's hectic dealings. But today the silence was no friend. The recorded speech delivered, only the whir of the machine remained. Frances switched it off and sat back in her chair and swivelled slowly to her left. Her eyes scanned the room. The paraphernalia of the office, the photo-copier, the telephone, the typewriter, the new computer that Adrian had insisted on getting and which nobody knew what to do with, silent witnesses to her condition. As yet the human inhabitants of the office were ignorant of the fact. Soon, however, they would have to know.

The three weeks since her revelation to Father Donne had been remarkable only in their tedium. She had felt morning sickness just once more and there were, as yet, no other signs of the pregnancy, apart from the small addition to her midriff. But, until this day and due to an apparent preference for loose fitting woollens, her secret was shared only by the priest and the good Lord. She wondered how the news would be greeted by her colleagues and feared the worst. Frances considered just leaving the job, handing in her notice without any explanation. But that would be impossible. Her only income was her salary, most of which disappeared into the coffers of the building society within the first few days of the month. Without this steady income how would she manage? Father Donne had mentioned the father of the child and, of course, he ought to take some financial responsibility for its upbringing. But where was he? *Who* was he? How could it be that even his name was erased from her memory? She could ask Adrian, he would surely know who the man was that she went off with at the party. He might even know where he could be found. But then there would be questions and two and two would inevitably make four, especially when her little problem was big enough for all to see. 'What? Frances O'Donnell, preggers? And she doesn't even know the name of the bloke that put her in the club!' She could imagine the barely subdued sniggers and gossip of the girls in the office to whom Frances had always appeared aloof and unfriendly, and the sly, knowing grins of the dealers. She put a hand over the as yet modest bulge in her stomach and wished it away, but of course it refused to go. She looked in turn at the machines, pleading with each one to help her. They were obstinate in their silent denial.

Frances jumped as the Telex machine clattered into life. Her face reddened as she moved towards it, fancifully expecting answers to the many questions still occupying her thoughts. When she reached the machine on the far side of the office, it was silent again. It sat squat and self satisfied. Frances stopped before it, peered into the white of the near naked page, clad only in the few words of a short message. Her heart skipped a beat and her eyes widened as they made out the first word of the message. 'GUILT…'. She stepped back from the machine, convinced that she must be many miles along the road to madness. She knew already that her memory was going. Now this, judged guilty by a machine. But why not? her confused mind asked as question begat question. If God created Man in his own image, then why not machines as well? Like the priests, the nuns, the laughing people of her dreams, the machines too were messengers of His judgement.

Frances' hand trembled as she reached towards the accusing paper. She tore it from its track and threw it to the floor as the office door swung noisily open and Adrian appeared.

"Bad news, old girl?" he said, picking up the crumpled sheet. "Christ, you're right. Gilts are bloody down again. That's going to put the cat among the pigeons!"

She looked up at him and she began to laugh, she could not stop laughing. The tears streamed down her reddened cheeks and she held her swollen stomach as the laughter took hold. Adrian watched the spectacle, astonished and bewildered. Frances mumbled something inaudible and brushed past her boss and out of the office, out into the street. Still crying and laughing, she did not stop until she reached the small park where she often sat alone, eating her sandwich lunch. She found her favourite bench, empty at this time of the day, as was the whole park. She sat, holding the laughter and tears in her stomach and gazed into the still waters of the small pond.

* * *

The look of astonishment on his face told Frances that her pronouncement was not well received. It was too far to go, and she was still too young (naïve and innocent was what he was actually thinking) for her to think about leaving.

"But why d'you need to go to London? There's plenty of

other places nearby need lasses to work for them. Typists and secretaries and the like. You've no need to go all the way to London." Uncle Bill was putting his foot down as hard as he could, which was never too uncomfortable for anything slow enough to be caught beneath the sole. Still, Frances did not like the obvious anguish which was beginning to darken his features and she lowered her eyes, wishing that she did not have to hurt the man and woman who had been her parents for nearly seven years. Auntie Irene sat quietly as Bill continued the homely logic of his argument and she watched her dead sister's daughter blush beneath the pain of hurting others. She thought she understood. There was nothing in the small Derbyshire town to keep Frances with them, no boyfriend, not many other friends, come to that. Perhaps only the gratitude of a motherless child who had finally grown into a woman had kept her with them this long.

They had no children of their own and, despite the trauma and upheaval following Mary's death, they had been glad to look after the girl. But now Irene understood that it was time for Frances to go. Bill, evidently, did not.

"But what's wrong with the job you've got here. I thought you liked living here."

Frances did. Her Aunt and Uncle had always been good to her, in spite of the almost manic periods of silence and withdrawal she had suffered. They had been kind and patient and had accepted implicitly the doctor's and the priest's advice that such a reaction was only to be expected after such a tragedy. The period of bereavement would not last forever; within a year, maybe even six months, Frances would have come to terms with her grief and would be a normal, well-adjusted teenager once more.

She was now almost 23 and the lines between grief and guilt still contoured her mind. Irene had been able to read only one side of the map.

"You speak to her Irene, will you? Maybe you can make her understand."

She would not tell Aunt Irene that living here, with her mother's sister, going each Sunday to Mass and confession, wanting to explain why she wrote that letter, but never being able to do so, it had been impossible to bury the memory of her mother's death and her own blame for it. Frances had to go, and the prospect of a good job in London was an excuse she could not throw away.

* * *

A small duck splashed into the grey surface of the pond, sending an easy ripple outwards. The distraction was enough to bring Frances out of her reverie. She had stopped laughing some time ago, but tears still clung to her cheeks as she thought, consciously now, of her foster parents. She wished that they were not dead, not just because of her affection for them, but because they would surely have been the people, perhaps the only people, she could turn to now. Auntie Irene would understand and Bill would be sympathetic and patient in his desire to be kind. But they, like the rest of her family, were no longer alive and Frances, at the age of forty, felt more keenly the loneliness of an orphan than she ever had before.

The bird lifted effortlessly out of the pond and Frances watched it rise into the air, droplets of water showering from its beating wings. She thought how lucky the bird was to be able to rise so swiftly from the surface of the pond and she made her third wish of the morning. She waited for a few moments, then as no wings materialised, she gave a last, envious look at the bird now high in the sky, and made her way back to the office.

* * *

Adrian was on the phone when she entered the building. A couple of the dealers were hovering around him. They glanced up at Frances as she moved towards her desk, nodding a curt hello. She sat down, determined to speak truthfully to Adrian and to let him know the reasons for her odd behaviour. He would be shocked, then amused. But what other choice did she have?

"Okay, Jack. Leave it to me. Might be a bit dicey for a couple of days but I'm sure things will settle down soon," she heard Adrian say, as he put the phone down and turned to the young men hanging on his every word. He noticed Frances sitting at her desk opposite. He mumbled some instructions to the dealers and they left the office, closing the door behind them. Frances looked up at him, feeling intimidated but still undaunted, knowing what she had to do. She opened her mouth to speak, but before a word emerged Adrian cut in.

"Look Frances, I'm glad we've got the chance to talk alone for a few minutes. All hell's likely to break loose here later on today. That telex you took this morning is no joke. But that's not what I wanted to talk about." Frances listened, intrigued. Did he know her secret already?

"Except that, in a way it is. You've been acting a bit odd lately. I've noticed, and so have the rest of the staff. Now I know you've always been a little, what shall we say, standoffish, even eccentric, and normally the way you do things, as long as it doesn't affect your work here, is up to you. But let's face it

Frances, you're beginning to be a bit of a square peg in a round hole here."

He stopped, perhaps expecting some reaction from the seated woman, but none came. She looked at him, unblinking, knowing that there was more than a grain of truth in what he was saying. She had been with the business a long time. It had changed, adapted to the demands of the new financial era. Still greater changes were on the way. Now they were bringing in computers. What did she know about computers? Adrian continued:

"I'm sorry to say this Frances, but the business is changing. We're in the market for people who can adapt to that change. Young people with ambition and drive and frankly that's something you have always lacked. You're an intelligent woman and there have been chances. But you've always been content, apparently, to take a back seat. You're not a bad secretary, but these days we need more than that." He stopped again, unsure of how much more he needed to say, a little surprised at the lack of reaction.

"What I'm getting at is that we're going to have to let you go."

Frances swivelled on her chair, turning her back on Adrian, envying more acutely than ever the little duck in the park. She did not miss the irony of the situation. She was being saved the embarrassment of having to reveal her condition, but at what cost? As if to pour a little soothing oil over this particular worry, Adrian went on.

"I know this is going to make things difficult for you, financially I mean, but we'll see that you don't go empty handed. Frances, did you hear me. Please turn round and at least say something. Call me a bastard if you like, but it'll be best for the both of us, in the long run."

Frances allowed herself only a cynical smile, revealing little of the turmoil inside her. She said nothing, simply rose from her seat, as effortlessly as her still concealed condition would allow, and flew from the room, showering her interim boss with a torrent of silent indignation.

* * *

The park was now populated with the occasional dog pulling at its owner's lead. Frances had always been amused at the perversity of taking a dog for a walk. Clearly the reverse was true. Today was no exception as first a large poodle, then a larger Alsatian dragged their human cargo behind them. Frances watched them pass, little appreciating the humour she had previously enjoyed.

The bathing bird had not returned and the surface of the pond remained sombre and unbroken, reflecting only a grey and murky sky. Frances left the bench and the mirrored waters of the pond. She walked towards the little wood that formed a leafy crescent at one end of the park, letting this new twist in the nightmare sink in.

'No job,' she, thought. 'Why?' Because she had not taken her chances? Did everybody have to be ambitious, grab every chance that came their way. So what, if she was a bit of a stick-in-the-mud, she did her job well enough. She thought hard about the chances that had come her way. Chances for advancement at work. In truth, there really had been few of those. Chances to make new friends, a boyfriend, marriage?

* * *

The taxi drew up outside the basement flat in Kilburn. She had said that he could come in for a coffee so Tommy paid the fare and followed her down the short flight of stairs and in through the blue door whose paint puckered and blistered as if it had been shaved by the cutting edge of a fire. Inside, the flat was dark and a little musty, but Frances had shown some taste in its decoration and it looked comfortable enough. She ushered Tommy into the living room and went off into the small kitchen to make the promised coffee. She could hear the folk guitar chords of a Lindisfarne song; one of her few concessions to the Pop music explosion whose reverberations could often be heard through the walls of the Edwardian building which topped her basement. Tommy must have been a little frustrated at not finding a Beatles or a Stones album among her collection of mainly classical works. Still, although their taste in music might differ considerably, she liked him and had been happy to share his company for the evening. They drank their coffee and chatted, he sitting on the settee and she in the comfortable Windsor armchair that Bill and Irene had brought with them on their first visit to her new life in London. Frances said little, content to let Tommy exhaust his enthusiasm for the career he had embarked upon as a junior dealer in the company they both worked for. He was ambitious, he said, and had plans. He was going places and would soon be dealing his own portfolio. Frances smiled at the clichéd rhetoric, not sharing his euphoria but a little excited by it, not sure how much was fired by the quantity of vodka he had downed in the hour spent in the pub after the cinema.

"Why don't you sit over here?" he said, patting the cushioned seat on the settee next to him. She did as he suggested, her empty mug placed on the coffee table in front of the settee. Tommy had also finished his coffee and he clinked his mug against its dissimilar companion on the table. A languid arm found its way to the back of the settee. He spoke softly to her and began to stroke her hair. She stiffened a little. Tommy felt her stiffness and was encouraged by it, taking it as a sign of arousal. He felt her breathing hard, her eyes were wide and he drew her towards him, searching out her lips. His free hand reached for her breast and he squeezed hard, his own breath heavy and laced with vodka. He felt the reaction of her nipple to his touch and stroked it through the soft cotton of her blouse.

"Don't Tommy, no!" Frances moaned, standing up, her small hands forcing themselves against his shoulders. He ignored her protest and climbed quickly from the settee, holding her more tightly, grabbing at the buttons of her blouse. She pushed harder, confused and tearful, feeling herself drowning in the wash of his fervid breath.

"No!" she screamed, flinging her arms against him. Tommy lost his balance, his legs striking the coffee table, sending the mugs crashing to the floor, spilling the dregs onto the carpet. He fell backwards, pulling at the cotton blouse in a vain effort to save himself. Three or four buttons broke their threads and Tommy saw the white lace of her bra as his head hit the wooden leg of the Windsor chair.

He lay motionless. Frances pulled the flapping wings of her blouse around her, unable to prevent the motion of her own trembling body. She could not take her eyes off the boy and wondered whether she imagined the moan coming from his lips. She had not. Tommy moaned again, his hand feeling the back of his head.

"Fuck you!" he screamed, seeing the red smear on his finger tips. "They're bloody right about you, you know." He stood, still feeling the back of his head, trying to determine the extent of the damage.

"I'm sorry, Tommy," Frances began to say, "I didn't mean..." He cut her off, brushing past her, a handkerchief now stemming the trickle of blood staining his ear.

"It's true what they say. You are bloody frigid. Frigid Franny that's what they call you. Fucking frigid Franny." He repeated the insult as he swept out of the room. Frances heard the door slam as Tommy screamed the obscenity one more time.

She collapsed onto the settee, the foul litany ringing in her ears, repeating over and over. She wanted to repeat it, like a blasphemous tongue twister that she must get wrong. It was wrong, she was not frigid. How could she tell Tommy what she really felt, that his caresses did excite her, that she wanted him to kiss her. She did not want the image of her dead mother, dressed in the dark habit of Sister Bernadette, brandishing a flailing, tattered umbrella handle, forcing itself between her and the touch of a man.

* * *

"Park's closing in ten minutes, Miss." She looked up at the man standing over her, the peak of his park-keeper's cap catching the last dull rays of the setting sun. The whole day had slipped by in her painful review of lost chances. Since Tommy, there had been no-one. She was not unattractive, but soon the invitations to dinner or the cinema ceased. The men in the office even began to avoid her. At least, that's how it seemed to Frances. Her recovery from the incident with Tommy was slow and it was not until he left the company, 'going places', as he might have said, that she began to put it behind her. Except that it never did go away completely and an aura of coldness surrounded her dealings with men. She wondered now whether Tommy had been right. Maybe Adrian had felt this all along and her recent eccentricity was a good excuse to get rid of her.

The fact was that now she was about to leave Adrian and the ambitious young men who, she had no doubt, were Tommy's successors. But she was not 'going places' and her plans were, to put it mildly, uncertain. Until now she had always been able to cope and her self-imposed solitude, relieved from time to time by a visit to the theatre or a concert, had not been a problem. She liked, preferred, her own company, or the surrogate company of a good book or record. Now she felt the need of a companion, a confidant who could listen and understand. Understand how sorry she was for the trouble that stupid letter had caused, explain the irony of the punishment she now endured. If only she could speak to her mother.

* * *

She had not been back to the cemetery since the funeral. It was a long journey from Bill and Irene's place in Derby. They would have taken her, but Frances always made some excuse whenever it was suggested. Her foster parents were never insistent, but hoped that the intense period of grieving would, as they had been assured, soon pass and that Frances would want to visit her mother's grave. Now, a quarter of a century later, she was back. The cemetery was small and much overgrown, thick vines of ivy clinging to the headstones and climbing the trunks of the oaks and yews. The paths were mostly obscured by the spreading vegetation and Frances took care to avoid the snagging thorns of bramble. She had no clear memory of where her mother's grave was and there had been no superintendent to ask. Evidently the cemetery was all but abandoned, only the occasional splash of colour from a bouquet of fresh cut flowers against the constant green background suggesting that its occupants received visitors.

Frances was beginning to doubt that she would be able to trace the grave. It did not help that she had no idea what the head-stone was like. Bill had shown her a picture of the one they had chosen, but she had not really looked at it.

The light was beginning to fade and she decided that she would have to abandon the search and return in the morning. Perhaps even phone the local council. She was sure there would be a plan of the cemetery and the plots in it somewhere at the town hall.

She turned towards the exit, some way off beyond a small copse of ancient yew trees. Her eye was caught by the vivid blue of a fresh bunch of sweet williams, their slightly sickly scent beginning to pervade the air. The grave on which they lay had clearly been looked after. No rampant vine covered the headstone and she could read without difficulty the inscription. She noticed the year, 1955, and was struck by the thought that someone still brought fresh flowers to the grave after 25 years. She envied the person whose husband, father or friend lay beneath. She was also struck by the realisation that 1955 was the year in which her mother had died. Her grave might, therefore, be somewhere nearby. Frances looked at the other headstones, dismayed that almost all of them had been invaded by the plethora of green, their epitaphs obscured. A cold shiver shook her spine, carpets of green vegetation threatening to envelope her thoughts again, only this time the ivy was not imaginary. She approached the grave to her left, reluctantly leaving the order of

Sweet William's tomb. She reached a trembling hand towards the leafy shroud covering the headstone, hesitating before pulling the ivy aside. The vine broken reluctantly from its stony anchor, colonies of ants and beetles scurrying from their tiny apocalypse. Frances coughed against the dust of many years of neglect and the inscription slowly revealed itself on the granite slab.

She was not surprised to see her mother's name on the stone. She stood, unmoving before it for many moments, trying to order the tangle of thoughts in her head. There was so much she wanted to say but she was silenced by the desolation of the grave. The inscription had been badly savaged, eroded by the wind and rain and ivy of a quarter of a century. Frances could still make out the detail however. She read the name again, saying it out loud. She read the simple epitaph, again chosen by her aunt and uncle. The date was a little more difficult to read, as if time had called in its own more quickly than the other words 'Born 7.6.1915', Frances could make out in the fading light 'Died 12.12.1955'. She repeated the last date, when she was sent home from school in disgrace, just a few days before the end of term. Then the horror of the accident.

There was something else about that date which would not let go. Frances considered it again. December 12th. What was it about this date that spoke to her, that said something she didn't really want to hear. She looked at the stone again, peering closely and squinting to make out the last few words. 'Aged 40', she read. 'My age', she thought. Then she understood the significance of the date. The shiver repeated its chilling path down her spine and her mind spun in panic. She looked around seeing only the darkness of tombstones and the bony knuckles of branches of poison yew, swaying in a sudden cold breeze. She ran towards the exit, no longer caring about the snags in her stockings, imagining that the bramble, the dog-wood, the ivy were deliberately trying to trip her up. She was soon breathless, her swollen stomach seeming to pull her downward, into the swarm of ants and beetles that her interference with the past had dislodged. At last she reached the rusted iron gates of the cemetery and was out. She staggered another fifty yards from the gates, drunk with fear and exhaustion before gratefully sinking onto the bench beneath a nearby bus shelter.

"What's happening to me?" she screamed, her lungs burning with the effort of running. There was no-one to answer her anguished question, to tell her that it was just coincidence, that December 12th was also the date of the fateful party, of her meeting with ...The name had gone, but the date remained etched on her memory.

* * *

It had been impossible to return to work since her panic stricken flight from the cemetery. She had phoned Adrian, incoherently trying to explain that she was unwell and did not know when she would be back. He said he understood and that she need not worry about working out her notice. There would be a cheque for three months pay in the post. His callousness on the phone confirmed her suspicions that she was not liked or apparently needed at the office. Where was she needed? Where were the friends she ought to be able to turn to at this time of abject crisis? Frances faced the truth of her situation. She was on her own.

* * *

Frances sat in the last pew, watching Father Donne complete

the Eucharist, giving the host, the wine and the sacrament to the last of the small queue of believers, and for the first time in her life, she felt apart from the ritual. She had been badly shaken by the inscription on the headstone of her mother's grave. The 'coincidence' of dates, of age, had removed another brick from the already crumbling wall of sanity which threatened to give way completely. She dare not take communion. She imagined the white sphere of the host burning her lips and the red wine turning into real blood. But she had to speak to Father Donne. He was her only hope.

The final communicant genuflected before the altar, turned and made her way down the aisle, passing the empty ranks of oak-wood benches, towards the great gothic doors of the church. Frances followed the woman's frail procession and felt that if God really did exist the old lady would not have to wait too long to meet him. She almost envied her. Despite the threadbare blackness of her clothes and her ridiculous hat, despite the arthritic crack of each joint which was audible in the silence of the building, the woman's eyes were bright with a still burning faith.

Frances bowed her head as the woman reached the last row. She hoped that the old lady would not turn to look at her; she feared those bright accusing eyes. But the shadow passed and Frances was alone with the priest in God's house. Father Donne was kneeling at the altar, his head bowed in silent prayer. He heard the slow click of a woman's shoe on the ancient stone floor and thought that Mrs. Carmichael had returned. He stood and turned just in time to see Frances O'Donnell collapse in a ragged heap on the carpeted steps of the altar.

* * *

It was dark when she opened her eyes. The only light came from the far end of the long room. A single lamp cast a yellow orb around a table and chair. Frances turned her head towards it and winced, screwing up her eyes against the offending pain. She instinctively reached a hand to the point of the hurt and felt the bandage encircling her head. She opened her eyes again, allowing some minutes for them to adjust to the darkness of the room before turning, more cautiously, towards the illuminated table and chair. A figure moved into the light and sat down, the starched white of her cap unnaturally bright. Frances moaned as the pain in her head took another stab at her. The nurse looked up and moved on squeaky shoes down the length of the aisle separating the rows of beds, checking her fob to note with a frown that there were still several hours to go before the night shift was over. Frances watched the young woman and vaguely remembered something about absurd hats.

"Hello, Miss O'Donnell. Is the pain bad again?" the nurse whispered, adjusting the three pillows behind Frances' aching head. "I'll give you something that'll help you get back to sleep. We don't want you waking the other patients at this time of night, now, do we." The young woman smiled affably, despite the hour, and Frances was grateful for the concern in her face. The nurse returned within a minute with the promised relief. Within two more minutes Frances was asleep again and the ward nurse back at her desk, whiling away the remaining hours of her shift in the pages of a library borrowed romance.

* * *

She was running, her heart pounding and the breath in her chest rushing out more quickly than she could pump it back in.

41

She was sure that she could hear dogs matching the baying wind, their howls echoing through the rain lashed trees. A white swirl of mist curled at her feet, covering the tangle of vegetation that clothed the path. Her hair dripped ice cold rain onto her bare shoulders but she was hot and sweating with the effort of running. She saw ahead of her the iron gates, their huge stone pillars topped with grinning gargoyles. She trips, a snaking tendril of ivy catching her flailing ankle. The ground rushes up to engulf her and her scream is muted by the litter of leaf and mist. She coughs out the rotting mess that threatens to choke her and raises her eyes towards the exit. The gates are still far away but she scrambles to her feet, determined to be out. At last she reaches them and grabs at the great iron ring which is their handle. She pulls but the gates do not move. She pulls again, straining her body against the weight of the immense door. She feels the pull of the empty grave behind her; her eyes are red with tears, her hands grazed red by the pitted iron of the ring. Still the gate does not budge. Now she hears footsteps from behind. They click, loud and clear. They become louder still until the stiletto jabs fill her head. She dare not turn round.

Suddenly the gates open outwards and she falls through them. She feels the rush of wind through her wet hair. The ground has gone and she is falling still. She looks down but there is nothing. The abyss is eternal. She tries to scream but the wind pushes the sound back into her throat. She tries again. Her ears detect the feeble cry and she pushes the breath from her lungs as hard as she can. Light now blinds her still closed eyes and other noises can be heard. The sound of frenzied talk. She hears her name, 'Frances! Frances!'. She keeps her eyes closed but feels the grip of strong hands on her arms.

"Open your eyes, Frances. It's me, Uncle Bill. For God's

sake, open your eyes!" She does as she is told and Bill is there, holding her tight, feeling the wetness of her nightdress and stroking the matted confusion of her hair.

"It's all right. It's just a dream, a nightmare. You're alright now," Bill said, turning a worried look at Irene. They both knew that it was not alright, that this nightmare was another frightening episode in a saga which should long since have run its course.

"She'll sleep again now," her aunt said, screwing the top back onto the bottle of sleeping pills which the doctor had said the girl would only need in the severest moments of grieving. The repeat prescription was now in its third year.

"When's it going to stop? That's what I'd like to know, when's it bloody well going to stop?" The light went out and the door closed. The question, as recurring as the bad dreams, remained.

* * *

"Now you've not been taking very good care of yourself lately, have you." The doctor unhooked the chart from the end of the bed and studied it, occasionally glancing up at Frances who stared meekly at him, the dose of sleeping pills still fuzzing her brain. He smiled at her and approached the side of the bed.

"Your blood iron count is really quite low, apart from the nasty cut on your head that your fall caused," he continued as sensibility slowly returned to Frances' still sore head.

She wondered how much the chart was telling him. Did he know that she was pregnant? That she was 40? That she was unmarried? She tried to remember the sequence of events which had brought her here. She could not remember being asked any questions last night, but she knew that she had been conscious when the ambulance arrived at the hospital. The youthful features of the houseman gave nothing away.

"In your condition it's vital that you eat properly and that you don't go around fainting." His admonishments were gentle and he showed an exemplary bed-side manner which his senior consultant would no doubt have approved of.

Of course he knew that she was pregnant. Father Donne had been with her in the ambulance. He would certainly have given all the necessary details, answered all the relevant questions. Silly to think that you could keep pregnancy a secret in a hospital.

"You're pretty lucky you know. A fall like that could have caused some real damage. You might even have lost the baby. But fret not. All is well and your pregnancy is proceeding as normal and there are no complications." He smiled his disarming smile again, safe in the knowledge that he was the harbinger of good tidings. His reassurances did not produce the expected result. His patient remained silent and morose, the only sign that she had received the doctor's message a discernable tightening of the grip on the bedclothes that Frances had maintained since she awoke.

The young doctor, clearly not used to such a reaction, blushed as he realised that his hurried scan of the medical chart had failed to pick out the 'Miss' which preceded the name of his patient.

"Oh, I'm terribly sorry, Miss, eh, O'Donnell. I didn't realise. I take it this is not a planned pregnancy?"

This time Frances blushed. She was tempted to tell the young man that, of course it was planned. But not by her. Someone, something must have planned all that was happening to her. But he would not understand; how could he? He only dealt with the ills of the body, not the soul.

The doctor turned away and spoke softly to the nurse standing next to him. The nurse nodded a reply, took the clipboarded chart from the young man and replaced it at the end of the bed. Having regained his composure, the doctor smiled again, said something to Frances which she did not register, and left her bed to attend to the next patient on his overfull list.

"You have a visitor, Miss O'Donnell." said the nurse, but Frances gave no sign that this attempt to communicate with the patient had been any more successful than that of her doctor colleague. She tried again. "Miss O'Donnell, the nice priest who was with you last night is here. It's not normal visiting time but, seeing as he's a priest it will be alright. I'll bring him in now. Is that okay? Yes?"

Frances nodded her agreement.

* * *

"Do you think we could have the curtains drawn, nurse?" The nurse obliged as Father Donne sat down on the chair next to Frances' bed. Frances watched him do this and, although her head had cleared the foggy residue of sleeping draught, she had the sudden irrational thought that he had come to deliver the last rites. She almost wished that he had, that the doctor's innocent reassurance of 'no complications' was merely an attempt to hide the truth. The poor doctor knew little of 'complications'.

"Now, Frances, how are you feeling? Is that right what they're telling me? You've been starving yourself for the last few days. Now what kind of a carry on is this? No wonder you fainted in the church. And wasn't it lucky that it was there and not in the street or alone in your flat." He stopped and waited for some reply from Frances, patiently allowing for the diffidence he had come to recognise in her. He decided to do the simple thing and repeated his opening question.

"Tell me, how are you now?"

This question may have been simple, but Frances had gone to the church last night intending to lay open some of the more complicated questions. She wanted answers, from the priest, from the Church, from God. She took a deep breath, determined this time not to let tears or fainting prevent her from seeking the help she needed.

"I wish I knew, Father." She began, looking not at the priest but at her hands still tight around the bed clothes. Her head was hurting again, but she continued. "I suppose it depends what you mean. Apparently I've done no lasting damage to myself. The cut will soon heal." She felt tears well up in her eyes again and she looked at Father Donne, his earnest blue eyes large and unblinking through the thick glass of his lenses. He said nothing, but waited for her to go on, feeling that whatever had prevented her from speaking openly to him before had now been removed. "I can't remember anything about the night the baby was conceived. I only remember the date; December 12th. I can't remember what happened or why or who. Just the date. There must have been a man involved, but I can't remember his name, his face, I can remember nothing about him."

"Surely the blow on your head, Frances. Last night when you fell down. You may have slight amnesia. You hear about these things all the time. It'll clear up in a few days." He smiled and took her hand, hoping to induce some relaxation in the tightness of the grip. She pulled her hand away.

"No, Father. You don't understand. I'm not talking about not remembering now. I couldn't remember before. That's why

I was at the church. I wanted to speak to you, to tell you what's been happening to me, to find out why." She was sobbing now, loudly, the sound impinging on the low hubbub of the early routine of the hospital ward. The young nurse drew the bed curtains aside slightly.

"Is everything alright, Father?" she asked, as the priest handed Frances a clean, white handkerchief.

"Thank you nurse. Yes, it's okay. I wonder if you could just get Miss O'Donnell some pain killers. Her head is hurting again," he said as convincingly as possible, unaware that he was not telling an untruth. The nurse closed the curtains and left.

"Go on, Frances. Tell me what you mean," continued the priest.

"Father, do you know when I was born?" she asked; the priest's puzzled look the only answer to the question that the poor man must have thought incongruous if not irrelevant. "Of course you don't," Frances went on, feeling some pity for the man in his ignorance of the importance that this date, many dates, had assumed in her life. "I was born on the day the war began." Frances sighed heavily as she uttered the fateful line and looked away from the good priest, clutching ever more fiercely the white linen blanket, drawing it up to her chin. The name of the hospital, stitched firmly in bright red cotton along the top edge of the cover, lost its shape and meaning. Father Donne's expression, had Frances noticed it, would have told her that the revelation of her date of birth was also devoid of meaning to him.

"I don't understand, Frances," he affirmed after a momentary pause. "What difference does that make to you? There must have been hundreds of children born on that date. In that respect it must have been no different to any other day. God does not, in his wisdom, suspend all the ills that trouble mankind on a particular day so that children can come into a blameless world. There can be no connection between your date of birth and the outbreak of war. It's just a simple coincidence. Surely you know that Frances." Frances sniffed and dabbed the tears from her red-rimmed eyes.

"Do I know that, Father? I've prayed to God to give me answers to that question and to many others in the past few weeks. I've told myself over and over again that it was coincidence. Each time a misfortune has occurred in my life, I've ignored the coincidence of dates. I can't ignore it any longer, Father. There are too many coincidences."

Father Donne had taken his glasses off, the way he always did when he wanted to see things more clearly. Frances dabbed her eyes again, perhaps clearing the final remnants of uncertainty about her condition. She continued:

"I never really knew my father. He had joined up by the time I was born. I only remember the letters my mother received from him. She'd read them out to me, even when I was too young to understand what was in them, she always read them out to me. He was home from time to time, when I was very young, but not often, and I don't remember him very well." She stopped speaking for a moment, but not to allow the priest to respond to her. Her attention was focused elsewhere, elsewhen. Father Donne looked at her, recognising the remembrance of better times in the eyes of this woman whose suffering he did not understand. The flush in her cheeks had returned a little; the sallow white of her face which so shocked the priest when he first arrived reddening into a youthful pink.

"Go on, Frances," said the Father. His words shook the reverie from her and the colour seemed to drain from her face again.

"I'm sorry Father. I was just…" she stopped again, unable

to put words to her feelings, to describe the few years in her life when she was happy, when her mother was alive, when her father was away.

"It's alright, Frances. I'm still listening. You were telling me about your father. What happened to him?"

"He was killed. My mother never did tell me the details. I was only five years old. I remember the day very well, blow on the head or not, Father. It was funny. I couldn't understand why my mother was so upset. Outside, in the street, everybody seemed so happy and excited. There were banners and bunting everywhere. I remember at one point there was even a brass band playing. It was the day the war ended, you see. I found that out later. The day we should all have been happy."

"I'm sorry Frances. I didn't know that," the priest said unnecessarily. "That's a terrible cruel day to receive such news. But, I still don't see that it's anything more sinister than extreme bad luck. It's still just coincidence."

"Yes, I suppose it might be. But how much bad luck does there have to be, how many coincidences before you stop and say to yourself, 'why have I been chosen for such treatment?'"

"What else can you tell me, Frances? I'm still not sure I understand what all this is about."

"After my father died my mother changed. She had been very happy, even when he was away so much of the time. It was as if the memory of him, the promise that he would soon be back home, was all the happiness she needed. I was happy too. I didn't know what it was like to have a father, so I didn't miss him. I must have shared my mother's feelings of promises that would soon be met. But he didn't come back. Not even his body came back. There was no grave for my mother to grieve at, no sign that he had ever existed."

"Were there no photographs, Frances?"

"If there were I don't remember them. Perhaps my mother put them away after he died, but I don't think so. I just don't remember seeing any photographs."

"You were saying that your mother changed. After your father's death. How did she change?"

"She wasn't happy any more. That's obvious, isn't it Father. But it was more than that. She withdrew into herself and she became...well, just older. I mean, straight away, she was an old woman with a young child. I didn't realise any of this at the time of course, but now it seems crystal clear. I was sent away quite soon after, to a girls' boarding school, a convent school, naturally. From then on I only saw my mother during the holidays, but we would never really talk about anything. She only wanted to know whether I had been a good girl and had been to confession regularly." Frances looked directly at Father Donne as she said this but the priest averted his eyes from hers, not quite understanding the accusation in them but feeling its sting nevertheless.

"She was being eaten up by her faith, Father. At the same time, I suppose it was the only thing that kept her going at all. I think I just became a nuisance in the end, a reminder of her dead husband. But so long as I was a 'good girl' it didn't matter, I didn't matter, one way or the other. That's why she was so annoyed you see, with the letter I wrote. It's funny, all this time, I've never understood why I wrote that letter. But now, you know, I think I do." She stopped again. The dull green curtains surrounding the bed formed a confessional shroud, numbing the noise of the ward, now busy with scurrying nurses and sedulous junior doctors. Her mind raced, at last arranging the words of the confession which she had never previously been able to make.

"I'm sorry, Father," said the young nurse, pulling the curtains aside again and clutching a fresh jug of water. "We've been so busy this morning, I've only just this minute had time to get these pills." She handed them to Frances and poured some of the water into the plastic glass on the patient's bedside table. "There now, Miss O'Donnell, the pain should be gone again in no time." She said to Frances, who took the pills and the glass of water from the nurse and sank back into the pillow, her eyes focused on the ceiling.

The nurse turned her attention back to Father Donne.

"I am sorry, Father," she said again, "but you'll have to leave for the moment. Doctor Bambridge will be making his rounds soon. I'm afraid he doesn't approve of visitors outside proper hours. I'm not sure he approves of visitors at all, thinks they get in the way." She said this with a forced smile, opening the curtains completely, exposing Frances and the priest to the curious indifference of the rest of the ward. Frances felt vulnerable and unsure again, the lucid words of her 'true confession' dislocated and disordered in her mind. Father Donne saw this and regretted the nurse's unavoidable intrusion. He took Frances' hand. This time she did not draw it away from him.

"Don't worry Frances. I'll be back as soon as I can. You get some rest and I'll be here this afternoon, during proper visiting time, despite what Doctor Bambridge thinks." He exchanged a smile with the young nurse who was now adjusting the bedclothes around Frances in readiness for the tyrannous visit.

"3 o'clock, isn't that right, nurse?" Frances heard him ask as he left the ward, in the wake of the nurse who was busying herself elsewhere. Frances was still focused on the ceiling, seeing shapes come and go in the lines and folds of its badly painted surface.

* * *

Sister Bernadette rose from her seat in a rush of black habit, dragging the wooden legs of the chair angrily across the parquet flooring of the raised dais. The silence of the great, cold dining hall, usually broken only by the metal scrape of cutlery on plates, was violated. Tall and big-boned, Sister Bernadette appeared even more grossly statuesque as she overlooked the ranks of tables and benches at which the convent girls were seated. All eyes were on her and the silence had returned emphatically; no scraping knife disturbed the judgmental hush. She held the sheet of paper that one of the novitiates had just given her. Her face rapidly changed colour from its usual cool pallor to a hot red, made hotter by the contrasting white of her starched wimple. The Sister brandished the paper in her left hand, the offending script held high above her head. Her right hand was held straight out in front of her, the index finger sweeping menacingly across the lines of wide-eyed girls. The pointing finger stopped, many pairs of young eyes straining cautiously to follow its path. Before any of them had time to work out the target, Sister Bernadette's booming voice left no-one in doubt as to where the accusation was aimed.

"Frances Mary O'Donnell, leave this hall and wait outside my office! This instant!" Frances rose from the bench, the girls on either side of her looking up in astonishment at the quiet, timid girl who, in the ten years she had been a pupil at the school, had been conspicuous only in her anonymity. What could she have done that had caused such an apoplectic response from the good Sister?

The accused shuffled past the three girls who sat to her right, almost stumbling over the last, who quite possibly, Frances thought, had deliberately tried to trip her up. She moved awkwardly from the table and down the central aisle between the dinner tables, her eyes not daring to look at anything but her feet and feeling the burning skin of her cheeks. She regretted the newness of her shoes, an early Christmas present from her mother, as the hard new leather of the soles clicked noisily on the wood floor. At last she reached the heavy oak doors of the entrance to the hall and she was out into the corridor.

Sister Florence, a young novitiate whose timidity almost matched that of Frances herself, had opened the great doors and now closed them as quietly as she could, following Frances into the corridor. Neither spoke, but Frances could sense the same embarrassment and shame in the novice nun in the afterglow of her own blush. She looked at Sister Florence and noticed the tear in slow descent down the young woman's round face. She thought of the suffering that Jesus experienced on the cross and how Sister Florence had given her own life to God so that wicked girls like her might be forgiven. The shame overwhelmed her and she collapsed in an undignified heap at the feet of the nun.

* * *

Father Donne had returned, as he had promised, at the 3 o'clock visiting time. 'Thank God for Father Donne', Frances had thought, watching him approach her bed. She was immediately surprised by this silent affirmation of her faith. Yesterday, just before she had fainted in the church, she had been convinced of her rejection of God. He could not exist and she had gone to the church to tell Him so! But now, lying in this hospital bed, with the priest stepping confidently towards her, ready to hear the final truths of her confession, she realised the absurdity of such a thought. Her only hope was in God and belief in his existence. Father Donne was real and, therefore, so was God. The only alternative was that God had rejected her. Frances shook visibly at this thought as the priest pulled the iron framed chair around to face her.

"You're not cold, are you, Frances?" he said, sitting down and adjusting his glasses. "They usually keep these wards pretty warm, you know. I hope you're not getting a chill." The concern in his face was genuine, France knew, and she smiled at him in gratitude for this. Surely God was good. "So tell me, how is the headache. I hope those pills worked."

"It's much better," Frances lied. Not a good start, she thought, to this second round of the confessional. She said no more, but continued to look into the priest's bespectacled eyes, searching for a way to pick up the threads of their earlier conversation, hoping for a sign from him that might help. He took off his glasses and returned her smile.

"You were telling me this morning about yourself, about your mother and father. About that letter you wrote. Do you feel well enough to carry on?" As if answering his own question, he got up and pulled the curtains around the bed once more, closing off the rest of the ward and the growing clamour of visiting time. He sat down again and put his glasses back on. Frances remained silent for several moments, but the priest was in no hurry, realising that the lucidity of a few hours ago would not return easily. He, nonetheless, broke the silence:

"I have been thinking a lot about what you told me. Would you like me to find out about your father. There are bound to be army records of him, maybe even a photo somewhere that you could have. Should I do that for you, Frances?"

'He still doesn't understand,' Frances thought. Why should he? It was not a question of resurrecting her dead father, of replacing the years without him with a photograph. Frances said nothing, but gently shook her head. The priest tried again:

"You have told me about your own birth and the death of your father, the tragic coincidence of the dates. What about your mother, Frances, tell me more about her."

Frances turned her head away and stared blankly at the dull green surrounding the bed. She held her hand to the ache in the side of her head and winced with the pain. It would hurt to tell Father Donne about her mother, but she had to do it.

"Do you know how old I am, Father?" she asked, still looking into the green blur.

"Yes, Frances, I do. You told me that you were 40. But I don't see…"

She cut him off before he could finish:

"My mother was 40 when she died."

"That's terrible young, Frances, but I still don't see why it should be so significant."

"Did I tell you when she died, the date I mean?" she asked, turning to look at him.

"No, I don't think so."

"My mother died on the 12th of December. I had forgotten myself until the day I went back to the cemetery. I went to look for her grave so that I could talk to her, really talk to her for perhaps the first time in my life. It wasn't until I found the grave and the headstone that I realised." She stopped and took a deep breath and looked down at the bulge in her stomach. "The only thing I remember about the night this baby was conceived is the date. December 12th. Don't you think it's strange that nothing else from that night remains? I can't remember anything about it, not where, not who, not how, just when; the 12th of December during my fortieth year. The same day my mother was killed by a skidding car, the day I was sent home from school because I wrote a letter. A stupid letter to an imaginary lover because I was jealous of the other girls and their constant talk of boys. And maybe because I wanted my mother to notice me. It wasn't any surprise that Sister Bernadette was handed the letter, you know. I left it where I was sure it would be found. I wanted to be sent home but I didn't think it would end in my mother's death."

Father Donne removed his glasses and pinched the bridge of his nose. Frances wiped her eyes on a clean white handkerchief that she had taken from the small draw of her bedside cabinet.

"Is all this normal, Father, the dates, I mean. Is it all just coincidence?"

The priest considered her question for a moment, then replied with one of his own:

"Now let me get this straight. Are you telling me that you believe you're responsible for your mother's death because of some letter you wrote and that all these dates are some sign that you're being punished for it?"

Frances did not reply.

"Come now, Frances, in the name of the Holy Mother of Christ, who do you imagine is punishing you? Is it God you think that's doing it? Have you not learnt that ours is not a vengeful God, but a God of forgiveness. Did I not say the same when you first told me that you were pregnant, when we agreed that the Church could help to arrange an adoption for the child? Have you forgotten our conversation then, Frances?"

"No, Father. That's something I haven't forgotten. But I

had not been to the cemetery then, I didn't know about the dates. Father, there is something else about the dates too. This baby will be born on the 3rd of September. That's the day I was born, when the war started." Frances attempted a smile but did not succeed. The anguished grimace that appeared left the priest in no doubt that the significance of this new coincidence was real enough for Frances.

"I'm sorry, Frances, but I can't accept what you're saying, what you're implying. Besides, you're telling me that the baby was conceived on December 12th. Surely your child is likely to come into this world a little earlier, in August." The statement was a question to which Father Donne expected a ready answer.

"It will be born late, on September 3rd. Don't ask me how I can be so sure, I just know I am right. The baby will be born on the same day that I was." Frances answered with cast iron certainty, looking the priest straight in the eyes. "It will also be a boy." She surprised herself with this remark. Until now she had not even considered what sex the child might be. She had hardly considered the child growing inside her at all, except as the tangible evidence of her punishment. Suddenly, she knew its sex.

It was not the cosy warmth of the wards which caused beads of sweat to prickle the priest's forehead. He looked at Frances in astonishment. She was no longer crying and the unshakable belief in what she had just said seemed to have lifted a dark shroud from her. She looked different. The priest's mind raced in search of a word to describe her. She was now… rested?… comfortable?… relaxed? No, that wasn't it. She was divine.

In his thirty years as a man of the cloth, Father Donne had never doubted his own faith. He was a good priest and a true believer. But in all that time he had never encountered the joy of a truly religious experience, had never had his faith confirmed by a voice from God, a vision of the Holy Mother, or a validated brush with the dark side in an exorcism which stemmed from anything more than human fear. Now, by the side of this woman whose life seemed not to be her own, he felt humbled. There was an aura around her. Nothing that could be seen, he was sure, but nevertheless it was there and he felt it. He slid off the chair and knelt on the floor at the side of the bed. He took Frances' hands into his own and he prayed.

* * *

Adrian was as good as his word. A cheque for considerably more than might have been expected arrived by the hand of a motor-cycle messenger during her third day in hospital. There was even a 'Get Well!' card signed by most of the people from the office. Frances allowed herself a rueful chuckle at this and thought again about the 'illness' with which she was afflicted. The rueful chuckle soon vanished, however; replaced by the migraine frown for which she was still demanding pills from the nurses.

No-one from work, her former colleagues, had been to see her, of course. She might have expected one or two of them, those she'd worked with for a number of years, to show an interest. But no-one came, not even Adrian. Typical of him to let money do the talking.

Chapter Four

Father Donne helped her down from the taxi and took the suitcase from the driver after paying him off. The rest of Frances' limited possessions would follow later and be stored in a disused room at the rectory. Alice Donne, the Father's sister, waited at the door of the house to greet them. Frances was grateful for the priest's arm, extended for her to hold as they made their way through the wrought iron gates and down the short gravelled path to the house.

"How are you, dear?" Alice said, taking Frances' other arm and helping her through the door into the wide hall. "I've got the kettle on and we'll have a nice cup of tea. Peter will take your case to your room, won't you dear." She said, looking at her brother as she ushered her house guest into the lounge.

"Let me take your coat and I'll just go and fetch the tea."

Frances was glad of the chance to sink into one of the four comfortable armchairs which were placed with studied nonchalance around the large room. Despite the warmth of this late August evening, there was already a fire in the grate. A real log fire whose flames were caged by a heavy, brass guard. Frances chose the chair furthest from the fire and sank into its cosy cushions in as dignified a way as she could manage. She felt tired and uncomfortably heavy, her small frame longing to be rid of the extra weight, to deliver the child at last. She closed her eyes and rested her hands on the round bulge of her stomach.

Alice returned with a smile and a silver tray which bore a china tea-pot and three delicate cups. A small plate of rich-tea biscuits accompanied the drink. Frances opened her eyes and watched through a haze of half sleep as the priest's sister carefully placed the tray on the small oak table near Frances' chair.

"Thank you, Auntie Irene." Frances murmured, closing her eyes completely again. Alice looked up at her as Peter came into the room. She turned to look at her brother, a puzzled expression asking her brother what the mistake meant. The priest simply returned her puzzlement and shrugged his shoulders. He saw that Frances was asleep and signalled to his sister to leave the room.

* * *

The ardent flames of the fire were now faint ghosts, dimly red in the darkness of the room. She wriggled in the chair, pulling the checkered woollen blanket up to her neck and lifting her stockinged feet onto the seat. Despite the blanket she felt cold as her senses recovered from sleep. The chair was comfortable, but she must have been asleep for some time. She began to feel the wetness on her cheeks and an ache in her back. From outside the room, through the closed door, she could hear the vague murmurings of conversation coming from the hall. Dim, yellow light seeped through the imperfect frame of the door, faintly illuminating one side of the room. Frances' eyes opened and strained to adjust to the half-light. She could make out the tall standard lamp with its large shade. She knew it also had a tasselled fringe, but she could not see it. Beneath the lamp stood the small cabinet with its collection of glass miniatures that always fascinated her on her occasional visits. She remembered where she was and why she was there. She started to cry, softly at first, but then in great sobs which found their way through the living room door and into the hall.

Auntie Irene came in, an apron around her waist. The standard lamp was switched on and lit the whole room.

"There, there, lovey. You have a good cry," she said, hugging the distraught teenager as closely as the wings of the Windsor chair would allow. She knelt down and wrapped the blanket more tightly around Frances.

"I've made us a nice hot stew, with dumplings. You know how much you like dumplings," she said, stroking the girl's blond hair away from the wetness on her cheeks, feeling tears well up in her own eyes. It had not been easy since her sister's death, but they had not hesitated in offering to take Frances in. The funeral had been a trial for all of them, but now they were back in Derby and Frances had come to live with them. How long, Irene wondered, would it take the poor child to get over the tragedy?

The living room door opened again and Uncle Bill came in carrying a mug of hot, sweet tea and a plate of chocolate digestives.

"I thought you might like a cup o' tea, lass," he said. "Come on, now, wipe your eyes and 'ave a cup o' tea. I hate to see you cry."

* * *

Frances wiped the sleep from her eyes and stirred in the deep comfort of the chair. She felt the child kick inside her, as if reminding her that she had no right to comfort, no right to forget that he would take his place in the world in precisely one week. During this remaining week she would live in the rectory where Alice, the priest's sister, would look after her and the unborn infant.

It had been a hard decision to relinquish the flat, but, generous though Adrian's pay off had been, common sense dictated that the money would not last long with a mortgage to be paid every month. So, when Father Donne made his offer, Frances could hardly refuse. Besides, there was a natural logic to the move made even more curious by her first meeting with Alice. She allowed herself a rare smile at the thought of how startled she had been. But then, it was almost natural now for such coincidences to permeate her life. Why should it be even worthy of note that the priest's sister should so resemble her dead Auntie Irene? Now she was here, in the quiet comfort of the rectory lounge. The priest had made no enquiries about adoption for the child. He and his sister would happily take on the role of foster grandparents, looking after both she and the infant.

The lounge door opened on hinges trying desperately not to squeak. Father Donne put a benevolently spying head around it and saw that Frances was no longer asleep. His benevolence broadened into a smile and he entered fully into the room.

"You must have been exhausted, my dear," he said, taking the poker and provoking the dying fire. The provocation was not enough and he added more logs. "Alice has made a fresh pot of tea," he continued, "I'm sure that will revive you some more." He poked the fire again, satisfied at the healthy glow now issuing from the hearth, happy in the knowledge that God had once again shown him the way and he had known what to do about Frances O'Donnell and the child. Alice came into the room carrying the same tray, but with the delicate spout of the china pot exhaling steaming proof of the freshness of the reviving brew. She laid the tray on the occasional table and spoke softly to her brother as she knelt to pour the tea.

"We've a lovely stew tonight, Peter, with dumplings. You know how much you like dumplings. I hope you do too, Frances."

* * *

She felt a trickle down the inside of her thigh. There was no discomfort, no pain, just the warm wetness of the fluid sticking to her legs. She looked towards the window. It was not yet light outside, though through the net curtains she could make out the shape of the heavy boughs of the old yew tree swaying in a stiff breeze. She was fully awake and had been since just after midnight. She looked sideways at the red glow of the alarm clock on the bedside table. The light dazzled for a moment, her unfocussed eyes straining to make out the numbers. It was 4 o'clock and it had started. Soon there would be pain, but she did not mind that. For now, there was just wetness and a feeling that it was going to be a difficult day.

She tried to remember the advice of the ante-natal sessions to which she had reluctantly gone. Father Donne had insisted that it was the wise thing to do and he was right, of course. But he did not suffer the curious stares of the other mothers-to-be, all of them much younger than Frances, all of them, she was sure, at least acquainted with the name of the father of their as yet unborn offspring. She looked at these men when they occasionally came to the classes with their wives or girl-friends. From time to time she heard their names; John, Michael, Andrew, and irrationally hoped that a name, a father's name, would jog her indolent memory. But no name recalled the father of her own child.

No-one said anything to her, of course. Her natural stand-offishness allied to her self-consciousness about her condition made certain of that. She felt the paranoia of the outcast, imagining that each guffaw and chuckle was at her expense as the other mothers gathered in their excited, jabbering groups, sowing the seeds of lasting friendships, intent on drowning the promised pain of delivery in base humour, their confinement underwritten by the proffered pethadine, gas or epidural. Frances needed no such succour. Pain was to be expected and was a necessary part of her punishment.

She felt the stab in the pit of her stomach, like a long knife, twisting and cutting. She gulped in air and a stifled scream emerged as a thin cry. It pressed weakly against the bedroom door but did not penetrate. Condensation ran down the window-pane as the warmth of the room resisted the cold of the night. Frances shivered, feeling the dampness of cold sweat on her forehead. She fought hard against the temptation to panic and remembered the advice of the midwife. She took in another, deeper and more controlled breath and looked at the clock, noticing only the red minutes. She must count the interval between the contractions, she must wait for the pain to come again. The red figures clicked silently on, growing fainter as the pallid light of the risen sun began to illuminate the area around the window. She was hot now and pulled the bedclothes away from her distended body, stretching out her arms and stiffening as she did so. She remembered that this was wrong and tried to relax. The knife hit her again, but she was prepared for it and noted the minutes on the indifferent face of the electric clock. The contraction was short and she let the pain wash over her, taking deeper and deeper breaths, trying to concentrate on the growing light filtering into the room. She counted four seconds and sank back into the softness of the bed as the spasm left her, relaxing her grip on the bedclothes. Soon it would be time to summon Peter and Alice Donne, to be taken to the hospital where the child would be delivered. But not yet. Frances turned towards the clock once more, watching the colon flash away the seconds, seeing the minutes idle forwards, killing the time between the pain. The mechanical ring of a clockwork alarm faintly permeated the thick walls of the bedroom. She watched the digits on her own clock change from 4:59 to 5:00. Twelve minutes since the last contraction and Alice Donne was getting up a little earlier than her customary 5:45. Soon she would be knocking on the door, bringing Frances the early morning cup of tea and digestive biscuit which had become a staple of the ante-natal diet. Alice had taken her role as surrogate grand-mother very seriously and had put the physical welfare of her enigmatic guest and her unborn child above all else. Her zeal in this endeavour was matched only by her brother's vigil and his attention to Frances' spiritual needs. Frances thought she understood what he had been trying to do and she felt both gratitude and a little pity for his efforts. She had for several months been unable to attend the Mass which had been her unfailing habit for as long as she was able to remember. Not even her move into this house built on consecrated land, this rectory within view of the Mother Church, was enough to persuade her back into the heart of the Catholic ritual. She had remembered, how ironic she thought, far too clearly the last time she had foolishly believed that God was willing to share with her the secrets of his mysterious ways and how frightened she had been of the white host, the red wine and the black coated old woman. Frances touched the side of her head and fancied that the ugly bandage still swathed her aching skull, that the nurse was busying herself behind the green curtains of her bed searching vainly for aspirin to kill the pain. But it was not the nurse, of course, who knocked gently on the door and the tea and biscuit, welcome as they were, would do nothing to blunt the cutting edge which brought Frances back from her distraction. Her 'come in' rushed from the pit of her stomach as she tried vainly to hide the pain.

"Is it time, Frances my dear?" Alice asked, the slap of spilled tea on the metal tray the only hint of the excitement contained beneath her cool exterior. Frances did not answer but gripped her hand and arched her back, trying very hard to suck in the controlled breath which would ease the pain.

"Try to relax, my dear. Go with the pain and breathe deeply." Frances did her best to obey and to concentrate on the length of the contraction. She had forgotten to look at the clock and to count the seconds but she was sure that this contraction was longer than the last.

"When did the contractions start?" said Alice, feeling the grip on her hand relax as Frances sank back into the bed.

"About four o'clock," Frances replied, still breathless despite the efforts at controlled breathing. Alice had taken out a large white handkerchief and was gently mopping Frances' brow. She also rearranged the two well-feathered pillows so that Frances could sit up a little more comfortably and take some of the magical tea.

"You should have called me earlier, Frances. Here now," said Alice, "sip some tea. It's nice and hot, better than any pill." Frances did as she was told and was thankful for the hot liquid which she traced all the way down to her stomach. She thought of the overworked nurse returning to her bed with the pain-killers and telling Father Donne that he would have to go. Soon she would be in a hospital bed again and before the day was done she would be a mother.

* * *

Frances refused the wheel chair, despite the ache in her back, insisting that she was able to walk into the delivery room without mechanical assistance but gladly feeling the comforting hands of Peter and Alice Donne under each arm. The hospital was still quiet and the maternity wing especially so. Only the muffled scurry of a porter or nurse breaking the stillness of the morning.

"Mrs O'Donnell?" said a young nurse, her starched uniform making a noise like rustled paper as she approached. Peter and Alice flashed glances at each other worried that the error should have embarrassed Frances.

"It's Miss O'Donnell," said Frances, not in embarrassment nor anger, but impassively, resigned to her role as mother to this child that she had not wanted. The nurse looked hurriedly at the manila folder she was carrying, the insignificant looking circle around 'Miss' suddenly obvious.

"I'm sorry, Miss O'Donnell, I should have looked. Please come this way; are you sure you don't want a wheel chair?"

"Thank you, I'd prefer to walk, but can we go straight away?"

* * *

The mid-wife took the baby and wrapped it in disinfected towelling.

"It's a boy, Miss O'Donnell. You have a beautiful baby boy."

She placed the child in the white plastic bowl of the weighing machine. The hand moved quickly and settled with conviction on a point beyond 7 pounds.

"7 pounds 3 ounces," she announced, noting the fact on a form. The baby gurgled then cried, its hand searching the air, looking for its mother's warmth. Frances lay back on the sticky wet sheets, her hair wringing with sweat. She had refused the pethadine, the gas, the epidural, had endured all the pain of a 15 hour labour, her only succour the encouraging words of the mid-wife and a damp towel to wipe the sweat from her overheating brow.

Both Peter and Alice Donne had wanted and offered to remain with her in the delivery room but Frances had also refused this comfort. Both, however, were still at the hospital, sustained by a constant stream of hot tea, living the role of expectant grand-parents and enduring with almost as much discomfort as their surrogate daughter the anxiety of the final moments. The pair were alone in the bright waiting room, its walls decorated with painted nursery rhymes and story book pictures. Peter wondered whether the juxtaposition of 'Ring a Ring a Roses' and a poster warning of the dangers of non-inoculation against childhood diseases was deliberate and had decided that this was probably not the case when the door opened and a dark-haired young nurse walked in.

"Would you like to go in now, Father Donne. Frances has had a little boy."

"Everything is all right, isn't it nurse?" asked Alice anxiously as she got up stiffly from the chair she had half fallen asleep in.

"Yes, of course," replied the young woman, smiling. "Both mother and baby are doing well. He's a beautiful little boy. Please, come through and you can see for yourselves."

* * *

The priest knelt before the child and its mother and his sister followed. Their prayer was barely audible; only the occasional 'Amen' echoed around the walls above the discreet noise of the two nurses clearing the room. The baby had been lain next to Frances and she cradled the now sleeping infant in her left arm. Her right arm stretched towards the small table which remained by the delivery bed and she seemed to be reaching for something, but the surface was clear save for a kidney shaped bowl which contained a sterilised syringe made ready for the moment of unbearable pain which never came. Frances' hand swept across the table, dislodging the bowl and the empty syringe. A last 'Amen' was drowned as they hit the sterile floor with a clatter.

"I'm sorry, mother, I'm so sorry," Frances sobbed in great gulps and enfolded the tiny child, holding him to her so tightly that he awoke startled and fighting for breath in the warm valley of his mother's breasts. Alice and Peter still knelt by the bed, their hands now joined in silent witness to this sublime tableau. The nurse who had ushered the Donnes into the delivery room dropped the pile of white, sterile towels she was holding and rushed the few feet to the bed. Taking the baby by its shoulders she tried to prise him away from his mother.

"Miss O'Donnell! Frances! Sarah, come and help me quick!"

Sarah left the monitoring machine she was about to disconnect from the wall socket and came to the bed, the swish of her student nurse's uniform making a noise like the laboured breathing of an asthmatic. She all but pushed the stupefied Donnes to one side as she helped her colleague release the child. Frances was still mouthing her enigmatic lament, the tears streaming down her flushed cheeks.

"I'm so sorry, mother. I didn't mean it, I promise you, I didn't mean anything by it."

Father Donne seemed completely unaware of this ranting, his expression radiating only beatitude in the glorious coming of a boy-child. Alice looked anxiously at her brother, as concerned now about him as she was about the danger to the baby. She started to call the nurse but her alarm was cut short.

"Please Father, Miss Donne. I must ask you to leave. Would you, please." The young nurse ushered the two out, forcefully taking their arms and leading them through the double doors and into the waiting room. She left them there, concerned at their apparent stupor but more worried about the infant and its sobbing mother. She returned quickly to find the mid-wife cradling the baby who was crying heartily, but seemingly none the worse for its ordeal. Frances was still weeping, although with less vigour than a few minutes before. A doctor was taking her pulse while the nurse prepared a sedative. The prick of the needle stung Frances and she sucked in air. The tears stopped abruptly and she called out, weakly but calmly:

"Where's my baby?"

Chapter Five

The child lay in its cot among a sleeping array of fellow newborn. The boy was awake, but not crying. His tiny hands still wafted the air and his pale blue eyes tried hard to focus on the blur of the world he had come into.

"Are you two alright?" the dark-haired nurse asked as she joined Peter and Alice Donne by the viewing window of the small nursery. "You must have had quite a fright in there. The baby's fine, though. No lasting damage. I'm not sure about Miss O'Donnell though. I mean…, I think our Doctor Bremmer would like a word with you. Is that all right? Do you feel up to it?"

"Of course, nurse," Alice replied for both of them. She wasn't sure whether Peter had heard the question or even the nurse's approach. His attention was focused completely on the child in its cot. "Peter, we can see the doctor now, can't we," she urged, gently tugging at his sleeve.

"Sorry Alice, what were you saying?"

"The doctor, the nurse wants us to have a word with Doctor Bremmer, about Frances. Lead on nurse, will you.

* * *

By the time the mid-wife and the student nurse were wheeling Frances to the recovery ward the sedative had done its job. She was calm as the stiffness in her thighs and back relaxed and she drifted into dreamless sleep.

* * *

"Come in Father, and Miss Donne, won't you please come in. Here, sit down. Nurse, would you please fetch some tea?"

"Yes, Doctor Bremmer, three cups?"

"Now then, let's see." The doctor, searched through a pile of untidy files and papers on his desk top, eventually extracting one from the morass. He nodded an almost imperceptible reply to the nurse's enquiry as he looked up from behind an improbable pair of pince-nez spectacles clinging ferociously to the broad bridge of his nose. It was tempting to think that the redness which, beyond the tiny lenses of the pince-nez, framed the whites of his eyes was due to a stifled desire to scream rather than to the lateness of the hour. However, Alice suppressed the thought and sat patiently with her preoccupied brother, waiting for the obstetrician's deliberations to bear fruit. Doctor Bremmer cleared several more files from his chair and sat down. He read from the notes.

"I see," he said to himself, turning a page and looking up and over the clamp on his nose. Alice hoped he would not notice the stupefaction which had bathed her brother's features since the child's birth and had apparently deprived him of all power of rational thought or speech. "Miss O'Donnell is going to return to live with you in your house, Father, is that right?"

Peter made no attempt to answer the doctor's question and Alice shifted uneasily in her chair. She looked from her brother to the doctor then back again, hoping that the question might be dragged through the space between them by this simple movement. The silence continued and it was the doctor's turn to shift in his seat.

"I'm sorry, Doctor, but my brother has found the last few days quite a trial. You'll have to forgive him but I'm sure he'll be alright soon."

"Perhaps the tea will revive him. Put it down here, will you, nurse." More paper found its way to the floor as the nurse put down the tray and went out as unobtrusively as she had come in. Doctor Bremmer, handing a cup to Alice Donne, picked up the conversation:

"But she will be returning with you, to live with you and your brother?"

"Yes, Doctor. That shouldn't present any problems, should it? I mean, I don't really know where else Frances might go. She doesn't seem to have any relatives and... well... my brother and I seem to be the only people she will trust."

The doctor picked up a second cup from the tray and offered it to Father Donne. Quickly Alice took it from him.

"Peter, have some tea, will you? You'll feel better with some tea inside you. I don't think he's eaten properly since yesterday," she offered feebly to the doctor. "Come on, Peter, take the tea."

"I'm sorry, Alice. Yes of course, I'll have some tea, please." Alice breathed an audible sigh of relief as her brother at last reacted and took the tea in a shaky hand. A few drops spilled into the saucer but he managed to grip the handle of the cup and bring it to his lips. He closed his eyes as the hot brew stung slightly but it seemed, miraculously, to do as prescribed.

"Yes, Doctor, Frances and the child will be coming home with us, when she is released from the hospital, of course. That won't be a problem, will it, Doctor?" he unknowingly repeated his sister's earlier question.

"No, no, I don't see why not, Father. Besides, it's really nothing to do with us. She'll be visited, of course, but that's not our territory. No, no, that won't be a problem, but considering Miss O'Donnell's reaction to the baby a short time ago there are a couple of things you might be able to help me with, before I can give Frances the medical all clear."

"How can we help you, Doctor? Please, what is it you want to know? There are no complications, are there?"

"There are certainly no physical problems. Frances seems remarkably well, considering her age and her refusal to accept any analgesic at all during labour; rather rare these days. But, as I said, we are a little concerned about her apparent reaction earlier and, as you seem to be the only people she knows and as far as we know the only people who know her, I wanted to ask you about her feelings towards the baby. I see from the notes here that there is no record of the child's father. Can I take it then that this was not a planned pregnancy?" Doctor Bremmer paused a moment and looked first at Peter then at Alice Donne but neither returned his gaze nor an answer to the gently probing question.

"I'm sure that with you and your good sister's help she will be able to cope but...what about her general mental state, Father?" Whatever answer might have been offered to this more probing question was lost as the door to the office sprang open and a breathless nurse burst in.

"Would you please come quickly doctor, it's Miss O'Donnell, she's...well, just come and take a look, would you?"

Doctor Bremmer offered a quick 'excuse me, won't you a moment,' and hurriedly followed the already retreating nurse, carrying the folder of notes with him. The veiled invitation to wait in the office for his return was ignored by the Donnes and an exchange of anxious, almost telepathic glances, was enough to send them after the pair and the two cups of half finished tea spilling onto the green linoleum floor.

Peter and Alice followed the sound of muffled conversation as Doctor Bremmer and the nurse disappeared around a corner of the short, half-lit corridor. It was now late and the hospital was quiet, just an echo of assorted night noise fraying the hush.

The few hospitalised mothers to be were sound asleep, some snoring gently, sending sibilant messages to their unborn infants. In the post-natal ward all was quiet too; tired mums fast sleeping in their beds, dreaming of nappy rash and flat stomachs. All except for Frances. The Donnes caught up with Doctor Bremmer as he emerged from the ward a little red in the face from this unaccustomed haste. He charged the few steps towards the nursery, the white wings of his coat disturbing the still air of the ward, the pince-nez refusing to loosen their grip on a now wildly bouncing perch. The Donnes did their best to keep up with the flying doctor, as did the nurse, but it was he who arrived first at the nursery. He stopped at the viewing window and scanned the cots. Four were full, their young occupants with consciences clear and empty sleeping the sleep of the truly innocent. The fifth cot was vacant. The Donnes saw this and panic sent its cold steel fingers through their aging bodies, cutting through the sinews in their knees and threatening to send them falling to the ground. Peter closed his eyes and mumbled a prayer while Alice gripped his arm and chorused his words. They leant against each other, supported each other as they had always done, like the frail walls of a playing card house. The nurse stifled an expletive while she subconsciously prepared her defence; 'the shifts are too long, there's never enough staff. Christ! are we expected to be everywhere at once?' She ran past the Doctor and the Donnes, through the wide double doors of the nursery, to where her irrationally accusing mind told her she should have been all the time. Doctor Bremmer followed and switched on the overhead lights. Sharp shadows danced from the angles in the room, from the cots and the tables, from the comfortable chairs where mothers fed their infants and the cupboard where the practice bath was kept. Instinctively the nurse opened the cupboard. A life-size doll fell out and she swallowed a scream. One of the sleeping babies turned in its cot but did not call out. There was no sign of Frances or her child. Doctor Bremmer pulled off the pince-nez and scratched his scalp through the thinning hair of his large head.

"You'd better call security, nurse. And get them to call the police. Christ knows where she's taken the baby." He looked back out through the window at the Donnes, at the anguish in their faces and hoped that if Christ didn't know, maybe the Father would. The nurse hurried to the phone on the desk just outside the nursery as Doctor Bremmer made his way out of the room, to ask Father Donne whether, maybe, he knew where Frances might have taken the child.

The nurse picked up the phone and dialled the first two digits of the number that would connect her to security. She stopped before dialling the third. Doctor Bremmer was about to ask the Donnes to return with him to his office but he didn't. He too stopped. They all listened to something that was not the crying of babies or the snoring of mothers or any of the other little noises of the hospital night. It was a song, coming from somewhere at the other end of the corridor. It was still faint but now undoubtedly getting louder. Suddenly a stronger light filled the far end of the corridor as a door on the left opened.

"Hush 'a bye Baby, on the tree top, when the wind blows

the cradle will rock..." Frances emerged from the room, switching off the light as she came out into the corridor. She was holding the baby in her arms, gently rocking it from side to side, her right breast still exposed and the nipple wet and red from the child's suckling. She continued the lullaby, soft and true, as she made her way back towards the nursery. She did not notice the four bemused people staring at her through the renewed dimness of the corridor.

"When the bough breaks the cradle will fall. Down will come baby, cradle and all."

But the cradle did not fall and the baby did not come down. The loud crash that woke the sleeping child was the sound of Father Donne and his sister finally giving in to the laws of physics and gravity.

Chapter Six

The sky above was blue-black and the stars in it shone faintly. There was a smiling crescent of moon low on the horizon, scything the top of a purple coloured hill. Far above and to the east was a much brighter object whose light eclipsed the frail moon and stars and flooded the scene below. The star was huge and its brilliant rays formed distinct points, the lowest of which almost touched the yellow desert behind the stable. From time to time the braying sound of a donkey punctuated the stillness of the tableau. A young girl sat on the scattered straw of the stable floor, her back leaning against a bale, a baby cradled in her arms. The light from the enormous star seemed to focus its power on them, compelling the undivided attention of all who were present. Kneeling before the infant, three bearded men extended gifts to him and his mother, the colour and finery of their dress contrasting sharply with the simple robes of the girl and the swaddling clothes of the infant. Another man, bearded and tall, stood by the girl, his right hand gently touching her shoulder, his eyes fixed firmly on the sleeping child.

The church was full as the organist played the opening bars of the hymn and the congregation stood. Father Donne led the singing, still directing his attention to the wonderful scene that the Sunday school group had worked so hard to perfect this Christmas. Amongst the throng of worshippers in the crowded front pews Frances watched too, her eyes reflecting the bright glow of the arc lights. The idea to use her son instead of the usual doll had been Peter Donne's and Frances had now to admit that it had been a very good idea.

The boy had been perfect. In fact, he had been perfect since the day he was born. Frances wondered now, seeing the whole congregation focus its attention on her child, hearing the rousing chorus of the carol, feeling the warmth of the light from that make believe star, she wondered how she had ever doubted her faith, how she had even contemplated not loving the child, not loving the God that had given him to her. The agonising guilt that had threatened her very sanity had at last been buried and this ceremony, this Christmas celebration was as much a requiem for the fears and doubts of the past.

What nonsense to believe that a school girl prank, an adolescent attempt to draw attention to her pubescent self, should make her responsible for the death of her mother. Even more ridiculous to imagine that the gift of a child should be a punishment. Okay, so the coincidences of dates still remained, but Father Donne had been right, they were just coincidences. Her son had been born on the day she had predicted, he had been conceived on the anniversary of her mother's death, there was no denying that; and yes, she was forty, the age at which her mother had died.

"What of it?" her thoughts formed into words and were out before her mind could slam the door shut. No-one heard or paid any attention to the incongruity. Even the old couple at her elbow were not derailed from the lines of the Christmas hymn whose music poured from the gathering and like soothing balm bathed any remaining wounds of festering doubt. Frances laughed out loud. She could not remember ever having done that before so she laughed again. This time her neighbours on the front pew did notice and gave her a sideways glance but carried on singing. The carol reached its final chorus and Frances added her tiny voice to it. The volume rose disproportionately, filling the little church so that the very air seemed thick with the noise. Through it all the child slept.

* * *

She called the boy Alec. Frances didn't know why, but the name seemed to belong to him and there was no-one to disapprove or to make claims for another title. She had thought of calling him William, after her uncle Bill, but she didn't like the sound of William O'Donnell and babies shouldn't be called Bill, she thought. Besides, the name Alec had an insistence all its own, a good name for a baby boy and one that he would be able to carry into adolescence and adulthood with no problem at all. So, Alec it was and he was now a little over 3 months old, a golden haired infant who, despite his overdue arrival into the world, was perfect. Peter and Alice Donne, were, of course, completely enchanted by the addition to their already enlarged household, insisting that Frances and the child should remain with them for as long as they wished.

The child grew fast, physically and intellectually. His blue eyes deepened becoming almost black, contrasting sharply with his blond hair, and giving him a countenance that commanded attention. As Mrs Sykes, the Donne's cleaning lady remarked, 'he really pays attention when you speak to him, almost as if he knows what you're saying to him'.

It wasn't long before this remark took on a prophetic quality. A few weeks after the Christmas pageant, on January

12th to be precise, the boy uttered his first word. It wasn't 'mum', and not 'dad', of course. It wasn't a name, Peter or Alice or even Frances. It wasn't a plaintive 'more' as he was being fed too slowly for his hunger to accept. No. The boy's first word was 'star', as clear as a bell. He was sitting on Frances' lap at the time and she was reading to him from a picture book about the three wise men. The picture showed the three kings on their way to the manger in Bethlehem. They were riding camels across the cold desert night. The sky above them was a deep dark blue, as deep as the blue of the boy's eyes, and to the east was the star.

Frances had paused for a moment in her reading as she allowed her thoughts to drift back to the church in December, to the marvellous tableau with Alec as the centre of attention and adoration. She looked at her son sitting cosily on her lap, enjoying her warmth and the warmth of the winter fire in the generous hearth of the rectory's living room. He looked back at his mother, his eyes reflecting the flames of the fire, shining as brightly as the light in the picture above the emissaries in the desert. His tiny mouth arched into a smile which revealed his pink gums through which a first tooth was already showing. His small hand reached out toward the open book that his mother held, his index finger stretching to point.

"Star!" he said, clearly and deliberately, shaking his little pointing finger gently at the page. "Star!" he repeated, just to make sure that his mother had heard him. Frances had, of course, heard him the first time, but it had taken a second or two for the event to register. She had for some time suspected that her son was unusually bright and perhaps even a little advanced physically for his young age. He seemed to know what to do all the time, whether it was how to put his body, his limbs, in the right place to help his mother dress him, how to take his food so that there was no mess, how to take her breast milk so that it didn't hurt. Just recently he had begun to crawl and had even made an attempt to stand, using the arm of the softly clad settee in the living room to prop himself up. He had not quite made it but had managed to fall sufficiently gently not to hurt himself. Now he was talking. Not only was he talking but was apparently associating words with pictures in a book. Frances had not yet read the word star to him, nor pointed it out. The boy had recognised the image and had used the correct word for it. Frances didn't know precisely at what age babies were supposed to do this but she was sure that it wasn't usually this early. She decided to reopen the baby books that had been bought for her by the Donnes and which had lain mostly unread for most of the child's young life; after all, he seemed to know instinctively what to do even if Frances didn't.

The door to the rectory living room opened and Alice popped her head round it.

"I've run the bath for Alec," she said, "Would you like to bring him up in a minute or two?"

"Thanks, Alice. Yes, of course, I'll bring him up now." Frances closed the picture book and put it down on the table beside her, cradling the child in her other arm. She stood carefully, coping with the weight of the boy against her body. He was heavy but not overweight, but she determined to check the expected height and weight graphs in the baby book. She did not say anything to Alice about the boy's first word. It made her feel uneasy, perhaps confirming her growing suspicion that there was something unusual about Alec. She refused to sanction the word 'abnormal', but it was there, in the back of her mind, as she walked towards the door and the smiling Alice. Frances returned the smile and was grateful that the older woman did not seem to have noticed the flash of concern on her face as she stood up from the chair.

"Would you like me to take him up? You look a bit tired, dear," Alice enquired gently, obviously not as insensitive to her concerns as Frances had imagined.

* * *

Two weeks later Alec did walk. He was playing in his room as Frances tidied his cot. On the carpeted floor lay the pieces of a puzzle, a big chunky puzzle of about a dozen pieces that formed a picture of a spaceship, one of the rescue vehicles from Thunderbirds. Alec liked watching the television and he had quickly learned how to turn it on and which channel to select for Thunderbirds. He also seemed to know when to do this. Frances again said nothing about it to the Donnes, although she had begun to keep a note of this and a number of other events that her reading of the baby books convinced her were evidence of her son's 'unusual' qualities. The puzzle on the floor was almost complete. It had taken Alec less than a minute to fit the pieces together. There had been no forcing, no attempt to persuade the shapes to coalesce against their will. One piece was missing. It lay beneath the cot his mother was still busily tidying a few feet away from the boy. Alec rested his hand on the large chest that contained most of his toys. He pressed down, firmly planting his feet beneath him, and stood. He did not wobble and did not stumble as he took his first assured step in his mother's direction, his eyes fixed on the last piece of the puzzle. Five small but sure strides later he was at his mother's side. She had not heard him and was startled by the little tug on her cardigan.

"Last piece!" Alec said confidently, holding the contoured puzzle showing the nose cone of a green rocket, smiling at his bewildered mother. He let go of her cardigan, turned and walked back to the unfinished picture on the floor. He knelt down to gently push the last piece home, stood triumphantly and said, "It's finished now."

Frances quickly walked over to the boy, picked him up and engulfed him in a long and tender hug. She also started to cry, not knowing whether to be delighted by this literal new step in her son's spectacular progress or be scared by it. He was already taller than he should be, had begun to put sentences together far sooner than could reasonably be expected, apparently understood the functions of the television controls and now was able to walk like a toddler at the age of 4 months! She would have to discuss this with the Donnes, who, it would appear, had not registered any reaction to any of these phenomena, yet had surely witnessed some of them. So too, thought Frances, had Mrs Sykes. What might her reaction be?

* * *

Alec was in bed and, as usual, he was asleep within a few minutes. He never woke up during the night, even during his first few days at home. He needed no night feed, yet suckled heartily from his mother's breast as soon as he could the next morning. Now he was on a more solid intake, yet the pattern remained the same. He would eat all his food with no fuss, no mess. His early teething caused no apparent distress and at 4 months and a few days he could boast with an ever wider and whiter smile at least half a dozen good strong milk teeth. His early steps had quickly developed into a sturdy gait and he outgrew his baby clothes at such a rate that the local jumble sales were a regular venue on his mother's occasional sorties.

The winter had been very cold and for several days the church spire and lead roof sported a topping of snow. Alec was rarely taken from the warmth of the rectory to accompany his mother on her visits and even on fairly warm days she preferred to leave him at home in the care of the Donnes. Why? Had she really thought about it Frances would probably have rediscovered the word "abnormal" which refused to abandon its perch in the rafters of her brain. She did not know many of the church's neighbours. Truth told, she didn't know any, but maybe they knew her, were aware of the baby born with no father. They must have known she was living at the rectory. Were they also aware of her son's unusual qualities, his rapid growth into a toddler of 4 months, his precocious linguistic ability? She was glad that the health visitor had come to the rectory early in the boy's short life. The woman, a district nurse in stiff blue uniform, had been coldly professional in her inspection of the child and his mother. To Frances, it seemed as if the nurse was almost passing judgement, that she knew that Frances had no idea who the child's father was and some of her old fears re-emerged. Perhaps she was just being a little paranoid, worried that the nurse might pick up on her son's 'oddness'. But she didn't. The boy had behaved perfectly normally and his size was, according to the nurse, only slightly off the scale.

When Frances thought about this visit later, Alec's normal behaviour struck her as in itself odd, as if the boy had understood that the nurse would be expecting to see a 12 week old infant doing the things that 12 week old infants do. That is to say, not very much. He did not crawl around his cot on his hands and knees, nor did he pull himself up by the barred sides of the cot and stand, holding on with one hand. With the other he would take hold of the plastic characters of the mobile hung above the cot and, apparently, count them; not in words but in still baby-like mumblings, each mumble matching the number of mobiles passed through his hands. At the end of the visit Alec and Frances were given a clean bill of health with the only feature worthy of comment the child's rapid but apparently healthy growth rate. As soon as Frances had said goodbye to the health visitor she returned to the bedroom to find Alec standing in his cot, holding on to the side of it, passing the mobiles through his tiny hand and mumbling his primitive count.

* * *

Steam hissed from the neat pattern of holes in its base like a sudden intake of breath as Frances placed the iron back on its stand. The last of the pile of shirts, mostly Peter's black ones, lay on the ironing board, smooth and shiny, except for the creased fabric of one sleeve. She picked up the hot iron again, the steam spitting this time as she worked the iron over the cotton of the shirt. Alice had finished putting the crockery away and turned, smiling, to face Frances.

"Thanks, Frances. I hate ironing and I can never get the shirts to look like that. I'm sure Peter will appreciate the difference, although he wouldn't tell me that of course."

Frances ignored the remark. For her the ironing had not been a chore, more a period of reflection, a time to think about the last few months and what she would say to Peter. As she folded the last shirt she believed that her thoughts were in order; that any kinks in the logic of her thinking had been 'ironed out'. She smiled at the pun. Alice understood the smile as a response to her compliment.

Peter was in his small study at the back of the rectory. This was where he did his thinking, normally with a bible and a notebook in his hand rather than an iron. He was, as usual at this time of the week, preparing his sermon for the next service. This ritual, the writing of the sermon, he had never found difficult, but since the boy's birth the words seemed to flow as if they were guided by another's hand and thought. The priest's belief in the boy was growing stronger. He knew that Alec was different. He had seen the changes in him, the physical and intellectual transformation over such a short period of time. Now that the boy was half a year old (much more appropriate than six months, he thought), and was using a vocabulary rarely seen in a 5 year old, something would have to be said, or planned, or… He didn't really know what. Now Alec walked, not crawled or stumbled clinging on to one piece of furniture after another, into his study.

"Hello, father!" said the boy. "What are you doing?

"I'm preparing a sermon for tomorrow's mass, Alec. Look, I'm writing some notes in this book."

Alec took the book from the desk top and turned a page or two. Peter brushed the boy's long blond hair with his hand as he did so. The boy's deep blue eyes burned into the page of the note book. They scanned the lines of neatly written script, stopping only occasionally to ponder an obscure stroke of the pen. He continued to look at the page for a moment or two then turned it over to follow the writing on the next page. Peter watched in admiration at the boy's curiosity about the shapes and symbols on the paper, but expecting him to tire of the activity and to quickly give the book back.

"What does 'dilemma' mean, father?"

A blurted 'what!' was the only reply as Peter took off his glasses to stare incredulously at Alec, who was still holding the book with one hand and pointing to the elusive word with the index finger of the other.

"Dilemma, Father, what does it mean?" Alec politely repeated his question, terminated this time by an obvious concern in his voice for the poor man's sudden lack of complexion.

"I'm sorry, Alec. Eh…Dilemma, yes, um, well it means… a problem, something that you are concerned about. When you don't know what to do next."

"I understand," Alec offered calmly, touching the seated priest on the shoulder, as if to ensure himself that he was alright. Satisfied that he was, he put the book carefully back on the desk, said 'thank you', and walked off again.

The priest took the book from the desk where it lay open, his hurried handwriting testament to the torrent that had filled his head earlier. Now he was lost for words. Except perhaps for one. 'Dilemma', was all he could think of as he turned the word round in his mind, examining, investigating it. A Latin word, of course, dilemma. How was Alec able to read the word, to say it correctly? How did he manage to pick it out from all the other words that, it would appear, he had been able to read and understand? The words of a favourite song gently nudged his thoughts, 'there are more questions than answers…' How true, he conceded, closing the notebook before settling back in his chair, his bible in his hand, in quiet, perplexed contemplation.

* * *

The days began to lengthen as Spring slowly uncoiled itself, chasing the snow from the rectory roof, replaced by the shine of April showers on the grey slate tiles. Alec was in the garden, looking first at the sky, then at the grass and early flowers that coloured the ground, then back at the sky. Frances watched him from the kitchen window, her head cocked to one side and her mouth arched into a smile, as she absent-mindedly washed the breakfast dishes. It was, of course, impossible to believe that in a little over 6 months the baby had developed the physical attributes of a 3 year old. As for his mental capacity, she dared not even think about it. What was he doing, out there in the garden? What was he thinking about? He had taken to watching television. Not just Thunderbirds, which, it seems, he now found too childish and implausible. 'But how can they keep it a secret for so long?' he had asked her one evening. 'People can keep secrets for a very long time, darling,' she had replied, stroking his hair, the stark irony of the reply lost on the boy but not on his mother. No, not just Thunderbirds. Alec had taken to watching documentaries, mostly about science and his particular favourite was Tomorrow's World. The programme would begin at 7 in the evening and Alec would sit, cross legged, on the floor in front of the television, his eyes not leaving the screen for a moment throughout the whole event. There seemed little point in Frances, or the Donnes for that matter, telling him not to sit too close to the screen. He would know whether it was safe or not, the adults of the house knew that. Neither was it necessary to tell Alec when to go to bed; when, or indeed how, to brush his teeth. Potty training? Alec had stopped using, needing, nappies at four months, at which time he declared himself fully house trained by removing a dry nappy, putting it into the bathroom linen basket and directing his amber flow into the toilet bowl. He then began to pull the handle but stopped to look at his astonished mother before completing the manoeuvre.

"I'm not strong enough yet, Mother," he said. This did little to nullify the stupefaction on her face. "Would you do it for me?"

Chapter Seven

The boy's physical and mental growth continued unabated, a fact that was evidenced in an extraordinary way on his first birthday. A week or so earlier Frances was helping Peter prepare for the first mass of the day. She held the silk sash that he liked to wear, waiting for him to don his black cassock, feeling the smoothness of the silk and bathing in a warm glow of contentment. The past six months, peppered by a series of astonishing advances by the boy, had passed without any particular comment. Somehow neither Frances nor the Donnes had found the moment to bring up the child's unusual qualities. This tacit agreement to ignore the blatantly obvious was in itself extraordinary; as if some compulsion had forced their minds and their tongues not to raise questions to which there were only difficult and improbable, perhaps even frightening answers. The contentment that Frances felt, caressing the silk between her fingers, owed much to the velvet shackles restraining a small army of 'whys' that fought endlessly to release themselves into the battlefield of her mind.

"Have you ever been across the Channel, to France I mean?" said the good Father casually as the cassock finally found its way over his head, gently dislodging his glasses on its way. At first Frances was not sure that the question had been directed at her, but it was and she answered calmly.

"No, Father, I haven't." She thought for a bit as the priest continued to adjust his glasses and his cassock, finally managing to achieve some equilibrium with both. "They once arranged a day trip at Adrian's place, you know, where I used to work. A sort of staff day out. I decided not to go. I'm not sure why but I was always a bit of a stick in the mud. I never really got involved in things like that."

Suddenly she felt her mood change as a 'why' pushed harder against its bindings in an effort to break through. One last push and it was out. Peter looked at her, a little perplexed in a struggle against a 'why' of his own. 'Why was she crying?' he thought but did not yet ask.

"I'm sorry father, I'm being a little silly, but I suddenly started thinking of what I was like, what life was like before Alec was born. Why didn't I want to go to France with the people from the office? You know my father died in France on the day the war ended, the day I was born." She paused, deep in contemplation, her face gently wet with the trickle of tears.

"Yes, I know your father died when the war ended but I didn't know it was in France. But that was a long time ago now, Frances and ..." She put a hand on his arm to stop him before continuing:

"You're right of course, but, I don't know, maybe I was afraid that I would come across the ghost of my dead father. Although how I would recognise him I just don't know. I've never seen a picture of him. My mother never kept any in the house. It's strange, isn't it, Alec has never seen a picture of his father either and I ..." This time it was Peter's turn to interject:

"Look, I think it's about time we laid this particular ghost to rest. Alice and I would like you and the boy to come to France with us for a little bit of a holiday. Just a couple of days in

Boulogne. Would you like that now? Besides, Alice is keen to practise the French she's been learning from those tapes of hers. You must have heard her."

* * *

Yes, Frances had heard her listening to and repeating from the cassettes that she had bought some months before. Alec had frequently gone to sit with Alice as she listened and mimicked the strange sounds the machine produced. He never said anything apart from once asking Alice what she was doing.

"I'm trying to learn some French," she said, smiling at him, not at all sure whether this rather prosaic answer would satisfy him. Her smile became quizzical as she turned her head to one side to look at the boy, expecting him to say 'what's French?', but he didn't. He just smiled back in the disarming way that his infant features had developed. In her subconscious mind Alice struggled to suppress a plethora of questions, but nothing formed itself into a coherent enquiry. "I've always wanted to," she continued, "and with mummy helping me a lot more in the house now, I have the time to do it."

The boy demanded no further explanation and sat back on the settee next to Alice as she repeated each phrase several times. "Je voudrais un kilo de bananes, je voudrais un kilo de bananes…….."

* * *

September 3rd soon came and an early start was the order of the day if the Donnes, Frances and Alec were to catch the 7 o'clock ferry from Dover. Alec did not need any encouragement to leave the warmth of his bed and was up and dressed as the alarm sang out at the side of his mother's bed.

"Come on Mother, we'll have to go soon," he said as she blearily peered out from under the covers, stretching her arms around him.

"Happy birthday, son." She squeezed him as hard as she could, forgetting that the birthday in question was his first.

* * *

The Donne's car joined the queue for the passport control box. Alec sat with his mother in the back seat, manifesting his excitement by the occasional question.

"Why do we have to show a passport, Mother?" he said as Frances took hers from her duffle bag and handed it to Peter in the driver's seat. Alec's question did not prompt an immediate answer from Frances, at least not an answer that was intelligible. A sharp intake of breath, as if she had been punched in the solar plexus was all that escaped from her lips. Alice turned round, a look of some concern on her face.

"Are you all right, dear?" she enquired sympathetically. Three other cars now separated the Donnes from the control booth. The first in line moved off, through the upraised barrier, a young child in the back waving happily to the car now fronting the queue. Ignoring the urgency of Alice's question, Frances finally blurted a reply to Alec's seemingly innocuous enquiry; a reply that was still not quite clear in its intent.

"The passport!" she exclaimed. Peter and Alice gave each other a rapid sideways glance. "Alec's age; he's only one year old!" Of course, he was only a year old and today was his birthday, his first birthday. Peter was gently nudging the car forward, just behind the car at the front. The impact of what Frances was saying had not struck him until now; it's importance provoking a literal knee jerk stomp on the brake pedal. The sudden halt threw Alice, Frances and Alec sharply forward in their seats. Thankfully they were secured by their seat belts. Nonetheless, the jolt shocked them all.

"What is it, Peter?" Alice gasped, rubbing her chest where the belt had bitten hard.

"The passport, Frances' passport. Alec is only one, but he isn't. I mean; he looks like a 5 year old. What will they say?"

The car ahead had been given back its clutch of passports and was cheerily revving its way forward. An impatient beep from a van behind the Donnes prompted Peter to move the group, now deep in troubled thought, alongside the control booth. As Peter took hold of the handle to wind down his side window, Alec broke the sombre silence.

"Don't worry," he said calmly, "The policeman won't even look at the passport." Before the three adults in the car had had time to respond to the boy's certainty, the window was down and a large, stubby hand thrust itself towards them in tacit demand of the passports. The arm on the end of the hand led to an equally stubby passport controller whose uniform fitted him as tightly as he fitted the narrow control booth. The man opened the first two passports, those of Peter and Alice Donne, bent his corpulent body so that he could scrutinise the faces at the front of the small car and made no comment. Peter wore civvies, of course. Any chance that the group would be hastened through on the wings of a dog collar had been left in the linen basket back at the rectory. Apparently satisfied that the faces in the front seats of the car matched those in the passports, the man handed them back, with the third passport unopened and unscrutinised.

Peter took the three passports and handed them to Alice at his side. He didn't say anything; neither did Alice. Neither did he move off towards the ferry and the car remained in neutral, the idling engine providing the only accompaniment to an otherwise bizarrely silent scene. The spell was broken by the noisy van behind whose horn found full voice, its impatient owner mouthing an obscenity as he depressed the klaxon once again.

"We can move off now, father," said Alec, maintaining his usual calmness despite the noise behind and the perplexed silence of the other occupants of the car.

"Yes," replied Peter, pushing the gear lever forward into a reluctant first and managing, just, to guide the car through the barrier.

* * *

The ferry crossing was pleasant and passed without further incident, except to say that conversation was intermittent if not completely absent. Alec still asked his myriad questions; 'why did the seagulls follow the boat all the time? How fast was the boat travelling? Did the wind speed make a difference to when they would arrive?' Somehow, though, he seemed to understand that his scientific inquisition would, for the moment, have to remain unanswered.

* * *

Even without his dog collar and priestly garb it seemed that God still recognised his loyal servant and Peter managed to find an unlikely parking spot behind the church.

The market lay a street or so away, easy enough to find by following the growing throng of locals and late season tourists. A few obviously very early risers fought against the flow, on their way home with bags replete.

Alice was particularly looking forward to showing off her French and essayed a silent practice in her head as the small group joined the throng. Frances held Alec's hand as tightly as she could, fearful that the boy might lose himself amongst the solid mass of people that funnelled into the ever narrower streets before emerging into a sunlit market square. The group stopped on the pavement's edge, not to wait for cars to pass before crossing because here, there were none; the market square spared the danger and pollution of the motor car on market days. They stood on the kerb, taking it all in, as the growing torrent of shoppers continued around them. The noise, the sights, the sheer vibrancy of the place excited them all. On the opposite corner to where they stood was a small café, awning down to shelter its customers from the sharply angled light of the September sun. The few tables and chairs outside on the pavement already hosted a mixed clientele, although there was one table free. The alluring smell of freshly ground coffee was too much for Peter to ignore and the group agreed to join the people watchers under the shaded awning.

* * *

"Garçon!" Alice called slightly self-consciously, raising a gentle hand to support her first foray into French for real. The waiter, iconically mustachioed and neatly dressed in black and white, strode quickly to their table with pen and pad at the ready:

"Oui, Madame. Que désirez-vous?"

"What would you all like to drink?" Alice interpreted, pleased that the waiter's question had been a simple one. Peter and Frances both wanted a coffee and Alice reminded them that if they wanted it with milk she would need to ask for it explicitly, otherwise it would be strong, black and served in a very small cup.

"Trois grand cafés au lait, s'il vous plaît," she ordered with polite confidence.

"Et pour le jeune homme?" said the waiter, turning towards Alec.

"Je voudrais une glace au chocolat, s'il vous plaît," replied 'le jeune homme' without any hesitation and with little evidence of an English accent.

"Très bien. Alors, trois cafés au lait et une glace au chocolat. Tout de suite, mesdames et messieurs," and off he went, disappearing quickly into the shade of the café, completely unaware of the mental mayhem he had left behind.

The three adults at the table fell once more into the same astonished mutism that followed the extraordinary happenings at the passport control point. Alec preferred to study the menu that lay on the table, noticing that the left hand side offered an English translation of the French displayed on the right. Unabashed by the stupor that his linguistic feat had provoked, he broke the silence with a smile and an observation:

"Here comes the waiter!"

"Voilà! Trois café au lait, et une glace au chocolat pour le garçon."

"Merci, monsieur," Alec replied amid the continued indolence of his adult companions as he picked up his ice-cream. "This is nice," he continued, scooping the dark brown mixture from the tub with the little wooden spoon.

"Good," said his mother at last, "I'm just going to find the toilets."

"Me too," said Alice hurriedly.

"Okay," Peter offered in weak response, mechanically reaching out for his coffee as if reaching for a straw to cling to in his troubled sea of emotions. He sipped the black liquid, not realising that the milk of his 'café au lait' remained unused in a small jug on the table. He continued to sip absent-mindedly, lost in confused and confusing thought.

* * *

"Les toilettes, s'il vous plaît?" Alice enquired at the bar.

"Là-bas, au coin, Madame," replied the barman, pointing to the far corner of the café.

The toilet was clean and, more importantly, large enough for the two women to enter together, with two cubicles side by side. In typical French fashion, there was no separation of the sexes and opposite the cubicles three urinals stood unashamedly against the tiled wall. Thankfully, there were no men making use of them at the moment, sparing any prudish English blushes, but also leaving them free to talk, the real reason why they had left the terraced table in such a hurry. Alice tried to begin, but her words were incoherent, making no discernible sense.

"I know, Alice," said Frances, seeming to understand the thoughts behind the babble of incoherence. "We've never talked about this before. Why? Why haven't we been able to even mention the things that Alec does? The fact that he is one year old but looks, and acts, as if he were much older. Why haven't you or Peter ever said anything? Why haven't I said anything?

How can he speak French, let alone English at his age?" By now she was almost shouting, with tears starting a steady stream down her cheek.

Alice found a clean white handkerchief in her pocket and handed it to Frances, grateful to have something to do, if not yet able to find an answer, any answer, to the many questions the boy's mother had raised. In truth, she could add a dozen more questions that defied a logical response. She put her arms around Frances whose stifled sobs were the only sound now to be heard until a self-cleaning gush of water from the urinals broke the reverie.

* * *

Alec had finished his ice-cream by the time Alice and Frances returned to the terrace table. The coffee was still warm, just, and the warmed milk in the jug helped to keep it from being too cold to drink, although in their current state of mind, the two women would not have noticed. Nor did they notice the man in the raincoat approaching the table from the other side of the street, until he spoke to them.

"Excuse the interruption," he said, putting a hand on the back of Alec's chair and leaning forward slightly. "I'm a journalist and I'm researching an article about English people buying property in France. You know, what they like about the French way of life. What they don't like about England. You know the sort of thing. I wondered if that's why you were here?"

He looked inquiringly at the three adults, one after the other, almost imploring an answer from them. At last Peter provided one.

"No, sorry, but we're just here on a short holiday. With our, er, daughter and grandson."

The journalist didn't catch the sideways glance that this voluntary falsehood provoked from his 'wife' and his 'daughter'. His 'grandson' ignored the remark as the man turned to him and said:

"And how old are you, son?"

"He's 5!" Frances roared, almost hysterically. Unfortunately, it was at exactly the same time that Alice exclaimed:

"He's 6!"

Thankfully, Peter was prepared to add to the tissue of lies by saying that the boy was 5 yesterday and it was his 6th birthday today. That's why they were in France, to celebrate the boy's 6th birthday; Peter drew another thread through the weave.

"I see," said the man, who seemed not to have noticed the hysteria in the women's voices. "Well, it's been nice talking to you and I hope you have a good holiday. And 'happy birthday' son. My name's Peter Sayers, by the way. Maybe I'll bump into you again while you're here. Au revoir!" With that, he turned and left them, unaware, just as the waiter had been earlier, that this seemingly insignificant conversation should leave the little 'family' in such confusion.

"Sorry!" Frances was the first to say. "I didn't think. It just came out that he was 5. I couldn't tell the man the truth, of course."

"Me neither," Alice concurred.

"Likewise," agreed Peter, a little mournfully. After all, he wasn't in the business of telling lies. At least, not ones he didn't believe in. "Let's go and find our hotel. This holiday is going to be more difficult than I thought."

Chapter Eight

It is six months since the French excursion and winter has given way to an early spring. Frances treads across the yellow-specked green swathe of grass which carpets the local park; daffodils pushing their flower heads towards the light. Her left hand is held tightly by her son who walks in easy step with his mother. She looks down at him and is no longer surprised to see that the top of his blond-brown head is now at her shoulder. The calendar would have her believe that he is 18 months old. Any passer-by would recognise a 7 or 8 year old. Were they to hear him speak he would pass for a young adult. He has no formal schooling; yet ... Frances tries to stop thinking about this, but she cannot. Her head fills with the boy's astonishing achievements; his ability to read, to write, to calculate, to speak French simply by sitting with Alice Donne while she listens to those language cassettes. Mostly, she thinks about where all this will lead and an ice cold shiver freezes her spine and their passage across the grass. She has decided that it is time to question the boy herself; the walk in the park an excuse to find time and space away from the rectory and the Donnes. Despite the brief catalogue of questions which found voice in a French toilet, the return to England merely provoked a return to mutism as far as Alec and his 'gifts' were concerned. Away from the 'family', perhaps Frances would find the determination to seek answers to the enigma that was her son.

"Alec," she says, turning towards him, laying both hands gently on his youthful shoulders, "I want to ask you something." She stops to take a deep breath, afraid that a next step will see her out of her depth, drowning in a miasmic sea of confused feelings and unanswerable questions. Her lips contort in an effort to find an opening gambit but before she can speak again another voice draws their attention.

"Hello!" says a man in a light raincoat, "I'm sorry to interrupt but haven't we met somewhere before?"

"I don't think so," Frances retorts, trying hard to keep her annoyance at this interruption under control. Alec looks at the man and Frances feels a discernable tightening of his grip on her hand. The man looks at Alec, a friendly smile playing on his lips in an apparent effort to temper the awkwardness of the situation, perhaps realising that his approach was less than appropriate. He decides to introduce himself:

"My name is Peter Sayers. I'm a journalist. I'm on my way to the tube station, then up to London."

Alec's hand tightens even further, almost cutting off the blood supply to his mother's fingers.

"I don't know why, but I am sure we have met before," the journalist adds in gentle prompt. "I remember now," he says triumphantly, in response to his own prompting. "France, last year. You were with your parents and your son. How is he by the way?"

"I'm sorry, but you must be mistaken. I've never been to France before. I must go now, we're late for school."

She turns her back on the man, pulling Alec in her wake, and heads in retreat towards the rectory, her long awaited tête-à-tête with the boy postponed once more. The journalist looks on as mother and child head off, back in the direction he had clearly seen them coming from. Had the woman somehow forgotten where the school was? Hardly likely he surmises, and is convinced that they had met in France when he was writing a feature about English people moving there. He looks again at the boy whose back is rapidly retreating towards the park exit. He can't be the same boy he had met in France, probably the elder brother, although he looks remarkably familiar, just as the mother does. 'She's hiding something,' an internal voice vocalises what he senses is now apparent. Journalistic instinct kicks in and he smells a story here somewhere. The tube ride to London can wait and he too changes direction towards the park exit, being careful to stay far enough behind his quarry so as not to be seen.

* * *

The coins dropped into the slot and Peter dialled the number, still looking out of the grimy windows of the phone booth at the large house next to the church, conveniently just fifty yards or so away.

"Hello, Maggie. Can you put me through to the boss? It's Peter." The line went dead for a while as Maggie made the connection to the paper's editor. A gruff but avuncular voice finally broke the mechanical silence:

"Peter, where are you? Briefing in ten minutes, old son!"

"Sorry, boss, but I won't be able to make that. I think I might be on to something. I'm not sure what yet, but it's a hunch that might be worth playing. Can you ask Jenny to look up something for me, probably in those medical dictionaries or the encyclopaedias we have in the library."

"Sure. What is it?"

"I can't remember the name, but there's some disease or

condition that children get that makes them age rapidly. I might be totally off track here, but it could be worth a look."

* * *

The mother and boy had walked quickly away from the park and down the tree-lined street towards a church whose brick-built spire climbed resolutely into the morning sky where a few greyish clouds threatened the odd spring shower. She had lied rather unconvincingly, she was sure, to the journalist and paranoia began to spread its pernicious tentacles in her mind. She was sure he had followed them. But why would he? What could he possibly suspect?

Father Donne opened the rectory door and Frances almost fell in, pulling Alec along with her. Doing her best to remain calm and unruffled, she began to explain to Peter Donne the encounter with the reporter in the park and his insistence that they had met before.

"He remembered me from our time in France, Father," she said, her voice just managing a thin veneer of composure. "He looked at Alec, but I don't think he recognised him. After all, he is several inches taller now. But I shouldn't have rushed off the way I did; I panicked Father, I didn't know what to say. He asked how Alec was, not knowing that he was looking at him." The veneer was beginning to show signs of wear and the priest decided it was time to interject.

"I'm sure there's nothing to worry about, Frances. You've done nothing wrong and what could he possibly suspect?" he echoed Frances' earlier hope. "But I think it wise to stay home for a while, keep the boy in."

"Yes, Father. But..." She didn't finish the sentence, once

again prevented from voicing the many questions and concerns about her son by something she could not grasp. The questions banged around in her head until it ached and a solitary tear rolled down her cheek.

"Come on, Frances. Time for a cup of tea and a sit down," said Peter as he led her and the boy into the comfort of the living room. Alec still held his mother's hand but said nothing as was always his way when he sensed that his mother was upset. He sat with her on the settee in the living room whilst the Father sought the palliative cup of tea. Frances stared silently through the wide bay-window which fronted the rectory. The threat of a shower had been realised as heavy spring drops, driven by a sudden squall, splattered noisily onto the panes of glass. Suddenly the boy stood up, provoking a quick intake of breath as Frances contemplated his physical presence. As she sat on the settee, this boy who should be crawling looked down on her. He took his mother's hands in his and lifted them up slightly before speaking:

"It's all going to be alright, mother, I promise you, it's all going to be alright." Frances said nothing in reply. There was nothing to say. The boy had been categorical in his assertion that all would be well, and why should she disbelieve him?

* * *

"Progeria, that's what it's called," exclaimed Jenny Bolton triumphantly, thrusting the large open volume of the Encyclopaedia Britannica on her young colleague's already burdened desk. "It says here that it's a genetic condition in which children show symptoms of aging when they are very young. It's very rare with only one baby in every 8 million born with the condition. Just as well as otherwise they'd all be claiming a pension before they were six!" Jenny's attempt at humour went unacknowledged by Sayers who was more interested in reading the article for himself.

"Go make us a cup of tea, will you Jenny. Oh, and thanks for finding this for me." The girl reluctantly did as she was told, mumbling something thankfully inaudible as she sulked off. Sayers read on … *most affected children had a life span of around 13 years… genetic condition …scientists particularly interested because it might reveal clues about the normal aging process… mental development is not affected …aging six to eight times faster than normal.*

By the time Jenny had returned with the solicited tea, the journalist had gone, as had the book.

* * *

"Come!" coughed Bill Tyne through a haze of cigarette smoke. "Ah, Peter. What have you come up with then? Anything we can use?" he continued as Sayers marched purposefully into the editor's office. He positioned the book on the desk, being careful not to dislodge the over-filled ash-tray which sat precariously close to the edge of the desk.

"Have a look at this, boss, I don't know whether there's anything in it but it might just be that we've stumbled across a very rare medical case that might be worth a page or two." He waited while his boss scanned the article, ready and eager to explain the connection between this rare condition and the mother and boy in the park. By now, he had convinced himself that the boy was the very same child whose mother and grandmother had excitedly exclaimed a 5th or 6th birthday just 6 months ago. "The boy looked at least eight years old, possibly even older," he said in support of his theory. "What do you think? I'm sure the mother has something to hide. Worth a knock on their door?"

* * *

"Answer that, would you Alice. I'm just in the middle of something," Peter Donne called to his ever obliging sister as the doorbell rang. Alice put down her mixing bowl full of shortbread dough that would soon turn into delicious biscuits, wiped her hands on a nearby tea cloth and willingly did her brother's bidding.

"Hello! I'm sorry to trouble you but I wonder if I could speak briefly to your daughter?" said the man in the raincoat. "Sorry, I should explain. Do you remember? We met in France, last September I think it was. You were with your daughter and your grandson at a café. I thought you might be looking to buy property in France, but you were just there for your grandson's birthday."

Alice hoped that the blood draining from her face wasn't as obvious to the man standing in front of her as it was to her from inside her skin.

"Peter Sayers," he continued, seeming to ignore the signs of stress on the woman's face and holding out a hand as a gesture of formal introduction. Alice shook the hand weakly and absent-mindedly, still silently searching for the right thing to say. She knew who he was before he announced himself, of course. She did remember him from France even before Frances had told her and Peter about the incident in the park. She remembered how they had almost got into a complete muddle over whether it was Alec's 5th or 6th birthday. Was she now going to lie to the man's face and insist that he was mistaken?

"Yes, hello," she said finally, rejecting the path of deceit. "I remember you. It was the boy's birthday," she added, regaining her composure momentarily now that the need for mendacity had passed. "I'm sorry, but my daughter is out with her son. They've gone to see a film," she lied, vaguely amused at how quickly our needs change, and also forgetting that most children of Alec's age, at least his assumed age, would be in school at 11 o'clock on a Tuesday morning. The man seemed about to say something but changed his mind. Alice seized the opportunity to take some control of the conversation. "What is it you want to speak to my daughter about?"

"Well, as I said, when I met you in France I was writing an article about the English buying property abroad, particularly in France, of course. I'd like to do a follow up on the English attitude towards learning a foreign language and I remember that the little boy spoke quite good French. I thought it might be useful to talk to your daughter, and perhaps your grandson, about how he has learnt French. Is his father French?"

Alice regretted her question and her assumption that it would be possible to take control of the conversation and the situation. Reluctant to add to the lies, she replied simply that the boy's father was not French.

"Right," he said, expecting a follow up which did not arrive. "Eh, he speaks very good French. Did he learn it at school?"

"No, he is learning with me, from cassettes we both listen to. He seems to have a knack for picking up words." This was no lie, more an understatement, Alice thought, pleased that the truth took centre stage once again.

"Very impressive! You must be very proud of him."

"Yes, we all are."

"Well, if she's not in now I'd better get going. When would be a good time to call back?"

"I'm sorry, but I don't think my daughter would like to be interviewed. She's really quite shy and I'm sure she wouldn't want Alec to answer any questions; he's far too young."

"Sure, I understand. Look, if she changes her mind or wants to talk to me about Alec, here's my card. She can get me on that number any time. Please pass this on. I really do want to talk to her about Alec." He stretched out his hand offering the printed business card to a reluctant Alice. "Please," he urged, "you never know. She may be pleased to talk to someone about the boy."

Alice took the card, intending to throw it away once the man had gone. But there was something about his demeanour that hovered somewhere between danger and help. It was clear to Alice that he knew, or thought he knew, more than he was letting on. But what could that be?

"Thank you," she said, "I'll pass this on to Frances, my daughter," she added with an involuntary excess of emphasis. The man thanked her for her time and turned to walk out through the iron gate that separated the house from the pavement. He glanced back before stepping through the gate and noticed that the woman remained on the door step. Her head was lowered and she seemed to be studying carefully the name and telephone number on the card, but the journalist could, nonetheless, make out the deep worry lines now etched on her forehead. He was more certain than ever that there was a story to be had somewhere in this suburban rectory.

* * *

"I'll be off now, Father," said Mrs Sykes as she closed the door of the small cupboard that housed the vacuum cleaner when it wasn't in use.

"Thank you, Mrs Sykes," replied the priest mechanically, his thoughts deep in the mire of the unexplained, the inexplicable puzzle that Alec posed. His faith told him to believe that the boy was a God-given miracle, whose gifts were not to be questioned but accepted unequivocally. After all, the Church that he represented asked as much of its devotees, expecting and even demanding a blindness of faith that defied logic and challenge. But now he felt challenged. He wanted to question and to talk about the boy with his mother. There were so many things that needed an explanation. Faith, it seems, was no longer enough. He took off his glasses and rubbed the bridge of his nose as if it were a magic lantern that would produce a genie to grant the simple wish that he, Alice and Frances would be able to discuss the problem that was Alec. It was hard to believe that the boy and his mother had come into their lives little more than a year and a half ago, but that was an empirical fact and no question of belief. Something now had to be done.

The arrival of the journalist had shaken them all. Then there was the problem of Mrs Sykes. Why, Peter Donne asked himself, had *she* not said anything. Although a woman whose constant focus was on keeping the rectory and the church as clean as a new pin, she was not blind and certainly not stupid. Yet, she, like the rest of the household, made no reference to the fact of an 18 month old toddler striding around in the skin of an eight year old. The priest had no doubt that Alec possessed an ability to throw some kind of psychological blanket over people he came into contact with, to maybe even control their thoughts. The recent incident with the passports sprang immediately to mind, but other occasions proffered their evidence now that Father Donne thought about it. The district nurse, for instance, whose one and only visit to the boy and his mother provoked no enquiry into his impossibly rapid physical and mental development.

Added to the mystery of the boy himself was the history of his mother. It seemed a long time ago now that she had made her confession to him about her own mother and the peculiar coincidences of dates that peppered her life. Was she truly chosen to be this boy's mother? Faith might say 'yes', but logic pushed its way ever further into the priest's consciousness. 'Surely not', he reasoned, letting logic gain the upper hand; 'surely the dates, bizarre as they seem, are a complete coincidence. After all, who would be doing the choosing?' Then he remembered the day the boy was born and the euphoria he had felt, certain in his belief that something miraculous had happened. Faith was not slow in providing an obvious answer to his question. He prayed that God would guide him now.

* * *

"The Lord be with you."

"And also with you." The small congregation chanted the ritual response, each turning to shake hands with their neighbour as Sunday mass came to an end. At the back of the church a rain-coated man sat alone, standing only as the gathering began its slow procession down the aisle towards the exit, watching the priest shake hands with all who passed through the high wooden doors and out into a bright Sunday morning.

"Excuse me Father," called the man, "I wonder if I could have a word with you?"

"Certainly, my son," replied Peter Donne in his priestly way, standing with his back to the open doors, the strong sunlight fringing his dark silhouette. "How can I help you?"

"It's about your, ehm, daughter," said the man, pausing to gauge the catholic priest's reaction. Had the light been in the other direction it would have been easy for him to note the sudden absence of blood in Father Donne's face. It was, however, impossible to miss the priest's flustered grab at the arm of the nearest pew as his legs threatened to give way.

"I'm sorry," he mumbled in reply, seeking desperately for a composed response. "I'm a catholic priest, young man. You must know that we are not permitted the luxury of children of our own."

He then realised that his interlocutor was the journalist who had followed Frances and Alec back to the rectory, the same journalist who had been told, as they sat drinking coffee in a French café, that they were celebrating his daughter's son's birthday.

"Look," said Sayers in an effort at conciliation, having made an evident breach in the wall of deception that, for some reason which was not yet clear, had been erected around this odd little 'family'. "I really just want to help. Okay, I'll admit, I'm also looking for a story, but please, could I just talk to you and maybe your daughter. I promise I won't do anything without your permission."

"Please, come with me," replied Father Donne, leading the man into the vestry at the back of the church. "It's Mr Sayers, isn't it?" he continued, gesturing for the journalist to sit down.

"Yes, your ... I'm sorry, I was about to say wife, but I don't think that can be right. The lady at your house took my card from me. I'm sure you must have seen it."

"Yes. And you are right, of course. Alice is my sister and Frances is not my daughter. In fact, she isn't related to us at all. We took her in as she was pregnant with no-one else to look after her. She now lives with us on a more or less permanent basis." He paused for a brief moment. "Before you ask me any questions, could I ask you one?"

"Of course, Father."

"What is your interest in Frances and her son?"

"Well, I'm sure you know that I bumped into Frances a short while ago. For some reason I remembered her from France, and I particularly remember her son because he seemed to speak such good French. Very unusual for an English child. Anyway, when we met again Frances seemed very agitated, as if she had something to hide. And there was something about the boy. It was as if he was the same boy who was in France with you, yet he couldn't be as this boy was much older. I suppose my nose for a story started itching and I decided to follow them back to here, to the rectory." He paused in expectation of a reaction from the priest, the tick of a wooden-cased clock on the small room's mantle-piece imposing itself on the brief silence.

"So," the journalist resumed in the absence of any prompt from Father Donne, his eyes fixed on his entwined fingers as if uncertain of his next line of reasoning, "I decided to check on a condition that makes children age rapidly." He looked up at the Father, noticing that now the priest's glasses were no longer in their assigned position. Instead, his thumb and index finger pinched the bridge of his nose and his eyes closed briefly. The journalist was surprised to hear him say very simply:

"Please go on."

"Right. Okay. Well the condition is called progeria and, as I said, it makes children age very rapidly. Apparently about six or seven times faster than normal."

"And you think that Alec, the boy, has this condition?"

"I don't know, Father. I'm not a doctor, of course. But I have done some research and some of what I have read does seem to fit. This is such a rare condition that, if this were the case, it would make a great human interest story. And it might help Frances and Alec to be able to talk to someone about it."

"Do you not think that if Alec were suffering from this condition he, and his mother, would be talking to doctors about it already?" Father Donne countered with a hint of irritation in his voice.

"Normally, I would say yes, Father. But, again call it instinct, I get the feeling that in this case this isn't happening. I'm sure Frances is able to talk to you and your sister about it though." He paused again, expecting the priest to confirm his assertion, and was surprised that the Father's previously agitated tone gave way to silent reflection.

"Father," the journalist prompted once more, "you have spoken to Frances about this, surely?"

* * *

Frances kissed her son on the cheek and ruffled his hair as he and Alice Donne said goodbye.

"Have a nice time!" Frances called with a wave as the pair walked off to the nearest bus stop. The cinema was not too far away but they would be gone for a couple of hours at least. This, Frances hoped, would be enough time for her to talk openly, for the first time, to Father Donne about the boy. The Father was waiting in the rectory's living room, the soothing balm of a cup of tea already prepared to help the flow of what promised to be a difficult conversation.

"Come in Frances. Sit down and let's be comfortable." She

did as the priest asked, reaching out for the tea as soon as she was seated, a look of fierce concentration etched on her face as she sipped the liquid. Father Donne said nothing, content for the moment to let the tea work its magic and for Frances to gather the threads of her many thoughts. He too needed a moment to think about how this heart-to-heart might begin and where it might lead them. Frances put her cup back on its saucer, the shaking of her hand causing the clink of porcelain on porcelain and a few drops of tea to splash onto the table.

"Is it really possible that we can have this conversation now just because Alec is not in the house?" she asked, slowly looking up from the table at the priest opposite her.

"If you mean that Alec seems somehow to be able to block our thoughts, then yes, I think that must be the case. We've all known for some time that the boy has some psychic power, an ability to at least divert the thoughts of others, if not to control what they do. I think it is quite likely that this is what is happening to us, when Alec is here. The question is whether it is done deliberately, and if so, why?

They both fell silent again, as if the enormity of this question and its implications had, just like Alec himself, stopped them in their tracks.

"I have to tell you, Frances," continued the priest, finally freeing himself from the weight of the question, "that journalist, Peter Sayers, spoke to me at the end of mass on Sunday." Frances looked up again, tears and concern welling in her eyes. "Don't worry, he's promised not to do anything without our permission and I believe he genuinely wants to help."

"But what does he think is happening? What did he say to you? Why does he want to help?" The torrent came to a stop only when Father Donne sat next to Frances, placing a consoling arm over her shoulder as she sobbed a final inaudible question.

"He believes that Alec has an aging disease," he said, pleased to be able to give an honest answer. "He says it is called progeria and that Alec is aging much faster than normal because of it."

"But Alec isn't ill, Father. If anything, he has always been incredibly healthy. Never even a slight cold."

"Don't worry, Frances. I've looked it up and I don't believe that Alec has anything like progeria. But we know that Mr Sayers is right in believing that the boy is not normal."

"We haven't even spoken to a doctor, Father. Why should we speak to a journalist? What good would it do to have all this in the papers?"

"None at all Frances, but I do think it might be good to speak to an outsider; someone who could be trusted and who would believe what we were to say to him. A doctor would no doubt want to speak to Alec himself and we know that the boy might be able to manipulate the conversation."

Frances shuddered at the word manipulate. Did Father Donne mean to imply that Alec had some evil intent that they were, as yet, completely unaware of? She was about to question this implication, but the priest continued:

"And we know that Mr Sayers is already aware of something."

Frances let go of her earlier question, replacing it with another:

"And you trust him, Father? You really think that a journalist can be trusted not to publish his story, whatever he thinks that might be, without our permission?

"Well, we can at least put him right on his progeria theory."

"Yes, but what else is he going to want to know? What else are we going to tell him? If we tell him the truth, is he going to believe it?"

117

"Perhaps that's the solution, Frances. We tell him the truth and he thinks we are all mad and leaves us alone!" A wry smile played on the Father's face as he said this, hoping that the injection of a little humour might lighten their load.

"You may be right, Father," Frances responded with a smile of her own. "Maybe we are all mad and this is some sort of fantasy we are living through. Do you remember how paranoid I was about dates and the events in my life? None of that seems to matter now. The only thing that matters is Alec."

"Of course, Frances. But we need to think about his future and what is likely to happen to him, especially if he continues to develop in the same way."

"You know what is worrying me most?" She turned her head to look up at the priest whose arm still comforted her, tears once more threatening to blur her view. "If Alec is growing at such a rate, will he die in a few years time?"

Father Donne stood up, searching for an answer which would again provide some comfort to the boy's mother.

"To be truthful, Frances, I have no idea. Logic might have us believe that by the time he is, in real years, 18 or 19, his body might be telling the world that he is an old man. But, then, what has logic got to do with all of this? I still have faith that Alec is a gift from God, a miracle child who will achieve great things. I hope you do too."

"Yes, of course, Father. What else could he be?"

The question hung in the air, another challenge to their faith and the belief that Alec was, indeed, a God-given gift. Apart from his apparent ability to divert the attention of outsiders away from his abnormal development, he had never done anything that would suggest a malignant purpose. For Frances, he was the epitome of the ideal child. But for how much longer would he be a child? Frances burst into tears, the thought of losing Alec to an aging condition, progeria or not, too much to bear.

"I want to talk to the journalist, Father. Please call him for me, would you?"

* * *

The cinema was not full, even though the lights had now been dimmed for the show to begin. The usherette shone her torch down the aisle and Alice and Alec followed the ellipse of light along the carpet to a couple of empty seats in a middle row. This visit to the cinema was a rare excursion for the boy whose movements outside the rectory had been scarce. He had seen many films, of course, spending much of his time watching the television in the lounge at home. He liked some of the films but thought many of them were a little silly and lacked any scientific validity. He preferred to watch the documentary programmes which showed him about the real life of the planet. Today, in the unaccustomed dark of the cinema, his attention fixed first on the beam of light coming from the back of the big hall towards the huge screen at the front. He wanted to ask Alice about this but realised that everyone else in the cinema was quiet as the screen came to life with a film about things that people could buy. He made a mental note to ask Alice why it was necessary to persuade people to buy things, but this could wait until later. Soon the main film began. It was called Popeye the Sailor Man, but it wasn't like the cartoon version he had seen on the television. This had a real man playing the part of Popeye. It was a funny film which made both of them laugh out loud, along with the other spectators. At the end Alec told Alice that he had enjoyed the film very much but thought that eating spinach was probably not enough to give you special powers. Alice was tempted to ask the boy exactly what it was that gave people special powers, but thought better of it. In any case, Alec was already asking his own question:

"How does the beam of light make the pictures on the screen, Alice?"

* * *

They agreed to meet in the park, where he had bumped into Frances and her son a week or two ago.

"That's great," he said, noting the time of the rendez-vous on his pad. "I'll see you and Frances there at 10 tomorrow morning. Thanks a lot Father. I'm sure I can be of some help, even if it is as a sounding-board." Sayers put the phone back on its hook, pushing open the door of the phone booth and pushing up the lapels of his raincoat against the blustery April downpour. He looked up at the grey sky above, blinking against the heavy raindrops that smeared his face and eyes, but he was pleased with himself, happy that he had found a way in and ever more certain that there was a story to be had.

* * *

The squally shower of yesterday had been usurped by a steady drizzle as Peter Sayers waited, collar turned up once more, for Frances and Father Donne to appear at the bench in the park where they had agreed to meet. He glanced at his watch; not quite ten yet, and then looked over towards the park entrance a hundred yards or so away. There they were, sensibly under a large black umbrella that the priest held over their heads. Thankfully, there was no wind to fight against and they soon reached the bench. Sayers held out his hand to Frances, which she shook, after a moment's hesitation. He then shook Peter Donne by the hand, repeating his 'thank you' of yesterday.

"I think we ought to find somewhere a little drier. Shall we go to the café by the pond? It should be quiet at this time of the day."

"Would you like a drink?" the journalist asked as they entered the tiny café which served as a watering-hole for the humans who made use of the park. The ducks and geese preferred the pond and didn't seem to mind the rain at all. Frances watched the birds as Sayers ordered drinks at the counter; tea for herself and the Father, of course, and a black coffee for himself. She remembered watching the bird in the park in London, the day she was dismissed from her job with Adrian. It seemed such a long time ago and so much had happened since then, it was as if it were a dream. But then, so much of her life now seemed unreal. Frightened by something, the geese honked loudly as they suddenly flapped across the pond, struggling to find the necessary speed and lift to get them airborne. They made it just before their watery runway gave way to the concrete edges of the pond. Once again, Frances envied their ability to fly away from trouble.

"Here we are," said Sayers, handing Frances and the Father their white mugged teas, then sitting down to sip his own black coffee. Putting down his mug, he reached into his coat and withdrew his note-pad, looking up at the pair again to ask, "You don't mind if I take notes? Memory like a sieve."

"Actually, Mr Sayers, we'd rather you didn't. Not at the moment, anyway. As you said yourself, we'd prefer you to be our sounding-board, then maybe… Well, we'll see." The priest shifted his gaze from the journalist to Frances, whose almost imperceptible nod signalled once again her approval of the line they had agreed upon before the meeting.

"I understand," replied the journalist, putting the note-pad back in an inside pocket of his coat. "Well, where shall I begin?" he asked, rhetorically. "Your son, Frances," he continued without pause, "firstly, I am right in assuming that he is the same boy that I met some months ago in France?

"Yes, Mr Sayers, Alec is the same boy," she stopped and turned to Father Donne, still not knowing how much she should be telling this man. The priest returned an assuring smile, deciding that he needed to take control of the conversation.

"What is it you want to know, Mr Sayers? What is the story that you think is here?"

"Well, if Alec is suffering from progeria, as I said to you before Father, I think this would be a story of great human interest for our readers. It is a very rare condition and most people won't even have heard of it."

"And what would be the benefit of this to Alec and his mother?"

"Well, to put it bluntly, Father, this is the kind of story our paper would be willing to pay for. Not a huge sum of money, of course, but enough to maybe make a difference."

Frances blushed red on hearing this, her lips pursed and her gaze fixed on the young journalist. She didn't need to speak, she didn't need to tell the journalist that payment was the furthest thing from her mind; the anger in her face was enough to convey sufficient meaning. The priest spoke for her:

"Mr Sayers, I really don't think that we would be interested in receiving money for providing your readers with a story about the boy, human interest or not."

"Alec does not have progeria," Frances interjected, managing to control her anger. "He is not ill at all."

Realising his mistake in suggesting money as an inducement to the couple, Sayers held both hands in the air as a sign of apology.

"Look," he began humbly, "the last thing I want to do is upset you. Okay, I agreed that I would not publish anything without your say-so and I promise I will stick to that. So, perhaps it's best if you just tell me what you want to. I won't ask any more questions. How's that?" He waited as the pair looked at each other again in silent enquiry as to what to do next. "It was you who called me, Father," he reminded the priest, fearing that the interview was about to come to an abortive end.

"Yes, that is true, Mr Sayers. But I want it to be absolutely clear that whatever we say to you remains confidential, between the three of us. Do you swear to that Mr Sayers?"

"Of course, Father. I give you my word."

* * *

"Come!"

"Hi boss. What did you think? Incredible, yeah?"

Sayers was in good spirits. He'd spent most of the night crafting his copy, sure that here was a story that would soon be front page news. He'd listened to the priest and the woman, he'd seen the boy with his own eyes, and he believed what they had told him. A true miracle child. He'd heard of children who had one extraordinary gift, like the autistic boy who could draw in exact detail anything that he had seen just once. Then there was another boy who could play anything he heard on the piano, chords and all, again just on hearing it once. From what his mother had told him, this boy was way beyond that and not just in terms of his mental abilities. How could he possibly have grown so quickly? There had to be more to complete the story, but for now he felt that he had enough to show the boss. If he could follow this up with more enquiries, then surely the whole truth would come out, and what a story that would make.

"You're right, Peter. It is incredible. In fact, it's so incredible that there is no way that we could run this. Apart from your interview with the parents, where's your proof?"

"Parent, boss. Just the mother," he replied, already fearing a small puncture in the bubble. "I'm convinced it's the same kid that I saw in France, only he's much older. But it is the same boy."

"Do you have pictures?"

"No, boss. I didn't have a cameraman with me at the time."

"Then again, Peter, what proof do you have that you were being told the truth. Have you even interviewed the boy yet?"

"No, because they say that he'll be able to… block my thoughts," He looked down at his hands as the last three words escaped his lips, unable to look his editor in the eye and realising just how unbelievable the story now seemed. In the cold light of a new day he was being forced to re-evaluate the worth of this tale which was beginning to sound as if it should be prefixed with the word *fairy*. But, determined not to look a complete fool in front of his boss and mentor, he found a new argument to throw into the mix. "I can't believe the priest would be lying, boss. They both seemed genuine and I'm sure they were telling the truth."

"So, you've got a single mother, bringing up this kid on her own, supported by a priest who will swear blind that the Virgin Mary is the mother of a child of God. He's not lying, of course, but do you think that that is the truth? He believes what he is saying, probably just as they both do when they talk about a miracle child, but without any proof we have to treat them as delusional." He paused for a moment, careful not to go too far in deflating the ego of one of his most promising young journalists. "Look, I'll tell you what. We can't use the story in our paper but you could try one of the tabloids. I've got a mate over at the Daily World. They're always looking for something a bit quirky, a bit way out there. They might be interested in running the story, but for God's sake use a pseudonym. There's no way I want this associated with us."

Sayers thanked his editor and picked up the five sheets of A4 paper that housed his story.

"You'll phone your mate, then; at the World," he beseeched, turning before leaving the office.

"If that's what you want, Peter, I'll give him a call. Can't promise anything though."

* * *

The underground was crowded with the usual mix of shoppers, tourists and workers eager to be somewhere else. A train was disappearing into the tunnel as Sayers made his way to the front of the platform. An announcement helpfully reminded people to stay behind the yellow line, away from the edge, and that the next train would be arriving in 3 minutes time. Behind him the platform soon filled with more of the rush-hour regulars until it was 5 or 6 bodies deep. It had been a warm day and the Northern Line was living up to its reputation as an oven on wheels, but Sayers hoped that by elbowing his way to the front, he might be lucky enough to be in exactly the right place when the doors of the next train opened to be first in and, even more luckily, to find a seat. He'd called the editor of the Daily World that afternoon and, thanks to the intervention of his boss, he'd been granted an audience with one of the World's sub-editors the following Monday. He'd polished up the story, toning down some of the claims of the boy's abilities, in the hope that it would find an outlet, even if it was in a tabloid and with a false name attached to it. He pondered on the name for a while, thinking about pseudonyms that he'd come across before; Adam Ant, Justin de Villeneuve, George Sand; who was in fact a woman, of course, he reminded himself. Perhaps he should give himself a woman's name. Maybe this would add something to the story. His meanderings were blown aside by the draft of slightly cooler air that was being pushed through the tunnel by the approach of the next train.

By now the platform was a heaving mass of sweaty humanity, each hoping that there would be enough room on the train for them. The level of noise rose as the train grew nearer, the roar amplified by the tunnel itself. He moved a little closer to the edge, determined to be the first in, and could see the lights of the train and the driver illuminated in his booth. He didn't have time to see much else. A sudden push from behind and he was gone. The horrified train driver slammed on the emergency brake as he saw the man fall, holding on to a folded raincoat, but it was far too late. The front of the train hit the man's head, sending a wave of blood onto the windscreen. The screams of the onlookers on the platform were drowned by the screech of the brakes as they dug into the metal wheels to eventually bring the vehicle to a stop. Somewhere beneath the wheels of the front carriages the story of a young reporter's life had come to an abrupt end.

* * *

Since the interview with the journalist, a state of anxiety pervaded the rectory and its inhabitants. Frances now regretted having opened up to the man, giving him far too many details of the boy and his 18 months of incredible development. Father Donne tried to reassure her that Sayers had promised to do nothing without their specific agreement and that he believed the reporter had been sincere. Nonetheless, the journalist's newspaper had been added to their regular read, eagerly scrutinised each morning as soon as it was pushed through the letter box by the paper boy. They hoped to find nothing, of course; to be reassured that Sayers had kept to his word. So far, so good. Almost a week had elapsed since the interview at the café with no mention of Alec, or any boy with unusual abilities. Feeling reasonably confident that his judgement of the young man's character had been correct, Father Donne picked up the two newspapers lying on the horse-hair doormat. He paid scant attention to the usual headlines which constantly reminded the priest of the troubled world in which he and a few billion other souls eked out their lives, some with God as their guide and some without. He put this paper on the hall chair, opening out the other folded broadsheet to begin thumbing through the pages in the hope and belief that no story would trouble his particular world any further. He noticed the headline; more problems in the Middle East between the Palestinians and the Israelis with a picture of tanks in the desert. Then his eye fell on the page's other picture. In the bottom right-hand corner was the face of Peter Sayers, looking even younger than the priest had remembered him. The headline, smaller than the one above but still prominent, read, 'One of our own killed in tragic accident.' Father Donne went on to read in disbelieving silence that the young man had been accidentally pushed in front of an underground train when on his way home from work. The fleeting thought that God works in mysterious ways was regretted almost before it formed its vile outline in his mind. He turned to the two women who had followed him into the hall, always as anxious as he to know that there was no news. The look on his face was enough to tell them that there was news and both expected to hear that the journalist had lied to them, that he had published his infamous story, their story. The priest said nothing, still trying to take in the import of what he had just read. He stretched out the hand that held the newspaper. Frances was frozen to the spot, fearful of what she might see. Alice took the paper from her brother, scanning the page herself before exclaiming, almost in union with his first, repented thought:

"My God!" She sat down on the chair, ignoring the other paper that lay upon it. Had she or her brother bothered to look at its front page they would have seen the same picture of Peter Sayers, a youthful smile playing across his lips as he posed for his portrait.

Father Donne finally found a voice, "It's Sayers, Frances. The young reporter. He's dead!"

Chapter Nine

Three months have passed since the accident and it is approaching the second anniversary of the boy's birth. It was impossible for the Donnes and for Frances to think about his birthday in any conventional sense. They would certainly celebrate it, but any presents would be for a twelve year old. The boy was almost as tall as his mother and topped Alice Donne by an inch at least.

Alec had by now learnt the ritual greetings and responses of the catholic faith. To all intents and purposes he was being raised as a catholic and was content to join in when prayers were said, each morning and evening, at the rectory. After the accident, they had prayed for the soul of Peter Sayers, with some sense of guilt in their recognition that his demise had relieved them of any immediate problem. Frances felt particularly guilty, finding it hard to believe that such a misfortune, so fortuitous for them in its timing, could really be an accident. She even wondered whether Alec had had something to do with it, but quickly dismissed this as being as ridiculous as believing that God had ordained it.

So for now, they were safe from the prying of the press and any thought of enlisting a sounding board to help them understand their peculiar predicament was put to one side, replaced by prayer and a belief that God would guide them.

Alec would, as far as possible, stay at the rectory, using the walled garden as his play ground and to ensure that he had access to regular fresh air. This didn't seem to be a problem for him and he accepted the constraint willingly. Schooling for the boy had never been seriously considered, partly of course because he didn't seem to need it. It was inconceivable that he could attend a normal school without a plethora of questions being raised by the authorities, none of which could be truthfully answered without the boy's 'family' being carted off to a house of mental correction. Did they still have these? Frances pondered, as she watched her son turn the pages of the latest book he had chosen to read. It happened to be Oliver Twist.

"Maybe that's what made me think of mental institutions," she said involuntarily out loud. Alec looked up at her, pausing for a moment before asking:

"Mother," he began in his earnest and quite formal way. He never called her 'mum' and certainly not 'mummy'. Perhaps it was because he had been used to calling Peter Donne 'Father', although he clearly did not think of him in any way as his biological parent. Alice though was always Alice. He went on, "is there a book called On the Origin of Species in the house?

Frances blinked but maintained an air of calm composure. She was by now quite used to such questions from her son, and whether he was chronologically two, physically twelve or mentally twenty-one years of age, she felt a sense of pride that this was her son, but despite the pride she could not free herself of the fear and dread of what all this meant. She would pray again for God's help.

"The Origin of Species, Alec?" she began, remembering that it was one of those books that most people had heard of, but very few had actually read. She doubted that there would be a copy in the rectory. After all, it was, she knew, a book that challenged the teachings of the church and the Bible in particular.

"It's by a man called Charles Darwin, Mother."

"Yes, I know son." She knew he wasn't being patronising, that this was just his way. "I don't think so, Alec, but I can have a look. Do you want me to look now?"

"No, it's alright. But I would like to read it. I saw a programme on the television yesterday which was about some islands called the Galapagos and a ship called the Beagle. Charles Darwin wrote the book after his voyage there. I think it might be very interesting."

"I'll have a look tomorrow, Alec. It'll be time for bed soon."

"Yes, Mother," replied the boy, turning another page for a final read about the Victorian England that Dickens portrayed.

* * *

There was quite a large library at the rectory, with books collected over many years by the Donnes. Alice was an avid and eclectic reader, mostly fiction with a penchant for the historical novel. The classics were also well represented with a particularly fine edition of Shakespeare, leather bound and gold tooled. The Donnes had found this at an irresistible price in a second hand book shop in Devon whilst on a short holiday one summer. There was also Dickens, of course, who was a favourite of Peter's. He sometimes believed that the thought of becoming a priest lodged itself in his brain because of the misery and the squalor often depicted in these novels which he loved to read as a child. Although 20th century England did not quite mirror the plight of the homeless and the poor of the previous century, there were times when the reflection was not at all favourable.

In short, as Mr Micawber might begin, he wanted to do something to help his fellow man. Peter smiled to himself at this thought, as he moved from these great stories to thumb the spine of the edition of On The Origin of Species that rubbed shoulders with the novels, the essays and the many tomes on theology that filled the shelves.

"Here we are, Frances," he said, turning to the woman, book triumphantly held in his right hand. "I knew I had a copy."

"I didn't know whether you would, Father. Have you ever read it?"

"Yes, I did. Just after I took up my first mission. It's as well to know your enemy," he said, a wry grin spreading across his face and the hint of a wink in his eye, discernable behind his glasses. Frances had become familiar with the priest's dry sense of humour during these last two years. She knew, also, that although his belief in God was unequivocal there was an acceptance of the scientific interpretation of the origins of the human race and a realisation that the bible need not be taken too literally.

"And you say that Alec asked for this book, Frances?" he asked as she took the heavy volume from him. "Extraordinary!" he exclaimed, "but now why should we be surprised, eh?"

* * *

"Happy birthday to you. Happy birthday to you. Happy birthday dear Alec. Happy birthday to you!" they chorused as Frances carried in the birthday cake which Alice had baked and skilfully decorated with red lettering confirming the message. There were no candles piercing the white icing as it had been impossible to decide how many to include. Two would have seemed ridiculous, given the boy's size, but more would have been at best incorrect and at worst deceitful and somehow sanctioning a bigger deception. Alec grinned broadly as the cake was placed in front of him on the dining room table.

"Would you like to cut the cake?" prompted Alice handing the knife to the boy. Alec took it and began to cut a slice.

"You should make a wish, Alec," she said, as the first slice of cake found its way onto a plate. His mother wondered what he might wish for. A long life and happiness? Would he live a long life? Her fears about his astonishing physical development surfaced again. It had helped to talk to that poor journalist, to tell him about Alec, although she wasn't sure that he had believed her. After all, who would? But now he was dead and again she felt the need to seek answers from someone. How old, she wondered, would Alec be on his next birthday?

"Are you alright, mother? Here, have some cake," said her son, offering a slice to Frances.

"Thank you, Alec," she replied, the smile quickly returning to her face. "Happy birthday, son."

* * *

Alec looked up from his book, waiting a moment before deciding that Father Donne's concentration on his latest sermon could be interrupted. He had taken to spending much of his time in the priest's company, asking the occasional question as he worked from the many books at his disposal. His birthday had been a good excuse to provide a full gamut of works on maths, geography, history and so on, from which he rapidly gained a more than adequate knowledge. He did not need to be taught but welcomed the opportunity to clarify or discuss a point with the Father.

"It's a pity Darwin didn't know anything about DNA, Father," he said, "so many of his arguments and theories would have been proven a long time ago, even when he published this book." He lifted the leather covered volume that had been his most treasured birthday gift, as if in evidence. "Father, do you think that Darwin is saying that God doesn't exist?"

Thankfully the sermon was more or less complete, allowing the priest to focus his attention on the boy and his question. He thought it best to try to gauge Alec's own interpretation of the Origin of Species, before answering him.

"What do you think, Alec? Do you think that is what Darwin is saying?"

"I'm not sure, Father. It's obvious that Darwin doesn't believe that God created the Earth and everything in it in six days and had a rest on the seventh. He talks about the fossils that were being discovered at the time and how they showed that many animals existed a long time ago that are now extinct. He says that animals are always changing, evolving, but we don't notice because it happens very slowly and over a very long period of time."

Father Donne was not at all surprised at how quickly the boy had digested the arguments in the book, or that he was now capable of expressing his views clearly and succinctly. He wondered whether he himself would be able to make such a cogent case for his own belief in arguing that both the scientific and the spiritual interpretation of life on the planet were compatible.

"That's very true, Alec. There is, I believe, no denying that life has existed on Earth for far longer than a literal reading of the Bible would suggest. And there are many people who believe explicitly in such a literal reading. In America I believe there are whole communities of so-called Creationists who believe just that; that everything in the Bible is fact. I don't believe that, Alec. For me, the Bible is an allegory. Do you know what that means?"

"Yes, Father. It's a story that carries another meaning."

"That's right, Alec. So, for me, what we read in the Bible is meant to make us think about the way we live our lives, and it provides us all with guidance as to what is right and wrong. Without such a moral code, I believe that we are lost in the wilderness."

"I see," said Alec, giving the priest his full attention. "So, are you saying that God is also an allegory, that he doesn't really exist?"

"Ah, now, that I am not saying. I believe that there is a God. I believe also that our holy Mother Mary gave birth to his son on Earth, that Jesus died on Earth so that our sins may be forgiven." He stopped here, suddenly aware that he was talking to a child who he continued to believe might himself be the issue of a miraculous birth. He thought for a while without speaking further. He wanted to confront Alec, to talk openly with him about how different he was from other children; to perhaps even suggest that the boy was sent to Earth by God to help the rest of humanity out of the mess that it was getting itself into. But as ever in the boy's presence, such thoughts proved transient; ephemeral ghosts that never coalesced into concrete words.

"Do you know, Alec," he said at last, "a French writer called Voltaire once said that if God didn't exist, he would need to be invented. So, one way or another, He is real. Don't you think?"

"Yes, Father."

"Now, what was that you were saying about DNA?"

* * *

And so life continued at the rectory with the boy's very existence kept hidden from the rest of the world. His rate of growth, both physical and mental, followed its familiar hectic career requiring an almost monthly change of wardrobe for the boy. Frances had not yet returned to any paid work. The idea had not even occurred to her, nor the Donnes, as their time and thoughts had been focussed so securely on the boy. The priest's stipend had just been enough to keep them all. Any pecuniary worry was relieved by the temporary borrowing of clothes donated to the church by its parishioners. The trousers, shirts, socks and jumpers all eventually finding their way to the charity shops once Alec had outgrown them. His books, mostly bought at church jumble sales, now filled several shelves of the wooden book-cases in his room. He had long outgrown the need for toys, although a microscope, culled from a recent jumble, was 'played' with endlessly by the boy, particularly since his reading of On the Origin of Species. An array of dead flies, spiders, and other insects found its way under the lens of the brass scope, with Alec ever eager to call for his mother and the Donnes to see his latest discovery.

He also began to take an interest in the opposite sex, commenting one day whilst he watched a television programme with Alice and his mother that the female presenter was very pretty. Alice and Frances looked first at Alec, then at each other, not sure how to react to the boy's throw-away remark. Was this the onset of puberty and another giant step in his physiological development? The glance between them was brief, but long enough to indicate added concern, more uncertainty as to where this latest development would lead. For the moment they said nothing, but each determined to speak to the man of the house as soon as possible. Perhaps there were a few things that would soon need to be explained to Alec.

* * *

Father Donne knocked on the bedroom door.

"Hello," said Alec, looking up from the microscope with its latest insectivorous specimen lying underneath the lens. The priest entered and sat on the bed as the boy turned his chair around to face him.

"What have you got there?" said the Father trying hard to ease his way into the talk that he thought he would never have to give. He had, of course, had occasion to give advice to married couples, young and old, but such discussions always centred around the emotional, the caring side of relationships. The mechanics of the physical aspects of married life were not, he felt, within his realm of authority.

"It's a 'small white' butterfly, Father. I caught it in the garden this morning. I think it's a female; you can tell by the markings on its wings."

"I see," said the priest, getting up from the bed and coming over to look at the insect. "What else can you see in the microscope?" he continued, peering into the instrument's eyepiece. "Goodness, that's wonderful," he added, glad to be able to share in the boy's enthusiasm and to delay a little more the inevitable purpose of his visit.

"Extraordinary how beautiful God's creatures are, Alec, especially when revealed in such close detail." He paused for a moment, considering carefully how he might broach the subject about to find its own place under the microscope.

"Talking about females, Alec, I wanted to speak to you

about them; girls I mean." He had taken off his glasses and was assiduously wiping them with a cloth he had taken from his pocket.

"Yes, Father," said Alec, filling the silent gap in the cleaning operation, a hint of puzzlement in his voice. Glasses now restored to pristine cleanliness and once more perched on the bridge of his nose, the priest continued:

"Yes, Alec. I wanted to talk to you about love, uh... relationships with the opposite sex."

"Do you mean sexual intercourse, Father?" the boy replied in his usual matter of fact way. Father Donne removed his glasses again, holding them in one hand whilst using the cleaning cloth to wipe the beads of sweat which were beginning to erupt on his forehead.

"Why, yes, Alec. That's exactly what I mean. What do you know about the matter?"

"I know how it is done, Father. I looked it up in the medical encyclopaedia that's in the library. It explained it really clearly with diagrams as well as the text."

Father Donne felt himself blushing, although he wasn't at all sure why. Was it due to the candour of the boy's response, his lack of self-consciousness in comparison with his own feelings of discomfort when discussing such matters? He began to feel that the roles in this particular conversation might well be reversed, as Alec seemed to have no apprehension in his ingenuous approach to the subject.

"Oh, I see," said the priest, his face slowly losing its flush of colour. "I'd forgotten about that encyclopaedia. Well, that's good. But is there anything you want to ask me about it, anything that you don't quite understand?"

"I don't think so, Father." He thought for a moment, as if

wondering if he should be asking more questions, but said simply, "No I think I understand it all."

"Fine, Alec, if you're sure now. But remember that you can talk to me at any time."

"Yes, Father, thank you."

Father Donne left the room with feelings that hovered between relief at not having to elucidate the detail of an act that his own experience did not encompass, and concern that the boy was fast approaching sexual maturity and was already inquisitive about it. The priest was well aware of the problems that often accompanied the onset of puberty; a normal and in recent years well documented part of growing up. But there was no manual to turn to, no research by some erudite professor of child development that would provide guidance to a family who instead of preparing to hear its offspring put together a first string of coherent words, was already facing the prospect of having an angst ridden teenager in their midst. 'Goodness!' thought Father Donne, 'the boy will be shaving soon!'

* * *

There were no spots or blemishes of any sort on the face of the youth reflected in the bathroom mirror. His blond-brown hair had been cut short, trimmed by his mother with clippers bought by the Donnes several months ago. His hair kept pace with the rest of his anatomy, growing at a speed which demanded an almost weekly cut. Outside it had started to sleet, a harsh wind driving the icy rain in waves onto the small bathroom window. He looked at himself, running a finger across the stubble that had appeared on his chin. He was more aware of himself than ever before. He had known for some time that he was very different from other children; that he was not, in fact, a child any more. His knowledge of the outside world, through the books he read, the television and radio programmes that he saw and listened to, as well as his discussions with Father Donne, had shown him a world that was very different from the cocoon in which he lived. He knew also that his chronological age matched that of a small child, a toddler, an infant still reliant on its mother to feed and clothe it. This was not the boy that stared back at him in the mirror. He had not questioned his difference, either internally or with the Donnes or his mother. There seemed no need to. He thought it odd, though, that no-one else in the house felt the need to question either. Perhaps, he considered as another watery rasp hit the window, perhaps they were under the same apparent constraint that he was. He thought again, this time contemplating the very thoughts that were passing through his mind and the ease with which he was able to find words to fit them. Did he really think 'apparent constraint?' "Yes, you did," he said out loud to himself, watching his reflected lips move in unison with the sound. He was aware of the physical changes taking place in his body and that these changes seemed to have brought with them a psychic companion, as if puberty had released a genie from a bottle that now sat on his shoulder, urging him to seek answers to questions that a month ago were buried deep within his consciousness. He spread the shaving foam across his face, taking the safety razor in his right hand, then pulling it slowly downward across his skin. The sensation was pleasing as the blade cut through the weak resistance of the straw-coloured bristle on his cheek. Another pass furrowed a new path through the foam, leaving the skin on his chin smooth and fresh. Soon he was done, the remaining foam washed clear with clean water. He would speak to his mother and Father Donne after the Christmas period was over. There were many things he needed to understand. He looked again at the face in the mirror, resolved to find out who he really was.

* * *

Frances pressed down on the shirt, smoothing out the creased cotton as her right arm moved the iron instinctively across the cloth. Her thoughts were, as usual when ironing, elsewhere. She considered what the new year would bring and how she and the people she had come to regard as family, would cope with her son's seemingly ever more rapid development from toddler to teenager. She finished the shirt, folding the collar over to give it one last press. The iron hissed steam at her as if to remind her that it had finished its task, that the boy's shirt was ready for wearing.

"The boy's shirt," Frances mouthed, her semi-conscious thoughts finding a voice. "The boy's shirt," she said again, now fully aware of the import of this short little phrase. She looked down at the white label stitched into the blue cloth on the inside of the collar; a size 15½ neck, a man-sized neck for a man-sized shirt for a man-sized toddler. She almost laughed at the litany; but this was no laughing matter. "What sort of a matter is this?" she asked herself, aware of a new determination to find an answer. She would speak to Alec as soon after New Year as possible.

* * *

"We really should discuss what Alec is going to do next year, Peter," Alice said casually to her brother as she pulled the blue thread through the canvas pattern stretched across the embroidery hoop. Peter looked up from his book, unsure of what his sister had said to him.

"I'm sorry, Alice. I wasn't listening. What did you say?"

"That we should talk to Frances and Alec about what he is going to do next year. After all, he can't be kept cooped up in here forever. He's a young man now, Peter, isn't he."

"Yes, Alice, of course, we need to discuss this with him." He began to read his book again as his sister's needle pierced the canvas once more to add another stitch to the picture that was slowly forming

"Alice," said her brother a moment or two later, "do you realise what is happening?"

"What do you mean, Peter?"

"I mean," he began, closing his book and taking a deep breath, "I mean that we are having this conversation. Why are we having this conversation? Why are we being allowed to have this conversation? Why now when for over two years we have avoided the very thought of questioning the boy, not only about his future but about he himself?" He paused for more breath, looking earnestly at his sister in the hope that she would provide an immediate answer.

"How extraordinary!" was her only response. And it was just that, extraordinary how they knew that this time they would be able to speak openly with Alec and his mother and to ask all those questions that had bubbled beneath the mirky waters of their situation since the boy's birth.

"I will speak to Alec and Frances in the new year," he concluded with a confident and determined air.

Chapter Ten

Thursday 1st January. The new year began with snow blanketing much of the country and temperatures struggling to break through winter's icy grip. Alice was first up and busied herself in the rectory kitchen, preparing the first cup of tea of the day. Their celebration of the night before had been quietly contemplative but nonetheless joyous in their collective prayers for a truly happy new year with each privately hoping that their resolutions to finally seek and find answers to all those muted questions would be kept. The white porcelain teapot was filled to the brim, kept snug and warm with a knitted cosy that Alice had made as a Christmas present to the house.

"Tea's just brewing," she said, seeing her brother and Frances come into the kitchen, both equally snug, wrapped in their dressing gowns against the cold of the morning. The rectory was never an easy place to heat and today the boiler seemed just as reluctant as they were to embrace an early start to the day.

"Thanks, Alice," replied her brother, stifling a yawn with the back of his hand. "We'll have it in the living room, shall we? It'll be warmer in there."

"Would Alec like a cup, Frances?" asked Alice as she poured the last of their three cups.

"He's still asleep, Alice," replied Frances, "I don't suppose he will be up for a while yet."

"Good," said Peter, more urgent in his tone than he had meant to be, "I mean that the young man needs his sleep…and it will give us an opportunity to discuss a few things before he is awake."

They set off for the living room, each aware of the importance of the 'few things' to be discussed.

As Peter had suggested, the living room was several degrees warmer than the kitchen, helped by the wood fire burning in the hearth. They sat around it, drawing their chairs forward, each staring into the fire, watching the flames dance and the thin wisps of smoke make their way up inside the stone chimney. For a moment no-one spoke; the only noises the cracking and spitting of burning wood competing for prominence with the tick of the casement clock sitting on the mantle-piece. Then they all spoke at once, drowning the clock and the fire in an eruption of questions, doubts and uncertainties. Father Donne held his hands up, seeking to calm the tirade.

"Now," he said quietly as they all fell silent once more, "let's just take this one step at a time." He looked from one to the other over the rim of his glasses. His sister did not return his gaze, preferring to focus on her intertwined fingers as they gripped and rubbed against each other. Frances stared back, like a rabbit caught in the glare of headlights, not daring to move a single muscle on her face.

"Frances," the priest continued, stretching out a gentle and encouraging hand that rested on the woman's shoulder, "you are the boy's mother, so I think it is right that you should be the first to speak, to say what is in your mind, and in your heart."

"Amen," said Alice.

"Yes, Father," Frances responded. She hesitated for a moment further as if she had forgotten her lines or missed her cue, now that she held centre stage. Alice looked up from the hands now still on her lap, adding her own support.

"Please, go on Frances, tell us what you are thinking."

Frances took a deep breath, about to ask the one all embracing question that had been etched on her mind since Alec was born; what did all this mean? The words formed and arranged themselves into a coherent question in her mind. Her lips moved to make the first sound, but before she could speak, before she could finally start to unravel the mystery that was her son, the door-bell rang loud and long. All three held their breath as they turned towards the intruding noise. Who could it be at this time of the morning on this New Year's day? The bell rang again.

"I'm sorry, Frances, I'll have to see who that is. Please, you and Alice finish your tea. We'll continue in a moment." He got up and headed for the front door as his sister and Frances picked up their cups in vague obedience, and sipped the tea that was now cold.

* * *

"Father Donne?" said the tall man in the dark overcoat whose collar was turned up against an icy wind that had picked up again. His head found shelter under a black fedora which he respectfully doffed with a leather-gloved right hand. Behind him stood a woman, hatless but wrapped in a thick woollen coat buttoned up to her neck. In her left hand was a black leather briefcase.

"Yes, how can I help you?" replied the Father, half wondering what Jehovah's witnesses were doing calling at his door on New Year's Day.

"Hello, Father. My name is Landon Foley. I wonder if I

might speak to you and your sister. It's a matter of some importance." He handed the priest an identity card as he made this introduction. "This is my assistant, Marcia Wells," he added, turning to the woman behind him who nodded an acknowledgement but said nothing.

The Father gleaned from the identity card that Foley was a senior ranking government official, although which particular branch of government was not clear.

"Please, could we come in for a moment?" Foley urged, taking a step nearer the threshold.

"Yes, of course," replied the priest as another icy blast suggested that closing the door might be a good idea. "Now, how can I help you?" he continued, politely showing the visitors into the hall, but uncertain as to how he would, in fact, be able to help them. "Please, come into my office, and perhaps you can tell me what this is all about. I'll see if I can rustle you up some tea."

He showed them into his small office, bringing in another chair so that all might sit down, then went back into the living room to find his sister and Frances standing behind the door.

"What's going on, Peter?" said his sister anxiously. "Is it about Alec?"

"Now why would it be about Alec, Alice? What would these people know about Alec? I'm sure it's nothing like that. Look, would you mind making them a cup of tea. When they are gone, we can continue our discussion."

* * *

"My sister will bring us some tea in a few minutes, Mr. Foley. Now, what can I help you with?"

"Thank you, Father," replied Foley, his hat lying on his lap and coat collar turned back down. His assistant had unbuttoned her coat, evidently enjoying the warmth of the little room they were in, compared to the freezing air outside. On her lap lay the now open briefcase. She reached in to take out a dossier as the priest sat down behind his paper strewn desk.

"You have a Miss O'Donnell staying with you, a Frances Mary O'Donnell?" The question leant towards an affirmation rather than a genuine enquiry and came from the woman. Her gaze was fixed on the dossier, now open in her hand, rather than on the priest as she spoke.

"Why, yes," replied Father Donne, beginning to feel a little less secure in his belief that this had nothing to do with the boy. "Is that a problem?" he offered, casting rapid looks from one interlocutor to the other.

"And Miss O'Donnell has a child?" Again, the same tone and the same refusal to make direct eye contact with the priest, who was by now feeling distinctly uncomfortable.

"I wonder if you could ask Miss O'Donnell to join us," added Foley.

A knock on the door postponed an answer, giving Father Donne a moment to reflect. What did these people want with Alec? What did they know about him already? He put these questions aside, reacting to a second knock on the door to bid Alice enter. She silently handed the teas to the visitors, glancing inquiringly at her brother, reading his flustered features like the banner headline in a newspaper.

"Thank you, Alice," said Peter before she could say anything. "Would you ask Frances to join us, please." He could not help the small tremble in his voice as he spoke, knowing how frightened Frances would be.

"Of course, Peter," replied Alice; these few shaky words enough to reveal her own level of concern.

The door closed, leaving an uncomfortable silence in the room, thankfully soon broken by a further knock on the door. Father Donne stood up to let Frances in and to fetch another chair which he put beside his own. Frances sat down, grateful that the desk provided a barrier, a shield between her and these people, but fearing their intent. She already sensed that this was about Alec, of course. What else could it be?

The woman spoke again, but this time her eyes met those of Frances and her voice suggested a gentler approach.

"Hello, Frances. I'm Marcia Wells and I am Mr Foley's assistant." She turned briefly to redundantly indicate the man sitting to her left. "We represent a government agency. I'm afraid we are not at liberty to say exactly which agency, but my identity card here will be enough to show you who we are."

She handed over the plastic covered card displaying a not particularly flattering photograph of Miss Wells with an official looking stamp impressed into it. Frances glanced at it for a brief moment, not really seeing anything as her mind raced with thought upon thought, trying to anticipate what was to follow.

"We are here to speak to you about your son," continued the woman, taking the card back and returning the lanyard to its place around her neck.

Frances reddened and instinctively gripped the arm of the priest at her side.

"What do you want with my son?" she said, as calmly as her thumping heart would allow.

"Mr Foley will explain, Frances, but I think you should prepare yourself for a bit of a shock."

* * *

The doorbell rang insistently, then a brief silence before it sounded again. The noise of footsteps in the hall and the front door opening. A few murmured words before the door closed once more, shutting out the cold and the wind of the winter outside. More steps in the hall and voices distinct; Father Donne offering a cup of tea, asking how he could help. Alec got out of bed, dressed quickly, hoping that the visitors would soon be gone. He had not forgotten his determination to speak to his mother and to Father Donne. For the moment though, that would have to wait. He wondered who the visitors were, suddenly realising that he didn't know. He should know, he thought to himself, but he didn't. Something had changed. In the past, whenever strangers were in the house, Alec would be aware of them, wherever he was. He would also know unerringly what they wanted. Most were there on church business; helping to run a charity bazaar, planning the Christmas mass, arrangements for a funeral. Some came to seek help and advice from Father Donne. Whatever the reason, whether he consciously thought about it or not, Alec knew. This time it was different and his very conscious effort to think about these people was in vain. This sudden and unexpected lack of clairvoyance troubling him, he quietly crossed the bedroom floor and opened the door to his room as silently as he could, wondering whether this would remove the barrier between him and the visitors. More noise as he heard a door downstairs open and close again, the muffled voice of Father Donne, footsteps heading back down the hall to the living room, the voices of Alice and his mother, both sounding worried. Another realisation. He too felt worry and anxiety for the first time, as if he were no longer in control. He heard the door of the priest's office close once more and then the heavy tread of Alice's footsteps on the wooden floor of the hall. He would go downstairs to ask her what was happening.

* * *

Landon Foley thanked his assistant as he took the dossier from her and removed some of its contents. The few seconds spent in a final scan of the information before him seemed eternal to Frances and Father Donne as they waited, not daring to breathe, for the promised shock. At last Foley looked up and spoke.

"Your son is a very special boy, Miss O'Donnell. I'm sure you know that already." He paused to let this truism sink in, hoping to prepare the ground for what was to follow.

"Every child is special, Mr Foley," said Father Donne, aware that Frances, whose fingers still dug into his arm, had not responded.

"Yes, indeed, Father. But I am sure you are aware of just how special the boy … Alec, is."

"Please, Mr. Foley, please tell us what you know about Alec," Frances interjected, unable to tolerate the tension any longer, her reddened eyes imploring the man to give them the answers to the questions they had for so long been unable to ask.

"Thank you, Frances. Let's begin at the beginning, shall we?"

"I'm not sure I know where that is, Mr Foley. Perhaps you can tell me."

"Well, there are always many beginnings, you are right. But the beginning I'm going to focus on concerns the night you met Alec Samuels." He switched his gaze from Frances to the priest, then back again, seeking to discover any hint of recognition, any sign that the name meant anything to either of them. The furrowing of the Father's brow and the blank expression on the woman's face told him that, as he had expected, the name did not register.

"You don't recognise the name, Frances, I can see. I wonder if you remember the party you went to, about three years ago, when you worked for Adrian Bryant?" He paused again, waiting for the positive response that this time he was sure would be forthcoming. Frances thought for a moment, a look of puzzlement still creasing her features, trying to understand the relevance of this question. She did remember going to the party, when one of her young colleagues was leaving.

"Michael, that was his name. He was leaving the company and there was a party for him. Yes, I remember that, but what has this got to do with Alec?"

"You left the party with a man who had offered to take you home. His name was Alec Samuels. He drove you home in his car and you invited him in to your flat for coffee." He saw that there was still no sign of recall, but continued nonetheless. "In some respects, Alec Samuels is the father of your child."

"Mr Foley!" exclaimed Father Donne, as Frances, her eyes beginning to fill, sat speechless and motionless next to him. "How in the name of God can you expect us to believe that Frances would not remember such a thing?"

"For the simple reason, Father, that she was drugged."

For a brief moment they were all silent, as Foley let this appalling revelation sink in.

* * *

Alec stepped out of his room and leant over the banister of the landing, trying in vain to make sense of the murmur of subdued voices coming from Father Donne's office. He crept quietly down the stairs, looking for Alice. He found her in the kitchen where she was trying to busy herself, preparing vegetables for a slow cooking stew for the evening meal. Alec could see that she had not made much progress as one lone onion sat half-peeled on the wooden chopping board. She turned towards the boy on hearing him come into the room, roused from her vacant gaze through the kitchen window at the garden beyond.

"Hello, Alec," she said, hoping to hide the concern that gnawed at her insides. "Would you like a drink?"

Alec ignored the question, preferring to ask his own.

"What's going on, Alice? Who are these people?"

"I don't know, but I'm sure your mother will tell you soon," she answered earnestly.

"Alice," said Alec inquisitively, "why do you think I am so different from other children?"

An audible gasp escaped the woman's lips and the sharp knife she was holding slipped from her grasp, bouncing onto the kitchen's stone floor. She had not expected this and had no idea how to begin to reply. Thankfully, a kitchen chair gave safe haven as she slumped into it, her heart thumping alarmingly.

"Are you alright, Alice?" asked the boy, moving towards her, a placating hand touching her shoulder.

"Yes, it's okay, Alec. Just a bit of a funny turn. Would you mind getting me some water?"

She sipped the water in small gulps, taking deep breaths between to try to regain some composure. Alec waited patiently, the consoling hand back on Alice's shoulder.

"Thank you, Alec," she said after placing the empty glass on the kitchen table, "I feel better now. Let's wait until your mother and Peter are back before we answer any more questions."

* * *

"I don't understand," said Frances through a sob, "how could I not remember being drugged, then presumably raped by this man? It doesn't make any sense."

"The drug you were given induces loss of memory, normally of events shortly before and a few hours after it has been ingested. In your case, this would have included the drive from the party with Mr Samuels and the events that took place in your flat," explained Miss Wells impassively, as if describing the side-effects of a flu vaccine. "The loss of memory for this period of time is more or less permanent. Some people are known to have flash-backs, vague visions of what might have happened, but this is rare."

"So, are you telling us that this man, this Alec Samuels, this rapist goes around drugging and violating women?" added the indignant Father Donne.

"Not exactly, Father. And no, Miss O'Donnell was not raped, at least not in the conventional sense," continued the laconic Miss Wells.

By now Frances was awash with tears and Peter Donne's indignation had breached its breaking point. He stood abruptly, waved an uncharacteristic fist in the air and bellowed:

"What in the name of God does that mean?"

"Please, Father, sit down and I'll try to explain further," said Foley, worried that the situation was rapidly deteriorating, making it potentially more difficult for the next phase of the operation.

"What did you mean when you said that this Samuels was in some respects the father of the child?" Frances asked, wiping a tear from her face, trying hard to come to terms with what she was being told and ever more fearful of what had not yet come to light. Nothing had so far been said about Alec himself. Father Donne sat down heavily in the chair, irately intrigued by Frances' unexpected question. Foley shifted uneasily in his chair, letting the paper dossier slip from his lap onto the floor. His assistant quickly retrieved it, keeping it on her own lap.

"Well, this is where we come to the crux of the matter, Miss O'Donnell, and I do want you to realise that this is a matter of vital national, one might even say global importance." He paused once more, leaving space for these sentiments to do their work, before continuing. "Alec Samuels is a scientist; a geneticist to be precise. He has spent much of his career working on the effects of changing or modifying the genes of various animals. Through his experiments with rats, he discovered a gene that seemed to switch on unused parts of the animal's brain. I am not a scientist so I can't explain exactly how all this works, but suffice it to say that as a result, the rats became smarter; much smarter."

Father Donne was about to interject and raised a petitioning hand to do so, but withdrew the hand and the unborn question, allowing Foley to continue uninterrupted.

"At about the same time, Samuels was also learning about in-vitro fertilisation, IVF for short. Well, Samuels wanted to combine the gene changes with a form of IVF. He successfully did this with rats, to the extent that the offspring of the genetically changed rats were also super-intelligent. He then moved on to primates, chimpanzees to be exact, our closest relatives on the evolutionary ladder. It worked with them too, except that with the primates the gene modification seemed to speed up their rate of growth, at least to puberty. Then it all slows down to something approaching normal."

Frances sat upright in her chair, staring intently at Foley, not sure whether to be completely horrified at what she was hearing, or delighted that there seemed to be a chance that her son would not die of premature aging.

"Do you want to ask a question, Frances?" said Foley, seeing the woman's reaction. Caught between her two opposing emotions, she declined the offer, urging Foley to continue.

"Now, you will both be aware, I am sure, that experimenting on animals is one thing, and even that is frowned upon by many people. However, doing the same thing with human beings is, of course, another matter entirely, and completely illegal in all civilised countries."

Foley stopped again, realisation that this really was the point of no return in trying to explain to this woman who or what her son was. He could see and feel her tension as she continued to sit upright in her chair, each hand now clasped around the wooden arm-rests, her back stiffly straight, refusing the comfort of the back of the chair. Her eyes were wide open, staring unblinking at a silent Foley.

"Go on, Mr Foley," said Frances, through gritted teeth.

"Well, the fact is Miss O'Donnell, Samuels decided to experiment on a human." Another pause before the final, inescapable truth that no longer needed to be uttered. "Yes, Frances, I'm afraid that your child is the result of that experiment."

The scream could not be heard. It was a silent, internal scream that rang in her ears. She couldn't hear anything else and her water filled eyes veiled the view of Father Donne standing once again, remonstrating with Foley, a torrent of accusation and opprobrium crashing down on the man. The door burst open to reveal Alice Donne, both hands raised to cover the gape of astonishment on seeing her brother, with Frances almost catatonic at his side.

"Mother, Mother, what is it? What's happened?" Alec shouted, more agitated than anyone had ever seen him. "Who are these people?" He pushed his way past Alice to hold his mother around the waste, a tear beginning a slow descent down his cheek.

"Please, Miss Donne, would you take Frances and the boy out of here. I'd like to speak to your brother a little more," said Foley, taking advantage of the moment, before the priest could add more to the diatribe. "Miss Wells will go with you."

"Come on Frances, we need to have you lying down. Would you help me Alice, please. Alec, please help your mother too, will you. They managed between them to manoeuvre Frances out of the small office and into the living room where she was made comfortable on the settee. Alec remained at her side but said nothing more, seeming to be as confused as they all were.

"I'll make some more tea," Alice mumbled to herself, not knowing what else to do, before trundling off to the kitchen. Marcia Wells stayed in the room, silently watching Alec with his mother.

* * *

"I know this must be a tremendous shock to all of you, Father, and particularly to Frances, of course," said Foley to the very evidently distressed priest now slumped in his chair. "And I am sure there are many questions you will still want answers to."

"Are you a religious man, Mr Foley?" came an immediate

and unexpected first question. Foley delayed an answer, gathering the papers from the dossier which had once more found their way to the floor in the commotion of a few minutes ago. He sat back in his chair, the dossier back on his lap, thinking for a moment.

"I am that clichéd human being, Father, a lapsed catholic. If I am pushed I would probably confess to being an agnostic now. The coward's way out I know; too scared to go the whole hog, to declare myself an atheist, just in case. Why do you ask?"

"I have been a priest for over 30 years now, Mr Foley. I have always been a devout believer, trusting in my faith and in the love of God. But in all that time I had never experienced a truly religious event, a spiritual experience that would confirm empirically my belief."

"I thought that's what faith was, Father, you believe without question, without the need of proof. Isn't that what religion is based upon?"

"Yes, Mr Foley, but also on the acceptance that miracles do, and have, happened. I said that I had never experienced such a miracle," he paused for a brief moment before continuing, "until the boy was born. On that day, for many reasons, I believed that the child was very special. What you have told us confirms this of course, but not in the way I imagined. You must forgive my outburst of a moment ago, but your story of this Samuels and his genetic experiments is monstrous. How could you let this happen?"

"You must understand, Father, that this is not something that we have sanctioned. What Samuels has done is highly illegal and he will be dealt with."

"He has been arrested, I take it?"

"Unfortunately, not yet. But we are making enquiries as to

his current whereabouts. We will find him, you can be sure of that. In the meantime, there is the boy."

"Yes, Mr Foley, there is Alec," confirmed Father Donne emphatically. A silence followed, as if both men were unsure, even fearful of the next step. It was the priest who broke the silence.

"Why Frances?" he asked cryptically, taking a step away from the boy in the belief that this would take them to safer ground for the moment.

"Ah," replied Foley, his tone hinting at his own relief at moving in this direction. "We believe that Frances was chosen by Samuels for a number of reasons. We have, as I am sure you will understand, made a number of enquiries concerning Miss O'Donnell and her role in all of this."

"I'm sorry!" exclaimed the priest. "Are you suggesting that Frances is anything other than an innocent victim in this affair?"

"No, of course not, Father. Please forgive me, but ... look, just let me explain what we think we know about why Frances was chosen to be the mother of the child."

He waited in the wake of the priest's indignant response before beginning to unravel the complex web of dates and coincidences, of religious belief and feelings of guilt that evidently led Samuels to believe that here was a woman who might just accept that hers was a pregnancy made in heaven.

"To a large extent he was right, of course," added Foley as Father Donne listened intently, recalling the same dates, the same coincidences that he had heard from Frances herself. He felt a little foolish in remembering that a part of him also believed that Frances had been the chosen one.

"But how did Samuels know all of this?" he asked.

"We are not entirely sure, but probably in the same way that we do. There are school records and such like. We know, for example, that Frances was expelled from her school and that her mother was killed when she went to meet her. The tragedy was reported in a local paper. The coincidence of dates of her own birth and her mother's death are also a matter of public record. As is her father's death on the last day of the war. It's astonishing what one can find out about people if one has the inclination. Samuels had both inclination and motive."

"What did Samuels expect to happen once the child was born?"

"Well, again, we can only speculate. My own belief is that his mind was made up for him by you and your sister coming onto the scene. I think he was happy to see the boy brought up as you have done; by that I mean in virtual isolation, with you all believing that he was a miracle child who needed protection from the glare of the public gaze."

"I don't understand, Mr Foley. How could Samuels know anything about the boy's development here?"

"Once again our information is sketchy, but we believe that he was content to watch from afar, not to intervene unless there was some reason to do so."

"Peter Sayers!" exclaimed the priest.

"Precisely," replied Foley. "We are pretty sure that Samuels was responsible for the journalist's untimely death."

Another silence followed this shocking revelation. Father Donne crossed himself and uttered a brief prayer before asking:

"Why have you come to us now, at this particular moment? Why have you waited so long?"

"Ah, well, this is where we need to turn back towards the boy himself," replied Foley, taking the inevitable step that would lead to further revelations.

"Yes, Mr Foley, what exactly do you know about Alec?"

"Well, we know that his physical development has been unusual in the extreme, as was the case with the primates."

"And how do you know this?"

"Observation, Father. Although you have been careful to keep the boy from public view, there have been opportunities to gauge his progress, his very evident and rapid physical growth. That we are clear about. What is not yet so clear to us is the extent of his intellectual progress. If the example of the animal experiments is anything to go by, there must have been phenomenal mental development over the past couple of years." He waited, hoping that the priest would pick up this cue and provide the missing information. Father Donne felt a curious sense of relief, to be able at last to speak openly about the boy. He picked up his cue willingly.

"It's difficult to know where to start, Mr Foley. The boy is a phenomenon. You have already heard him speak, and to all intents and purposes he is as fluent in English as most adults. He has also reached a passable level of French, studying the cassettes that my sister has used. She is still struggling with asking where the toilets are!" He paused to smile at this thought, glad to lighten the conversation a little. Foley acknowledged the ease of tension with a smile of his own. The priest continued, citing the many ways in which Alec demonstrated his intellectual ability which seemed way beyond both his chronological and physical age. "Do you know, he has recently read The Origin of Species, from cover to cover."

"Extraordinary," agreed Foley, before adding, "and are there any other signs of unusual ability in the boy?"

The priest knew what the man was getting at, of course, but wasn't sure whether to include his apparent psychic gifts in his eulogy of Alec's skills. He stalled for time with a counter question.

"What sort of abilities do you mean, Mr Foley?"

"Well, the primates for instance, we know from Samuels' notes that, although they had no speech patterns of course, they did seem to display an ability to know what their keepers were going to do before they did it. I suppose we are talking about a psychic ability. Does Alec have this?"

The hesitation in Father Donne's reply was enough to tell Foley that Alec did possess such a skill. He waited patiently for confirmation as the priest continued to consider his response.

"Yes, Mr Foley, I think he does," he said finally, realising that there would be no real purpose in hiding this fact and even glad to be able to say it at last.

"And can you give me an example of how this has manifested itself?"

Father Donne recounted the story of the trip to France and the incident with the passports, remembering that it was during this trip that they met poor Mr Sayers. Foley listened with great attention but made no notes. The voice recorder concealed in the inside pocket of his overcoat would take care of that.

"Thank you, Father Donne. This has been most useful. Shall we see how Miss O'Donnell is feeling now?" Foley rose from his chair, expecting the priest to follow him. Instead, he reminded Foley of an earlier question, one that had still to be answered.

"But you haven't told me why you have come now. Why are you telling me all of this now?"

* * *

Frances had fallen asleep. Her cup of tea, still full but now cold, lay redundant on the occasional table by the sofa.

"I'll just clear these cups away," whispered Alice, getting up from her armchair, the tension in the room palpable in the stiffness in her neck and shoulders. During the five minutes they had all been in the living room together she and Miss Wells had drunk their tea in silence. Alec sat on the carpeted floor, his back to the sofa, looking at the nameless woman in the chair opposite. He tried to imagine what she was thinking but could not get beyond the menacingly benign expression on her face. There was something amiss in her smile as she looked back at him; that he *could* sense. Why was she here? Why didn't he know what she and the man wanted?

"I'll just be a moment," said Alice, heading for the kitchen with the two empty cups, glad to escape the vaguely threatening mood that seemed to be engulfing the room.

Marcia Wells sat forward in her chair, her smile broadening to fall just short of a grin. Alec thought that it didn't make her any more appealing. She spoke to him:

"It's Alec, isn't it?" she said as amiably as she could muster. "My name is Marcia, Marcia Wells. Mr Foley and I are here to help your mother, and you, Alec."

"Why do we need any help?" replied the boy, unconvinced.

"Perhaps if I can ask a question of my own, you will begin to see why you might need a little support from us."

Alec said nothing, a little confused that his mind was not already telling him what it was the woman wanted to know. She spoke again, leaning even further forward in her chair to ask:

"How old are you, Alec?"

Alec gave no reply, so Wells prodded a little more.

"Do you know when your birthday is?

"Off course I do," he replied, his voice betraying his irritation at the triteness of the question, "it is September 3rd."

"Yes, but which year, Alec?"

The door opened as Alice walked back in to announce that Father Donne and Mr Foley were coming out of the priest's office towards the living room. Alec stood up and turned towards the door, relieved to break away from the penetrating gaze of his interrogator. A moment later the Father walked in, the troubled expression on his face impossible to ignore. Foley followed shortly after, his own countenance more difficult to read.

Frances began to stir on the settee, one hand moving to her right temple in an attempt to ward off the headache she knew was coming. She sat up awkwardly, turning round to see Peter and Alice Donne and the intruder, Foley, standing in the doorway. Alec was sitting on the floor with his back to the settee. The man's assistant was sitting in the armchair opposite, leaning forward, her hands clasped together on her knees.

"Frances," said the Father, moving towards the settee, "how are you feeling?"

"I'm alright, Father. I just want to know what all this means."

"Of course, Frances. This has all been a dreadful shock." He hesitated for a second before going on. "Mr Foley will explain more in a moment. In the meantime, Alec, would you mind helping Alice to prepare the vegetables for our supper tonight. Would you please, Alice?" he added, turning to his sister. Alice returned a puzzled look, but as usual did as she was asked.

"Come on Alec, you can peel the potatoes," she said as cheerily as the growing cramp in her shoulders would allow. Alec looked at his mother, his unvoiced question answered with a nod towards the door and a concealing smile.

"Go on, Alec, I'll be fine," she added, patting the boy on the back as she got up from her seat.

* * *

"Please, sit down Frances," Foley beckoned as he claimed one of the armchairs, gesturing to Father Donne to do likewise. The headache that Frances had expected did not disappoint her. She felt her heart thumping in her chest and in her temples with each beat heralding a measure of pain that raked her whole body; the fear of further revelations adding to the ache. She folded into the sofa again and looked directly at Foley.

"So, Mr Foley," she began, her voice choked with emotion, "am I to believe that my son is the result of some mad scientist's experiment, a Frankenstein monster, a circus freak?" She looked away from Foley to Father Donne who held his head bowed with his hands together as if in prayer.

Foley's gaze remained on Frances as he answered her question:

"No, Frances. Alec is no monster which I am sure you know already. There is, however, much more to tell you about the boy." He paused as Frances turned her eyes back towards him. "What I am going to tell you will shock you, but there is no way to avoid this. You need to know and try to understand what we intend to do." He stopped again, giving Frances the chance to digest this tasteless hors d'oeuvre before the main course was thrust down her throat. Her eyes reddened once more, taking the full force of the headache as they followed the movement of Foley's lips.

"You were not raped by Alec Samuels, Frances, as we said. But you were impregnated by him with sperm that had been genetically altered. The drug that you were given would have rendered you unconscious for a time while this, uhm, procedure was carried out. You would have no recollection of this or of events some hours before and after.

"Whose was the sperm?" interjected Frances, dispassionately, "was it Samuels; is he the father of my child?"

"That we don't know, I'm afraid, Frances. His notes relating to this are missing."

"And how long have you known about this?" she added, her anger fuelling the pain behind her eyes.

"We have known about Samuels and his experiments on animals for a number of years, but had little real interest in him. After all, he was doing nothing illegal, at the time that is. He always had the necessary permits to work with animals. He is, was, a well known and respected scientist in his field."

"So when did you first know about my case, about Alec."

"Well, luckily one of his lab technicians came across some papers which seemed to show that Samuels had already chosen a subject for the next phase, the illegal next step of experimenting on a human. Those papers related to you, Frances. He had evidently spent a great deal of time selecting the right person."

Frances closed her eyes and rested her head on the back of the sofa trying to come to terms with the realisation that this man had deliberately stalked her, had groped around in her history before choosing her to be part of his insane experiment.

She opened her eyes again to hear Father Donne ask if she was alright to go on.

"Would you like some water, Frances, and perhaps some aspirin?" he added, sensing her physical as well as mental pain. She paid no heed to the priest's concerns for her well-being, turning instead back to Foley to ask:

"So why didn't you stop him then?"

"Unfortunately, by the time the information came to light, it was too late. You were already heavily pregnant."

"But you have waited until now to see me, until my …," she hesitated, seeming to struggle to produce the next, simple word, "until my… son had grown up. Why?"

Foley shifted in his seat, as he had done when in the priest's office, as he always did when faced with a difficult question. He exchanged glances with the priest before turning back to meet Frances' expectant gaze.

"Let me explain, Frances, by telling you a little bit more about Samuels' experiments with primates. As was the case with your son, the females had normal, full term pregnancies. Then, again like Alec, the offspring developed very rapidly, both physically and mentally. They were evidently much more intelligent than their mothers. Indeed," he added quickly, careful not to suggest that the mother he was now addressing lacked intelligence, "they were much cleverer than any of their elders and peers." He paused, expecting a comment from his audience, but there was none. Accepting this tacit agreement to continue, he went on, "Well, very soon the young male chimpanzees reached puberty. In normal chimps this occurs at around eight or nine years of age, so you can imagine how soon it was before these chaps were sexually active," He said, more enthusiastically than he had meant. He stopped again, aware that his turn of phrase might have been inappropriate in the circumstances, but there was no further reaction from either Frances or the priest. He pressed on. "Well, there was less aggression between the males than might be expected in a normal family group. The young males seemed to cooperate with each other, as they mated with as many females as they could."

"What on Earth has this got to do with Alec?" she intervened angrily. "I don't understand. What is it you are suggesting?"

"Please, let me just go on a little further, then you will begin to understand," replied Foley before turning to Father Donne for some sign of support. The priest nodded his consent for the man to continue.

"Father Donne has told me about Alec's unusual gifts and particularly his apparent ability to control the actions, maybe even the thoughts of certain people. He has told me, for example, of the incident with the passports when you went to France last year. And I am sure there have been other, similar occasions. The chimpanzees too showed signs of some psychic ability, although nowhere near as advanced as with Alec. But this ability seemed to diminish as they approached adulthood; in fact, by the time they had reached puberty, if we are to believe Samuels' notes, it had disappeared altogether. Since we raided his laboratory and removed the animals, none have yet regained their psychic powers, as far as we are able to tell. It is for this reason that Miss Wells and I have been able to come now; to talk to you and Father Donne about your son. Three months ago this would not have been possible."

* * *

"Alec, would you peel the carrots for me? They are in a basket in the pantry. About six large ones should do; and you'll find a bag of potatoes in there too."

The boy headed for the pantry, still aware that he had not answered the other woman's question. He wasn't deliberately avoiding an answer, or seeking to give a false one. It's just that he had, for the first time, considered the absurdity of an honest response. He knew that he was chronologically less than three years old, and that, paradoxically, his mental age was that of an adult. But it was his inability to know what the woman's motives were that troubled him most. As he picked up the bag of potatoes and the carrots from the basket, he could hear Frances and the woman speaking. He hesitated before the closed pantry door, trying to decipher the words of the women.

"… old is Alec, Miss Donne?" He could hear the Wells woman asking Alice.

"I'd rather you spoke to my brother or to his mother about that, Miss Wells," replied Alice abruptly.

"It's such a simple question, I thought you would be able to tell me."

"Perhaps the answer is not as simple as the question," countered Alice, immediately regretting her impetuosity. "What is it that you and Mr Foley want with the boy?" she added defiantly.

"I'd rather you spoke to Mr Foley about that," retorted Wells in sardonic tone.

The pantry door opened, provoking an awkward silence between the two women. Miss Wells creased her face into that smile again in a clumsy attempt to put the boy at ease. Alice was stern-faced as Alec tried to read the latent message in her eyes. Despite his lack of clairvoyance, he understood the meaning and determined not to answer any more of the woman's questions, at least not until he was back with his mother and Father Donne.

"Thank you, Alec," said Alice calmly, "put them on the table and we can start to peel them."

There were no more questions and the awkward silence now engulfed them all, broken only by the negligible scrape of peeler against carrot or potato skin, then the chop of the knife as it sliced through the naked vegetables onto the chopping board. Miss Wells did not seem in the least put out by this burden of silence, apparently quite content to simply watch the two of them in their labour. Alice was sure she was taking mental note of Alec's behaviour and demeanour. What else was she there for?

* * *

"He means that Alec would have been able to think them away, Frances," said Father Donne, "as he seemed to be able to do with the district nurse, even when he was a baby. And there is Mrs Sykes too. She is our cleaning lady, Mr Foley," he said in explanation.

"Yes," replied Foley, "and Mrs Sykes has never mentioned the boy to anyone outside this house?"

"Strange as it may seem, I don't think she has. If what you say is correct about his psychic powers diminishing, I suppose it's quite possible that she will begin to talk, at some point."

"Indeed, Father. That, among other things, Frances, is why we have decided to intervene now."

"What other things, Mr Foley?" said Frances, her mind awash with conflicting thoughts. She had been told that her son was the result of an illegal experiment, that there was a father but he could be anyone, that these people now needed to 'intervene'.

"We talked earlier about the primates reaching puberty and the unexpected effect this had on their abilities, and also on their sex drive. This was unusually intense, even for adult male chimpanzees. It seems at least possible, maybe even probable, that Alec will also show signs of an exceptionally active libido."

Frances returned a puzzled expression in response to this

latest news about her son, once more struggling to grasp the implication.

"So, are you suggesting that my son is likely to start leaping on the first female he comes across to mate with her? That is just ridiculous, Mr Foley."

"Yes, I agree Frances, it does seem implausible, and I am sure you still think of Alec as a little boy, your little boy."

Did she, she wondered; did she still think of Alec as her little boy? Her initial reaction to these awful revelations had been one of rejection, as if her son had, in one single moment, metamorphosed from a gift of God into the devil's spawn. Yet, he was her flesh and blood, and she was still his mother.

"Yes, Mr Foley, Alec is still my little boy, and you are trying to tell me that he is likely to turn into some kind of sex maniac. I just don't believe it."

"Unfortunately, it's not something that we are able to take a risk with," said Foley, trying to pave the way for the next blow.

"What do you mean?" Frances asked, the hairs on the back of her neck suddenly standing to attention.

"Well, Samuels speculates in his notes that a human male with the same genetic modification as the chimpanzees would seek to impregnate as many women as possible. He believes that the drive, the motivating force would be to create a population of similar humans with the same abilities that Alec displays. This is exactly what has happened with the offspring of the chimpanzees. They are highly intelligent progeny of their fathers. In other words, Frances, the gene effect is passed on. In a human population, this would need to be controlled."

"And how do you intend to do that, Mr Foley?" asked Frances, her voice shaking in accord with the rest of her body.

"We want to run some tests on Alec, to get a better idea of

his mental abilities. We want also...," he began, but hesitated a moment, judging whether this was the right moment to reveal the end game, "we would like to keep Alec with us for a while, in a safe environment."

"Do you mean safe for him or for the female population of the country?" Frances spat the words out, unable to control her anger any longer. "Please, Father, would you tell him that this is all nonsense," she said more calmly, turning to the priest who had witnessed all of this in silence, only half listening to Foley's repeat exposé of this strange affair. In his office, alone with the man, Father Donne had been astonished at the story he was hearing. His long-held belief that Alec was truly a miracle child, gifted to Frances and to the rest of humanity, had crumbled into an acceptance that his creator was not God, but a meddling and morally corrupt scientist. Was his the casting vote here? If so, he was unsure how to use it. He decided to stall for time.

"Look, Mr Foley, this has, I am sure you can imagine, been a huge shock to Frances and to all of us. I think we need a little time to come to terms with it all, to decide what to do next, what is best for Frances and the boy." Foley listened in apparent indulgence, but his response left them in no doubt as to the outcome of their meeting.

"I'm afraid, Father, that the decision as to what to do next is not yours. As a matter of national security we will need to keep Alec in a secure environment for an unspecified period of time. There will be facilities there for his mother to stay with him and, of course, he will be able to receive visits from yourself and your sister."

"This is not what we discussed in my office, Mr Foley. You led me to believe that the boy's mother would have a say in what happens next," replied the Father, his own voice revealing a growing resentment.

"I'm sorry, Father Donne, but the decision has already been made, by a higher authority. It is the government's view that as the result of an illegal genetic experiment, the boy will need to be carefully monitored in a safe and secure environment," Foley retorted emphatically, leaving no room for further discussion or argument. Frances and the priest received this final edict in horrified disbelief, until a single word reluctantly escaped the Father's lips.

"When?" he whispered, just loud enough to break through the oppressive film of silence.

"You will have a week to prepare the boy, and yourself Miss O'Donnell. You'll need to pack some clothes and any other essentials that he might need. Although, I can assure you, he will be very well cared for."

"Can you tell me where you will be taking us?" asked Frances through a curtain of tears.

"I'm afraid not. I am sure you understand."

"Then how will Father and Alice be able to visit us?"

"Like you, they will be picked up by one of our vehicles and taken to the site, whenever visits are arranged." Foley stood up after this last sentence, signalling an end to the discussion.

He left the house with his assistant, having given final instructions that no-one in the household should speak about the meeting and what they had discussed. They would be contacted during the following week, when arrangements for the transfer of the boy to a 'secure environment' would be explained to them. Alec was to be told only that because of his level of intelligence he and his mother would be staying with some people who could help him use those talents and decide what his future should be.

* * *

It was now approaching midday. In the kitchen Alice and Alec had long ago finished preparing the vegetables and a substantial beef stew was simmering gently in the 'slow-cook' that her brother had bought her as a Christmas present. Miss Wells had left the kitchen on hearing the living room door open and the sounds of her senior's muted good-bye. Before leaving she offered her own good-bye to the boy, giving no hint of the arrangement to follow. A curt nod of the head was all she was prepared to extend to Alice Donne. Outside the thick covering of cloud had begun to release its store of snow once again. The heavy flakes quickly built upon the layers already lying on any surface they could find and the light, such as it was beneath the grey pall, reflected dimly off the whiteness. Inside the house the atmosphere was no less gloomy. Frances had wanted answers and now she had them. 'Be careful what you wish for, isn't that the proverb?' she thought to herself as she and Father Donne left the living room. The priest gently took her arm, stopping her before they set off towards the open door of the kitchen.

"Frances," he whispered, "I think we should tell the boy what Foley has suggested. I don't think we have any choice."

"But…," Frances began, responding instinctively, trying to find a valid reason to argue with the priest. She found none and finished her brief sentence with an acquiescent 'yes, Father,' almost followed by a reflex 'forgive me for I have sinned,' as if she were in the confessional.

* * *

The black limousine stood out sharply against the snowy

backdrop of the street, its dark tinted windows concealing any occupant. Foley and Wells approached the car, their footsteps marking a trail from the street corner they had just turned. The car's engine was running, the noise muffled a little as it always seems to be when snow is on the ground. A back door was thrown open before they reached the vehicle and they climbed in, glad of the warmth inside.

"Well, how did it go?" asked the well-dressed man in the back seat, almost before Foley and his assistant had parked themselves next to him.

"They bought it," said Foley, a thin smile breaking across his face. "We've convinced them that Alec Samuels is a wanted man. The woman has no recollection of you, Frank, and I'm sure she wouldn't recognise you even if she saw you. And would you believe that they thought, all of them, that the boy was a kind of miracle child, a gift from God, the priest called him. You were right, you chose the right person."

"Excellent!" replied Frank, evidently more than pleased that the plan had worked. "And they are happy for him to come to the facility?" he added, hoping for more good news.

"I wouldn't say happy, but I don't think there will be any problem. I think they realise there is little choice."

"And what about the boy himself? You saw him, of course."

"Yes, but Marcia here spent more time with him than I did, although I don't think she got much out of him."

"No, Sir, but just seeing him was enough. It's incredible to believe that he has grown so much in such a short time. And, although we haven't done any tests yet of course, I'm sure we will find out just how intelligent he is."

"And there was no problem... I mean, you were not blocked in any way?" asked Frank, already anticipating the answer.

"No, you were quite right Sir. If he did possess any psychic ability, it seems to have disappeared, just as you said it would. I think he was a little confused about that."

"That's not surprising. It would be a completely new experience for him," Frank added, "it's possible he didn't even realise he was doing it before it was no longer there."

"And you don't think it will come back?" asked Foley.

"Not if the boy follows the pattern of the chimps. So, you're picking him up when?"

"Last arrangements to be made, but we're planning for a week today. Okay, Higgs," said Foley, tapping on the glass partition between the driver and the passengers in the back, "let's get back to Whitehall."

Chapter Eleven

Most of the beef stew languished in its brand new electric slow cook as darkness replaced the gloom of the day. The snow had turned to sleet, blown across the flare of the street lights outside. No-one in the house was hungry although Alec was persuaded to pick away at his food by his mother. The events of the day had traumatised Frances and she sat in the living room, staring into the open fire. Peter and Alice too had been distressed by Foley's account of the boy's origins, not least because their belief in a celestial intervention had been blown away. They must all now come to terms with the all too human hand of interference in God's divine creation. Alec had been told that he would be spending some time away from home, with people who wanted to understand more about his special gifts, and that his mother would be going with him.

A gust of wind lashed the sleet against the living room window, drawing Frances out of her stupor. The room was dark apart from the glow of the fire, with the faint light of the street lamp on the pavement outside penetrating weakly through the sleet and net curtains. Frances got up to close the heavy voile drapes that would help keep the room warm. She peered out of the window as she grabbed the right sided curtain in her hand. Through the net and the sleet a dark shape could just be made out against the snow on the opposite side of the road and about thirty yards from the rectory. The church and the rectory were in a quiet road with few houses nearby, so it was unusual to see a car parked there. Frances moved the net curtain aside a little to get a better look. Yes, it was definitely a car. Maybe they have broken down in the snow, she rationalised, closing the curtains and thinking no more about it. She turned on the standard lamp that stood in the corner near the window and made her way out of the living room towards the kitchen. Alec had eaten his stew and was finishing a yoghurt to complete his meal. Frances looked at him, a little ashamed of her initial reaction to Foley's terrible message.

"Are you alright, Frances?" said Alice, "Would you like some stew?"

"No thanks, Alice, not at the moment. Perhaps a bit later."

"Well, there's plenty here if you want some."

"Thank you," replied Frances, moving towards her still seated son to give him a hug. She kissed him gently on the top of the head before asking, "have you had enough to eat, son?"

"Yes, Mother, thank you," he answered, putting the now empty yoghurt pot down on the table with the spoon in it, then turning in his chair to put his arms around his mother's waist. "It'll be alright, Mother, I promise." She looked at him, reassured again, at least for the moment.

"Alice," said Frances, still holding onto her son, "did you notice a car parked near the house a little while ago?

"No, I don't think so, but I've been in the kitchen most of the time. It's not our visitors come back again, is it?"

"I don't think so. It's probably nothing, maybe someone has broken down."

* * *

Sleep did not come easily to any of the residents of the rectory that night. When Frances did eventually succumb to her tiredness she dreamt fitfully of bizarre experiments with animals and people and woke up in a cold sweat as a pig with a human head was about to ask her for help. She looked at the clock on her bed-side table. Through bleary eyes she made out the hands showing twenty past four, then lay there wondering why the man-headed pig had found its way into her subconscious.

Alice and Father Donne had fared little better and both were up by the time Frances reluctantly left her bed at 6.30. All three adjourned to the living room where a fresh fire was lit. Alice drew the curtains in anticipation of the first light of the day and was glad to see that the sleet of the night before had abated. They drank their tea, huddled around the blaze, talking vaguely about the week ahead, about what Alec and Frances might expect from their time at the... what did Foley call it?

"The secure environment," said Father Donne.

"What does that mean, Father?" said Frances, fears for her son re-emerging.

"From what Foley told me, Frances, it's a place where Alec can be assessed safely, away from the prying eyes of the press, for instance."

"I'm sure you are right, Father," she replied, trying to sound confident. She put her tea down on the table and went over to the window to open the curtains. A weak sun had just begun to reveal itself behind the hazy winter sky. Her attention was drawn to the street light as it blinked off and beyond it the shape of the car still in its same position. She pulled the nets to one side again and could now see that the car was not abandoned as two hatted figures occupied the front seats.

"Alice," she called softly, "that car is still there and there are two men in it. Surely they haven't been there all night."

Alice left her seat to join Frances by the window.

"What car?" asked the priest, quickly following his sister. As they watched, the car started to move slowly away, its wheels slipping a little on the icy surface of the road. It passed directly in front of the house, causing Frances to instinctively close the net curtain and draw back from the window. She bumped into Alice who was standing behind her.

"Sorry, Alice," she apologised a little breathlessly. "Do you think they have been watching us?" she asked incredulously.

"Why would they do that?" asked the Father, unwilling to believe that such a thing could happen. As the black car disappeared from view another came from the same direction, back towards the house, but it was soon out of sight. "I suspect that the people in the car had come to collect it this morning. Maybe it had broken down yesterday, Frances," he added, glad to be able to reassure the two women that nothing sinister was going on. They looked out of the window again, towards the side of the road where the car had been parked. As they looked, a black car, the one that had passed them a moment ago, positioned itself on the opposite side of the road, thirty yards or so from the house.

Before any of them could articulate the question that each wanted to ask the strident ring-ring of the phone in the hall pulled their attention away from the window. Father Donne marched off towards the invading noise, a look of concern and puzzlement on his face. 'Surely we aren't being watched' he asked himself as he picked up the receiver. He put the instrument to his ear, absent-mindedly greeting his caller with a hollow:

"Hello, Father Donne here." Someone spoke on the other end of the line, but a mechanical click and buzz made their words inaudible. "I'm sorry, could you repeat that please. I think we have a bad line." The noise stopped abruptly, and Mrs Sykes was speaking.

"Hello, Father," she said, clear as a bell, "I won't be coming in this week I'm afraid. My daughter has asked me to look after my grand-son for a few days. I hope that won't be too inconvenient for you."

"No, Mrs Sykes, please go ahead," replied the priest, the sense of things not being quite right growing in his mind. "We'll be able to manage." He put the receiver back in its cradle before Mrs Sykes had finished offering her thanks and returned to the living room.

"That was Mrs Sykes," he reported to the two women, "she won't be coming in this week. Looking after her grand-son."

"Never mind," said Alice, "it's probably just as well given what's been going on."

"Yes," agreed Father Donne, his mind clearly elsewhere. "Alice, have we ever had any trouble with our telephone line?"

"What sort of trouble?"

"Any odd noises on it, a bad line; that sort of thing."

"I don't think so. It's always been pretty good."

"Yes, that's what I thought. Look, I'm going out for a short walk, across the park. I believe there is a phone booth near the entrance on the other side, isn't that right Frances?"

"Yes, Father, but there's the one nearer the house, you know, it's only about fifty yards away."

"Yes, I do know. But I want to be out of sight of our friends in the car." The women looked at each other, then at Father Donne, their faces lined with the apprehension that the priest's words had triggered.

"So you do think we are being watched, Father?" asked Frances timorously.

"I'm afraid I think that might be the case, Frances. Look, I'll find the phone box and I will call the house. When you pick up listen for some odd sounds before you hear anyone speak. I'll muffle my voice with my scarf. Just tell me I have a wrong number, then hang up. Frances, can you go into the vestry. I'll also call the phone there."

"What do you think is wrong, Peter?" Alice enquired, the worry lines a little more deeply etched into her face.

"What do they call it, in the movies, when someone is listening to your phone conversations? A bug, isn't that it. I think they might have put a bug on our phone."

* * *

Wrapped in his woollen overcoat and scarf, his hat pulled tightly over his head, Father Donne trudged across the snow filled road towards the park. He glanced to his right as he reached the opposite pavement and could clearly see through the windscreen of the car parked thirty yards away, the faces of two men. They looked back at him, making no effort to conceal themselves. 'If it is Foley's men', and by now the priest was sure it was, 'perhaps they want us to know we are being watched,' he thought as he crossed into the park. Halfway across he looked back, wondering if one of the men had followed him, but there was no-one, he was sure. The phone booth lay close to the exit and was unoccupied. Apart from the odd bit of graffiti scratched into one or two of the panes of glass, it was also relatively un-vandalised. He picked up the receiver and dropped some coins into the slot, then carefully dialled the number for the rectory. His call was answered almost immediately as no doubt Alice was hovering over the phone in the hall.

"Hello," Father Donne could hear down the line, over the enigmatic click and buzz. He raised his woollen scarf to his mouth, self-consciously attempting to anglicise his Irish accent and feeling foolish in the process.

"Hello," he said, "could I speak to Mr Flynn, please?" The noise on the line had quickly stopped and he could hear quite clearly his sister delivering her line.

"I'm sorry, you have a wrong number," she said a little stiffly. The priest made his own rehearsed apology and hung up. More coins dropped into the box and he dialled the number of the rarely used phone that hung from the wall of the vestry at the back of the church. This time it was Frances who answered, ready to act out the prepared scene. She picked up the receiver as soon as she heard the ring.

"Hello," she said, "St Augustine's Church. How can I help you?" Father Donne was relieved to hear her clear tones, unencumbered by any suspicious noises. He played out the charade, but was confident that this phone had not been tampered with. Perhaps Foley had not thought to check that the church had a line too.

He walked back through the park towards the house, still not entirely sure what the noise on the rectory phone was. He wondered whether yesterday's disturbing events had engendered a creeping paranoia amongst them; but there was the car. What was it doing there? He neared the southern exit. Should he approach the men in the car, ask them if they needed any help? They were still there as he left the park, but he decided not to speak to them and crossed the road to the house.

Alice opened the door, a little flustered and red in the face.

"I heard it too, Peter," she said excitedly. "Do you think Mr Foley is really trying to listen to our phone calls?"

"I don't know Alice. I could hear the noise too. It could just be a fault on the line. Perhaps I'll let the phone company know and they can check it."

"If they are listening, what do they think they are going to hear?" asked Frances as they all gathered in the kitchen. "And why do we need to be watched?"

"Well, maybe they are concerned that you and Alec will run away, or something like that," suggested the priest.

"But why should we do that?" She thought for a moment, struggling as they all were, to find an explanation for the surveillance which they seemed to be under.

Father Donne spoke, his voice hushed and guarded, as if the walls of the kitchen had ears.

"Unless they aren't telling us the whole truth," he whispered, a little surprised at the extent of his own suspicion. The two women looked at him, fear and foreboding etched ever more clearly on their faces.

"What do you mean, Peter?" asked Alice.

"I'm not at all sure, Alice. Maybe we are all being a little paranoid about this," he replied, stopping to consider his next sentence carefully, "but do you remember, Frances, when Foley told us about Samuels, he led us to believe that the scientist was responsible for the death of the journalist, or did I misunderstand what he said?"

"No, I'm sure that's the impression I had as well," confirmed Frances, "he said something about Samuels only intervening when necessary, and when you mentioned Peter Sayers, he said 'exactly', or something like that."

Alice put her hand to her mouth to stifle a latent gasp as her brother continued:

"Well, if that is the case, if Samuels is at least suspected of murdering poor Mr Sayers, then why haven't we heard his name mentioned, either on the radio or television news, or at least in the newspapers. The young man's death was reported on national television at the time. We heard nothing about it becoming a murder enquiry."

"And Foley said that they were looking for him, because of his illegal experiments," added Frances, holding back a tear as she forced these terrible words from her mouth. "Because of what he had done to me."

Alice put a comforting arm around Frances as the tear turned into a sob.

"Alice, do you still have that calling card that Mr Sayers gave you?" asked her brother.

"I believe so," she answered, thinking for a moment, "yes, I pinned it to the notice board in the hall."

"What are you going to do, Father?" asked Frances as she dabbed the wet under her eyes with a handkerchief Alice had passed her.

"I'm going to speak to the editor of Mr Sayers' newspaper. I want to know if he has heard anything from the police about the young man's death."

* * *

The vestry behind the south transept of the church housed an assortment of items used during the various church services, but today, the only item of interest to Father Donne was the black, bakelite phone hanging from the wall. The line from this phone differed from the one in the house and, as he picked up the receiver, the priest hoped that the absence of any unfamiliar noise would indicate that it was still not bugged. He put the receiver to his ear and breathed a sigh of relief as an unadulterated dialling tone greeted him. He looked at the card in his hand then carefully dialled the number. A female voice answered cheerily.

"Good afternoon, Daily Reader. How can I help you?"

Father Donne explained who he was and asked if he could speak to the editor.

"I'm afraid Mr Tyne is busy at the moment. Can I take a message?" replied the receptionist just as cheerily.

"It's rather a delicate matter," said the priest, wishing he had taken more time to think about what he was going to say. "Uhm, it's about that young journalist of yours, Peter Sayers, the poor man who died in that tragic accident. I'd like to speak to your editor about him."

The cheeriness in the young woman's voice gave way to a more sombre tone.

"About Peter? What do you know about Peter?" she said, forgetting herself in remembrance of the young man she'd had a crush on since he joined the newspaper. "I'm sorry," she apologised, "I didn't mean to be rude. It's just that, what happened to Peter is still a shock to all of us here."

"I understand completely," said an indulgent Father Donne.

"Let me just see if Mr Tyne is free now," continued the young woman, having regained a little composure. Father Donne waited patiently as the line went dead for a moment until a deep and smokey voice said:

"Hello, Bill Tyne here. How can I help you?"

"Hello, Mr Tyne. Thank you for speaking to me. It's about young Mr Sayers. I met the young man a few days before his very untimely death and... well, I just wondered if you had heard anything from the police about the, uh... accident?"

"Could you tell me what your meeting with Peter was about, Father?" said Tyne, not yet connecting the name to the story he had heard from his young journalist, and a little suspicious about the motives of the enquirer.

"It's rather a confidential matter, Mr Tyne, eh.. concerning one of my parishioners, so I'd prefer not to say, if you don't mind."

"I'm sorry, Father... Donne, is that right? There's really not much I can tell you. The coroner returned a verdict of accidental death as you probably know, and I have heard nothing from the police or anyone else since the lad's funeral."

"So the name Alec Samuels means nothing to you, Mr Tyne?"

"Should it?" Tyne asked, looking at his watch and thinking that his precious time was being wasted by this meaningless reminder of the tragic demise of his most promising protégé.

"Perhaps not, Mr Tyne. Just that I have been told by a government official that Samuels is suspected of being responsible for the young man's death."

"Perhaps, Father, you were misinformed," countered Tyne, the impatience revealing a less avuncular side to his character. "Now, if you will forgive me, Father, I have a meeting or two to attend to."

"Thank you, Mr Tyne. I'm sorry to have taken up your time."

The phone went dead and Father Donne put the receiver back in its cradle, trying to make sense of this latest twist. 'Is it possible,' he thought to himself, 'that the journalist's editor would not be informed of such a development? Perhaps Tyne was lying to him. But why would he do that?' Things were not adding up and the more he thought about it, the more Father Donne became convinced that if anyone was lying, it was Foley.

Bill Tyne sat at his desk, trying to remember where he had heard the name of the priest before. A knock on his door drew him from his thoughts. It was Jenny Bolton.

"Hi, boss," she said, pushing the door ajar, "I've finished the copy on the drug lords story. Do you want to have a look now or shall I give it to Fred?"

"No, leave it here Jenny," he replied, tapping the only free space that remained on his desk. The young woman put the few sheets of paper down and turned to leave the room. "Jenny," her boss stopped her before she'd grabbed the door handle.

"Yes, boss?

"Do you remember that story Peter was working on, just before the accident?"

"He was working on a few, boss," she replied, "which one do you mean?"

"He asked you to look up that disease, the aging thing."

"Progeria, you mean. Yes, I remember that. Seemed a bit odd at the time, but Peter was sure he was on to something."

"Did he ever show you the story he'd written?"

"No, boss, not at all. Although I do know he was quite excited about it. He wouldn't tell me what it was about though."

"So, you don't remember the names of any of the people involved?"

"Sorry, boss, he never said."

"Okay, Jenny. Thanks a lot. I'll look over your copy this afternoon."

"Thanks, boss." As soon as she had left the room, Tyne picked up the phone and spoke to the receptionist.

"Maggie, that priest that just called, did he leave a number?"

"Sorry, sir, he didn't," she replied, drawing the emery board she held in her right hand across her left index finger.

"Right," he said, pausing for a moment before adding, "see if you can get hold of Inspector Sheldrake at Holburn police station, would you."

* * *

Even in the cold of winter, the front garden of the suburban house looked well cared for. The snow of the last few days had melted, leaving the paved path to the front door clean and fresh, despite the verdant moss defiant in the cracks between the slabs. Bill Tyne had spoken to his old friend John Sheldrake who, after a few discrete enquiries, reported that he was sure there was no suspected perpetrator, that the journalist had died in a tragic accident. It was no comfort, and a little redundant, to hear from Sheldrake that such accidents, although thankfully rare, do happen from time to time. In his time as a journalist Tyne had reported on countless tragedies, both large and small, and in almost all of them a grieving mother or father, sister or brother, was left to pick up the pieces of a broken life. He rang the doorbell, surprised to hear the jovial tone announce his presence. Somehow it didn't seem in keeping with the tenor of his visit. A moment later the door opened.

"Hello, Mr Tyne, please do come in," said a small voice trying hard to sound as cheery as the door bell, but not succeeding.

"Hello, Mrs Sayers. I'm sorry to trouble you like this, but it could be important."

"Please let me show you where Peter's things have been put. It's all in what used to be his bedroom, when he was a child at home with us," she explained, leading the journalist into the hall then up the carpeted staircase to the first floor. She stopped at the door of the bedroom, deep in thought, with a trickle of tear escaping from the corner of each eye. "I'm so sorry Mr Tyne, but we're still finding it very difficult to come to terms with. It doesn't seem that long ago that Peter was playing with his toys in this room." She pushed the door open and stepped slowly across the threshold. The room was immaculately tidy with the bed made and a picture of a youthful Peter Sayers in a silver frame on the bedside table. In the corner, neatly stacked, sat a number of cardboard boxes.

"All Peter's personal belongings, his books and papers are in these boxes. One day we'll sort them out properly, but his father and I can't bring ourselves to do it just yet." She looked around the rest of the room, as if each corner provoked a particular memory from a happier time. "Can I get you something to drink?" she said, stepping out of the room again

"No, thank you. You've been more than kind already. I know how difficult this must be for you."

"Yes," she replied cryptically, closing the door behind her to leave Tyne to rummage through her dead son's belongings. Twenty minutes later he found what he was looking for.

* * *

A brief phone call from an indifferent Marcia Wells informed Frances that she and her son would be collected from the rectory at 10am the following Tuesday. They would have the weekend to prepare the few essentials that Wells listed. Her hand trembled as Frances put the phone down, the reality of the situation suddenly invading her consciousness. Until now it had all the qualities of a bad dream, a nightmare that would be gone if only she could wake up. But now it was real and in a few days time she would be taken with her son to some anonymous institution where he would be monitored and tested. As she turned to head back into the warmth of the living room the phone rang again. She picked it up, once again hearing the now familiar noise that Father Donne believed was proof of some bugging device. A gruff voice at the other end of the line asked to speak to the Father.

"He's not here at the moment. Could I give him a message?"

"Yes, could you ask him to call Bill Tyne at the Daily Reader. He has my number."

"Yes, of course," replied Frances, recognising the name as that of the man that Father Donne had spoken to a couple of days ago, the editor of the Daily Reader. The priest's suspicions about Foley and his assistant had not been tempered by the journalist's apparent unfamiliarity with the name Alec Samuels. If Tyne had been telling the truth then it did seem strange that he knew nothing about Samuels or any other suspect in the accident which caused the young man's death.

"I'll tell him you called," said Frances, putting the phone down once more. She went into the living room where Alice and Alec were both quietly reading. "Is Peter in the church, Alice?" she asked.

"Yes, he's marrying a young couple tomorrow. I think he's just having a final rehearsal with them now. He should be finished soon."

"Thanks, Alice. Maybe I'll just pop over to the church to see if he has already finished." She turned and left the room before a concerned Alice could ask if everything was alright.

The church was cold, despite the two electric fan heaters spewing out their warm breath on either side of the aisle. The young couple who would soon be man and wife stood before the alter, overcoats buttoned and collars turned up. Father Donne too wore a warm coat over his clerical garb as he finished the rehearsal with the inexorable 'you may kiss the bride.' The couple turned to each other and kissed a little self-consciously as the equally predictable Bridal March struck up.

"You then turn and walk slowly back down the aisle towards the exit. The congregation will follow you out starting from the front rows here," explained the priest. "And I'm sure tomorrow, with the church full of people and the central heating on, it won't be quite as cold," he added with a reassuring smile. Frances waited for the young man and woman to leave the church before approaching Father Donne. She told him of the call from Marcia Wells and how they would have to be ready to be picked up on Tuesday.

"There was also a call from the editor of the Daily Reader, Mr Tyne. He asked if you could call him back."

"Really!" said the priest, the sombre expression which greeted the earlier bit of news changing to one of surprised anticipation. "I wonder what's made him change his mind?" he asked, looking at Frances but expecting no answer from her. "He called at the house, obviously," he continued, still more in conversation with himself than with Frances. "If we are being monitored, that means that Foley will know the man has called. Did he say what he was calling about, Frances?" he asked, finally drawing her into the dialogue.

"No, Father, he just asked if you would call him back. But

he did say that he was from the Daily Reader," she replied, picking up the significance of the priest's question.

A worried 'uhm...', was his immediate reaction. "I'll call him now, Frances, from here."

* * *

The church was full, as was often the case with weddings. On either side of the nave the oak pews sported an assortment of uncles, aunts, cousins and friends of the bride and groom. Father Donne always enjoyed these days but regretted that more of these same souls were not seen on a more regular basis. Today, though, was a little different. His conversation with Bill Tyne had led to the editor of the Daily Reader being unexpectedly invited to a wedding ceremony, at the end of which Tyne would wait in the church to speak further with the priest. He would also talk to Frances and her mysterious child. In this way they hoped to foil any surveillance by Foley and his minions.

The ceremony proceeded without a hitch, despite Father Donne's sporadic scanning of his audience to try to spot his clandestine visitor. Could it be the tall man wearing a pin-striped suit in the back row? Probably not, he decided, spotting a more likely candidate in the right hand corner of the church.

Finally, the rehearsed words of yesterday echoed around the hushed assembly and man and wife kissed, provoking a spontaneous round of applause from the floor. Mendelssohn's immortal music signalled the last act of the unfolding drama and the couple duly turned to begin their march towards the exit, passing the smiling faces and congratulations of family and friends. The man in the corner played his part, applauding as the couple passed the final row of pews to pose for the photographer on the steps of the church. A few minutes later saw the building empty as Father Donne ushered the last of the wedding party out. The man in the corner had gone too.

The priest looked back towards the alter, wondering where Mr Tyne could be, then spotted a dark-suited figure leaning against one of the stone pillars of the church. He approached the priest.

"Hello, Father, Bill Tyne," he said, holding out his hand in greeting.

"Thank you for coming Mr Tyne. Give me five minutes or so, then I'll be back. I need to finish things off outside first. I'm sure you understand."

"Of course, Father. Please, take your time."

* * *

"I have to tell you that I was very sceptical when I read young Peter's story about your son, Miss O'Donnell," said Bill Tyne as he and Frances sat facing each other in the rectory living room. He had entered the house, shepherded across the walled garden from the church by Father Donne, in the belief that there would be no spies on high, perched atop the few tall blocks of flats which pierced the sky in the near distance. Frances returned the journalist's earnest gaze with a shocked expression.

"What story?" she asked cryptically before adding, "Mr Sayers told us that he would not publish anything without our specific consent, isn't that right Father?"

"That is right, Frances, that is what we were told. But please listen to what Mr Tyne has to say."

"Well, as you know, his story was not published. Frankly,

when he showed it to me I thought it was nonsense; and Peter had no proof at all. I believe he hadn't even interviewed the boy." He paused briefly, looking from Frances to Father Donne, accepting their silence as confirmation that Alec had not spoken to Peter Sayers. "I was not aware of his promise to you and, as he was very keen on the story, I suggested that he contact one of the tabloids to see if they were interested. According to his diary, he had arranged to meet someone at the Daily World, but he never made it, of course."

"I am sorry to hear that Mr Sayers lied to us Mr Tyne and it grieves me even more to think that it was his death that saved us from a humiliating exposure in a tabloid newspaper," said Frances indignantly. "But then, what should we expect from a journalist?" she added looking defiantly at Tyne.

"I'm not here to excuse Peter or the Press in general, Miss O'Donnell. But the story that Peter wrote was not sensational in the derogatory sense that you imply. He believed what you told him and thought, genuinely I think, that it was a good human interest story, and one that might in the long run help you and your son."

"Then why didn't you publish it?" asked Frances, a little taken aback by what was, in her view, a defence of the journalist and his profession.

"As I said, I didn't believe it. Without any proof, photographs, interviews with the boy, there was no way that we could go to press with it."

"So why are you here now?"

"Well, when Father here telephoned me to ask about this Samuels chap and his connection to Peter's accident, I didn't at first connect the name Donne with Peter's article. But I did think it odd that my old mate John Sheldrake, Inspector

Sheldrake, hadn't passed any information on to me. After the Father's call, I asked John to make a few enquiries and he came up with a blank. So I was left with a priest telling me lies or some sort of cover up. Then I remembered where I had heard Father Donne's name before – Peter's story, of course."

Frances sat listening to all of this with a little less hostility towards the newspaper industry and a little more doubt about the veracity of Foley and his fearsome sidekick. The journalist continued:

"Well, I decided to do some checking of my own and, with John's help, found out that the government has been involved in work on the modification of genes in primates and other animals. I could find no mention of any Samuels, but the top man seems to be a Frank Robson. He's been involved in this line of work for some time and my sources tell me that his paymaster is the Ministry of Defence. He's definitely a government man, Miss O'Donnell," he concluded with a flourish, sitting back triumphantly in the armchair.

"So who is Alec Samuels?" asked Frances.

"I don't know, Frances," replied the journalist earnestly before adding, "it's quite possible that he doesn't exist, or that he and this Frank Robson are the same person."

Frances looked at Father Donne, her eyes half closing into angry slits.

"I knew there was something wrong with that man!" she exclaimed, referring to Landon Foley. "I knew he was lying to us." She took a deep breath before continuing. "So, Mr Tyne, you know about Alec and you now believe what Mr Sayers wrote in his story, is that what you are telling us?"

"Well, let's not go too far just yet," he replied, holding up a hand in want of a pause in the rush of thoughts that threatened to engulf the conversation. After a moment he went on, "I believe that there is some kind of government involvement here that is, how shall I put it, not quite kosher. Sorry Father," he added, as if the use of the word might offend. Father Donne nodded benignly and urged the man to continue. "It worries me that Robson is a Ministry of Defence employee working on a branch of science which is both new and highly controversial. However, it's a step further to believe that he has moved on to experimenting with humans, and an even bigger step to accept that such an experiment has succeeded in producing a super intelligent child who has developed from infant to adolescent in less than three years. That I am finding very hard to believe, Miss O'Donnell, as I am sure you can imagine."

She did imagine and reasoned silently that this was why any story, especially if appearing in a tabloid, would lay her and her son, not to mention Father Donne and his sister, open to public curiosity and ridicule. Yet it was true, Alec was just as Bill Tyne had described him.

"And what will make you believe?" she asked, now wanting the journalist to understand her story, wanting him to provide a way forward before her son was taken away in just a couple of days time.

"I found Peter's article amongst his papers at his mother's house and I read it through again carefully. He had changed it a little, leaving out some of the more incredible details. But he did insist on leaving in your claim that the boy could somehow control the actions of some people. That, and the boy's astounding physical development, are the things that I am finding most difficult to accept. Now Father here tells me that this ability has left him, which is why this Foley chap was able to speak to you here." He paused again, letting Frances dwell a little on his scepticism, as he studied her face for signs of a reaction. She answered as honestly as she could:

"I can only tell you what we have experienced in Alec's presence, Mr Tyne. Perhaps Mr Sayers mentioned the incident with the passport in France." Tyne nodded a confirmation. "There have been other times; the health visitor, for instance, that checked him over when he was a baby." She paused again, thinking back to that and other incidents before explaining to Tyne that they themselves, Peter and Alice and she, had been unable to discuss the boy's remarkable attributes, despite being fully aware that they were far from normal, until now. It seemed that this was at least one thing that Foley was telling the truth about; Alec really had lost this psychic ability at the onset of puberty.

"As for his physical growth, Mr Tyne," she continued with a deep sigh, "unless you have witnessed what we have, I suppose you are bound to be cynical, and without photos, which we never thought to take, there is no proof."

"I think it is a matter of trust and faith, Mr Tyne," said Father Donne. "You have now met Frances and myself and I hope you agree that we are not people likely to tell lies or who live in some fantasy world."

"No, Father, I don't believe you are telling lies," replied the journalist, scratching the back of his grey-haired scalp. "Perhaps it is time I met the boy himself."

* * *

Bill Tyne stood up as the door of the living room began to open. From reading his late colleague's account, he might expect to see a boy of somewhere between eight and ten years of age.

So it was with some difficulty that he managed to cloak his surprise when confronted with the strapping adolescent who filled the frame of the door, now fully opened. Tyne raised a hand to his mouth, gently coughing to clear his throat and his mind. He thrust out a hand in greeting which the boy took after exchanging glances with his mother who had entered the room behind him.

"Hello, I'm Bill Tyne," said the journalist, shaking the boy's hand and noting the firm grip, "and you are Alec," he continued, almost gluing an involuntary question mark to the end of his sentence.

"Yes, Mr Tyne," replied the boy, "my mother says you want to ask me some questions," he added, his unaccustomed lack of precognition causing an equally unusual tremor in his voice.

"Yes, Alec, if that's alright with you? And please call me Bill," Tyne answered, trying to add a touch of amiability to his own gruff voice.

"What is it you want to know, Mr Tyne?" said Alec, ignoring the attempt at friendliness. The journalist also ignored the inference in the boy's insistence on the formal, anxious to press ahead with the many questions he wanted to ask.

"Let's start with an easy one, Alec. Can you tell me how old you are?"

Alec looked at his mother, now seated next to him, then at Father Donne who had taken his place in the remaining armchair

"Go on, Alec. You can tell Mr Tyne the truth," said the priest softly, suddenly aware of just how anxious he was himself to hear the answer that Alec would give, the answer to this and no doubt many other questions that, until now, no-one in the household had been able to ask.

"I was born on 3rd September 1979, Mr Tyne, so I suppose

that makes me not quite 3 yet," he replied ingenuously. Tyne took the curious response in his stride, quickly putting his next question to the boy.

"And you are aware just how unusual that is? Your rate of physical development, I mean, Alec?"

"Yes, I've been meaning to speak to my mother about it."

Tyne looked at Frances, noting the startled expression on her face as she in turn looked at her son. She was about to say something, but Father Donne's out-stretched hand on her shoulder and his shake of the head as she turned round suggested that now was not the time. She closed her mouth and her eyes, wondering what more would come out of this interview. She didn't have to wait long to find out.

"So why haven't you?" asked the journalist.

"I don't really know. Until recently I have never thought to. It just didn't seem necessary."

"And now it does?"

"Yes, I think there are many things which I am going to need to understand."

"What sort of things, Alec?" said his mother, unable to hold back her own need to comprehend. Father Donne decided not to intervene this time, again intrigued as to what the boy might say.

"If I am going to fulfil my purpose in life," Alec replied without any hesitation, as if a new knowledge and a new certainty had replaced his momentary period of doubt. The conviction of the statement induced a stunned silence in the room and it seemed to all of them that Alec himself was changing on the spot.

"And what is your purpose?" Bill Tyne eventually asked, his gravel edged tones resonating in the heavy atmosphere of the room.

"I think it's to breed, Mother," said Alec, addressing her rather than anyone else. The startled look on the woman's face turned to one of utter shock and incredulity. If Frances had had the presence of mind to look at the other faces in the room, she would have recognised the same horrified expression on each of them. Again, it was the journalist who broke the spell.

"Who with?" he said, trying to steady the shifting gravel.

"Healthy young women, Mr Tyne," replied the teenager with no less conviction than before.

Despite his many years experience in unearthing the weird and wonderful that lies beneath the thin crust that we call society, Tyne was visibly shaken by what he was hearing. He couldn't quite make his mind up as to whether this was all some sort of elaborate hoax, that this teenager was no more than his appearance would suggest. But the rising hackles on the back of his neck told him otherwise, as did the boy's absolute conviction. Unless they were all incredibly good actors, he began to believe implicitly what the boy had said and what he had read in his dead young colleague's unpublished story.

"This is extraordinary!" he exclaimed at last, in the absence of any other reaction. His mother seemed completely traumatised and hardly able to breathe let alone speak. The priest fared little better as he sat with his mouth agape, trying in vain to find a word to describe the turmoil in his head. His poor sister had more or less fainted and lay back in her chair with sightless eyes directed at the ceiling

"How do you know this, Alec?" asked the journalist as the boy caringly took hold of his mother's hand.

"Don't worry, Mother. It will be alright," he said, trying to comfort her before turning back towards Tyne.

"I don't know how I know, Mr Tyne. I just know that this is

what I am meant to do. And it's important for all of us that I do it."

"Do you know who your father is, Alec?"

"No, my mother has never told me. Do you know who he is Mr Tyne?" There was no pent up emotion in the boy's question, no evident emotional gap that needed filling, it was just a matter of knowing the fact of who his father was.

"No, Alec, I'm afraid I don't." He turned to Father Donne whose gaping mouth had now closed and whose head was in his hands. How many more blows was he going to have to take before the fragile walls of his sanity finally gave way? The boy who he had once believed was a gift from God was fast turning into the monster that Frances had feared when first she heard the name of the supposed mad scientist Samuels.

"Father," said Tyne, "perhaps you could check on your sister. I think she may have fainted. Maybe you could take her and Alec here out into the kitchen. They could probably do with some water."

With some difficulty Father Donne was able to rouse his sister and with Alec's sturdy arm around her waist they managed to transport her into the kitchen. Alone with Frances, Tyne spoke again.

"Look at me, Frances, please," he said, taking her hand in his. "I can see how shocked you all are with what the boy has said, and I must say that in all my years as a hard-bitten hack I've never heard such a story." She looked up at him with uncomprehending eyes, not knowing whether she wanted him to confirm or deny the truth of what the boy had said. Either way, her tiny world had been turned upside down again. She remembered what Foley had said about the chimpanzees and their enhanced sexual drive. But Foley had been lying, hadn't he? Through this new confusion of thoughts the sound of Bill Tyne's voice echoed in her brain.

"But somehow Frances, I believe that the boy is telling us the truth," he was saying. "What I want to know, however, is how is the Ministry of Defence involved. Did this Foley chap say anything to you about which branch of government he represented?"

Frances shook her head, still too confused to give anything more than this tacit response. Tyne wondered whether he should tell the woman what was now going through his mind. He remembered the time, just after the war, when as a young reporter he covered a story emerging from the darkest corners of the Third Reich. The Nazis had set up camps in a number of conquered European countries. These were not the concentration camps that became the hideous and grotesque icons of Hitler's 'final solution' to the Jewish 'problem'. No, these camps were for an entirely different purpose. The Nazis believed that it was possible, by careful selective breeding, to create the perfect Aryan race. Many women volunteered for duty in these camps, eager to produce a perfect child for Hitler and the Fatherland. However, in his research into the story, Tyne discovered that many other women were coerced or even kidnapped to become part of the Lebensborn (Fountain of Life) programme. In Poland alone it was believed that over 200,000 women were abducted for 'breeding purposes'.

In many cases, the fathers of the children born to these women were unknown, as was their racial background. Inevitably, the project failed to produce the pure-bred children that Hitler had hoped for. The story, though, had lodged itself deeply in the recesses of the journalist's mind and now, so many years later, the possibility, remote and illogical as it might seem, that the British government had embarked on a similar design filled him with dread. For the moment, though, he decided to keep these thoughts to himself.

Father Donne came back into the living room.

"Alice is feeling better now. She's having a cup of tea. I've asked Alec to wait in his room until we have finished here," he said, wiping his brow with a cotton handkerchief. "How are you feeling now, Frances?" he asked apprehensively.

"Probably as well as can be expected, Father," she replied, trying hard to calm the priest's apprehension, "in the circumstances," she concluded.

"Why don't you go and speak to Alec, Frances. I think you might be able to get him to explain himself a little more," suggested Father Donne, "God knows, we need some clarity in all of this!"

Frances stiffened at the priest's suggestion. How would she be able to talk to the boy about anything now, let alone a subject which she felt particularly poorly qualified to discuss. The boy, her young son, had said as simply and plainly as he could, that his purpose in life was to have sex, to 'breed' as he put it, not with a young woman with whom he might be in a loving and caring relationship, but he had said 'with healthy young women', plural. She shuddered at the thought as the nightmare closed in on her once more.

"No, Father. I don't think I can. What did he mean 'with healthy young women?' People just don't say that, do they?"

Father Donne could give no answer, and neither could Bill Tyne. Perhaps they should have the boy come back in to ask him directly what he meant, now that the shock of the revelation had lost some of its impact, thought Tyne; but for the moment, he really wanted to speak to the priest alone.

"I could murder a cup of tea," he said, looking at the priest and hoping he would read his purpose.

"Of course," replied the Father, pausing for a moment to allow Frances to pick up the cue, as he knew she would.

"I'll go, Father, she said, "I could do with one myself."

* * *

"Father," said Tyne as soon as the living room door closed behind Frances, "There have been attempts in the past to create a superior race of people. The Nazis during the war, for instance. Thank goodness they didn't have much understanding of genetics or we might be speaking German right now," he added, his gruff voice almost breaking into a nervous laugh.

"So, is that what you think is happening, Mr Tyne? Do you think the Ministry of Defence is involved in some programme to create a superior human being?" asked the priest with no hint of mirth in his tremulous voice.

"Hell of a story if it is true!" exclaimed Tyne, unable to rein in his journalistic instincts until he saw the anguished look on the priest's face. It wasn't the word 'hell' that bothered the Father, of course, but the inference that the editor's principle interest was in finding a scoop, a headliner for his newspaper. He began to suspect the same duplicity that poor Mr Sayers had shown. "I'm sorry, Father, I didn't mean to suggest that…"

"Look, Mr Tyne," Father Donne interrupted him before any excuse or apology was proffered. "We just want what is best for the boy. At the moment that is all I am thinking of, and I know it's the same for his mother and my sister. I'm sure there is a story here that one day will be worth telling, but for the moment can we concentrate on what we should do about next Tuesday?"

"Of course, Father," replied Tyne apologetically.

"Oh, and there is one other thing that we need to consider. Your phone call to me here. If my suspicions are right about the phone, it will have been overheard. Foley will no doubt be wondering why you called and will be expecting me to call you back."

"Yes," said Tyne, "and he'll also know about my connection with Peter, of course."

"Indeed."

Both men sat quietly for a moment or two, wondering what reasonable cause might be concocted for the journalist calling the rectory which would not involve a renewal of the link back to Peter Sayers. The priest spoke again:

"Do you think they know that Mr Sayers wrote and showed you his story, Mr Tyne?

"It's hard to tell Father, except that there has been no interference with me or the newspaper from the authorities. I can only imagine that they thought they had done enough to kill off the story when they killed off poor Peter. If that is what happened, of course."

"Well, whatever reason we come up with for you phoning me, I think you might watch your back in the next few days," said Father Donne, his anxiety manifest in his trembling words.

"As the editor of a national newspaper, I think it unlikely that they would dare to take such drastic action against me, Father. But I hear what you say," replied Tyne, trying not to look worried.

The two men thought silently again for a while until a knock on the door drew their attention away from their deliberations. Frances came in with tea and biscuits and Tyne, still thinking about the priest's warning, wished he hadn't used the word 'murder' to describe his need for a drink.

"Thank you, Frances," said Father Donne as she laid the tray with the two cups and a handful of digestives on the table. "How are you feeling now?"

"Better, I think, Father, but I don't want Alec to go with Foley on Tuesday. Do you think we can just say no?" she asked in hope rather than expectation. Her fears were confirmed as Tyne interjected.

"In my experience of anything involving what the government cares to call the 'national interest' I think it highly unlikely that you will have any choice in the matter."

"Then there is only one way forward," said Father Donne, discarding his earlier diffident tone, "we must take the boy away, somewhere safe where he will not be easily found."

* * *

"Hello, Father Donne. Thanks for calling me back," said Bill Tyne, picking up the call that Maggie, the receptionist had just put through to his office.

"How can I help you, Mr Tyne?" replied the priest, managing to keep his voice under control.

"Yes, we're back-tracking some of the stories one of our young journalists was working on, before he sadly died in a terrible accident. I know from his diary that he went to see you and I wondered if you could let me know what young Peter wanted to speak to you about. Unfortunately, he didn't leave any notes."

"Yes, I read about it in the newspaper," replied the priest, just as they agreed he would. "How awful for you all. We had met Mr Sayers in France last Autumn. I believe he was writing about the British living abroad but of course there wasn't much to tell him as we were there not to buy a property, just a birthday celebration for my house guest's young son."

"I see, Father. So why did he see you at your home back in England?"

"Well, it seems that he was also thinking of writing about the unfortunate decline in church attendances in recent times. He wanted to interview me about my view of the matter. I don't know whether he wrote about it after our interview, before his accident."

"No, it would seem not, Father. Well, thanks anyway for your help and for calling me back."

"You're very welcome, Mr Tyne."

The agreed dialogue delivered, both men put down their respective phones, neither convinced that the sham would work, but it was all they had and better than nothing. Much more important was the success of the plan to follow later that day.

Chapter Twelve

The church was almost full again, but the mood was in sombre contrast to the wedding celebrations of a few days ago. The congregation, clad largely in black, shuffled down the nave to take their seats on the pews on either side. The man who had passed away was a well known shopkeeper in the area whose large family and many loyal customers had come to pay their last respects. Amongst the mourners were three people that the deceased would have found hard to place. They sat in the back row, doing their best to look inconspicuous, to blend in with the rest of the assembly. The man and woman were both in their forties. The youth at their side a teenager.

The full catholic mass was long, but finally the heavy coffin was hoisted onto the shoulders of the six pallbearers and the recessional hymn intoned. Soon the church was empty and the convoy of cars, led by the hearse and the limousines of the chief mourners, set off on its respectfully slow procession to the shopkeeper's last resting place. The man and woman, with the young man at their side, each with a hat pulled tightly over their heads, climbed quickly into a dark blue Ford, anxious not to lose their place in the transfer to the cemetery.

"Hello, Frances. I'm Stephen," said the man, turning briefly towards the woman at his side. "Wait until we're further from the church before you take your hat off. You too, Alec," he continued, looking at the boy in the back through the rear-view mirror.

The plan had, at least until now, worked perfectly. Stephen Finnigan was an acquaintance of Bill Tyne's, a freelance investigative journalist who had frequently written articles for the Daily Reader and many other English language newspapers. It hadn't taken Tyne long to persuade him to take part in this subterfuge. 'Sounds like it's just up my street, Bill,' had been his response to the suggestion that he and a female friend should attend the funeral, taking with them a teenager, both of whom would be substituted by Frances and her son at some point during the funeral mass. Hats and coats had been swapped, making each pair difficult to distinguish from the other. Enough of a disguise, they hoped, to fool any clandestine scrutiny, and to give Frances and her son the chance to escape Foley's clutches. With luck, their disappearance wouldn't be noticed until tomorrow.

The funeral procession approached a large roundabout where other drivers had stopped to let the long snake of mourners' cars pass. Stephen began to lag behind, deliberately allowing other cars between him and the snake. At the roundabout he turned left, heading towards the west of London, as the funereal convoy turned right, towards the cemetery.

"We'll drive on for a couple of hours," he said, "then we'll have a short break, get something to eat maybe."

"So, tell me again where we are going, Mr Finnigan," said Frances, removing the pin that held her hat tightly fixed on her head.

"Please, call me Stephen," said the driver, smiling at his passenger. "We're going to Wales, Frances. To a small village near Tregaron, in mid-Wales. My cousin has a farm there. Lives there with her dad, my uncle George. He's a bit of a grumpy old sod, I'm afraid, but you'll like Helen."

"Do they keep animals there, Mr Finnigan?" asked Alec from the back seat.

"'Fraid not, Alec. They've sold quite a bit of land to neighbouring farmers and don't work it any more. Uncle George is retired, but Helen works as a nurse in a local hospital. Have you ever been on a farm, Alec?"

"No, Mr Finnigan, I haven't," Alec replied, beginning to notice the changing scenery outside the car window as they sped onto the M4 motorway, heading out of London. Frances wondered how much Tyne's acquaintance had been told about Alec. She figured that he must have been told something, in order to entice him to get involved with what no doubt Foley would consider a fugitive escape. She decided to find out.

"Why are you helping us, Mr Finnigan? What's in it for you?" she asked with unaccustomed directness. Stephen Finnigan didn't flinch, not even taking his eyes off the road ahead to look at his inquisitor. "I hope you don't mind me asking?" she added, realising that whatever his motives, she and her son were, for the moment at least, in his hands.

"No problem, Frances. Bill has helped me out many times over the years and it's a pleasure to repay the favours for once. He told me that you and your son were going to be taken to some government institution for questioning, or testing of some sort. I for one don't like the sound of that. Smacks of too much interference from our beloved masters, if you ask me." He stopped for a moment before adding, "he also told me that any story coming out of all this would be mine for the writing." This time he did look at his listener, his brief glance revealing a momentary pinch of the brow as the woman's relatively calm expression threatened to turn into a frown. "But," he added quickly, "we'll do nothing without your say-so, that's the deal, okay?"

'Where have I heard that before?' thought Frances knowingly.

* * *

Darkness had fallen by the time they reached the farm and the rain which greens the valleys had begun to fall heavily. Helen was looking anxiously out of her kitchen window and was relieved to see the headlights of the car illuminate the gravel courtyard in front of the house. She came out to meet Stephen and her anonymous guests, a large golfing umbrella held high to protect them all from the downpour.

"Helen, this is Frances," said Stephen as soon as they were all out of the car and on their way up the flintstone steps to the front door. "And this is her son, Alec."

"Hello," replied Helen, passing the umbrella for Stephen to hold and shaking hands with the newcomers. "Mind the steps as you go up, will you. This rain makes them a little slippy at times."

The house was warm and welcoming, with a big log fire burning in the hearth. Frances and Alec removed their coats which Stephen hung up to dry on the coat stand in the hall.

"It's really kind of you to let us stay like this, Helen. We really do appreciate it," said Frances earnestly.

"Oh, don't you worry now," said Helen, "my husband left me too, you know, when my young lass was only six. Lucky for me that Dad had this farm.

"You have a daughter?" asked Frances, trying to blunt the

edge of concern that had crept into her voice. "How old is she now?"

"She's sixteen now; lovely girl. She's sorting Dad out at the moment. She'll be back soon."

"Your father, is he unwell?" asked Alec, before his mother could react further to news of the daughter's existence.

"No, no. Sally sorts his tea out most evenings. He lives in the outhouse just across the yard. You might have seen the lights on as you came in. Done up lovely it is. Just right for him, it is."

Stephen came back into the room to properly greet his cousin with a hug and a kiss.

"Really good of you to do this, Helen. I'm not sure what Frances would have done otherwise." He took Helen gently under the arm and led her away from the fire to whisper in her ear, "husband's a bit of a brute, threatened all sorts of mayhem. At least your old man wasn't violent."

"Poor lass," said Helen with a knowing sigh, "she's welcome to stay here as long as she likes. You can stay here as long as you like, dear," she repeated loudly, turning back towards the mother and son, still huddled by the fire, each deep in their own thoughts.

* * *

Frances and Alec were shown to their rooms as Stephen braved the rain to retrieve a suitcase from the boot of the car. The clothing and other essentials in the bag had been lent by the surrogate mother and son, who, like Helen, had been told that the dramatic escape from the capital was provoked by a potentially violent and abusive husband.

"Hi, Uncle Stephen!" called out the young woman emerging

from the converted outhouse that stood across the yard from the house.

"Sally!" her uncle returned the greeting, "How's tricks?"

"Good thanks. I hear that you've been playing the knight in shining armour. Who is she then?" Sally asked, putting an arm around Stephen's shoulder and kissing him on the cheek.

"Just a friend, Sal. She needs a bolt hole for a while. I'm sure mum's told you."

"Yes, poor woman. Still, it will be good to have some new faces around here for a change."

They climbed the flint steps once more and went into the warmth of the house.

"I'll just take this case up to Frances and her son. I'm sure they'll be down soon and you can meet them," said Stephen, calling out as Sally went into the living room to join her mother.

* * *

"Do you think that Sally is beautiful, Mother?" Alec asked as Frances kissed him goodnight and tucked in the covers of the unfamiliar bed that he lay in. In view of what the boy had told them just a day or so ago, the question sent a cold shiver down her spine. She gulped in a mouthful of air, as if she had been winded suddenly, then released her breath in a long, controlled sigh, trying to contain her emotions. She felt the need to protect her son from the dubious intentions of Foley and Wells and their government overlords. But Alec's words, his stated purpose in life, had struck fear in her heart and mind. Maybe Alec wasn't the only person in need of protection.

"Yes, Alec," she said at last, "I think she is very pretty; and she is the daughter of our host," she added, hoping that the inference would be understood by the boy. Alec didn't reply, but lay his head on the pillow and closed his eyes. Frances tried not to think about what he might dream of that night.

* * *

Two black limousines pulled up outside the gate. Foley and Wells descended from the first and moved quickly through the gate to the front door. The occupants of the other car remained where they were. Foley rang the bell once, then again as no-one answered the summons. Now he could hear the shuffling of feet in the hall on the other side of the wooden door. At last the door opened and Father Donne stood at the threshold.

"Hello, Father Donne," said Foley, "I trust that Frances and the boy are ready."

Alice joined her brother at the door, her physical presence lending the support she felt Peter would need. He looked at his sister before relaying the news that he knew would make Foley a very unhappy, and probably very angry, man.

"I'm afraid I have some bad news for you, Mr Foley." He could see already the usually pale expression on the man's face begin to colour.

"Yes?" said Foley, very slowly and pointedly, already expecting the worst.

"Frances and Alec have left. She decided that she didn't want Alec to be tested, Mr Foley, so she and the boy have gone away for a while." He looked Foley defiantly in the eye as he gave this devastating news, ready for any backlash that it might provoke. Foley though, despite his unaccustomed crimson hue, remained outwardly calm.

"And where exactly have they gone, Father?"

"That I really do not know, Mr Foley. Frances said she would contact me when she was settled." The priest delivered this news in the happy knowledge that he was telling the truth. Tyne had not told him where his acquaintance would be taking Frances and the boy. Indeed, he had no idea who the acquaintance was, let alone where they were headed.

"Do you think we could come in for a moment?" said Foley, taking a very deliberate step forward towards the entrance, "there are a number of things we need to discuss."

"Of course, Mr Foley," replied Father Donne, standing aside to let the man and his assistant in. "But I don't have long this morning. Today is my day for the parish rounds, visiting my flock, as it were," he added, smiling, despite the aura of barely contained anger that now emanated from his visitors.

They sat once again in the living room, as they had done a week ago, but this time Alice's offer of tea was declined. Foley spoke again:

"Do you realise what this means, Father Donne?" he said, looking unblinkingly at the seated priest. Not waiting for an answer to his question, he went on, his tone rising as his anger began to take control. "If the boy is let loose, who knows where it will lead. Why have you let them go?"

"I'm sorry Mr Foley, but let me understand something here. I was not under the impression that Frances and Alec were under any obligation to go with you to this institution as you call it. Are you now telling me that that you have some sort of warrant for them?"

"No, Father, at the moment there is no warrant," replied Foley, the veins in his temples revealing the inner struggle to suppress his annoyance and frustration, "but that will change, believe me. It is essential that we get the boy back."

"Ah, now, Mr Foley, when you say 'believe me', I think that might be part of our problem," said Father Donne, lifting a finger to prod his glasses back onto the bridge of his nose.

"What on Earth do you mean, Donne?" asked the hitherto silent Miss Wells, obviously feeling that the situation necessitated a pruning of the accustomed clerical salutation. Father Donne looked at her with an expression he reserved for only the most abhorrent specimens of humanity that his priestly undertakings occasionally, but very rarely, exposed him to.

"What do you mean, Father?" Foley reiterated, drawing the priest's attention back from the political incorrectness of his overzealous assistant.

"Well, this Alec Samuels now. I made some enquiries myself about him, Mr Foley, and it seems to me that if, as you said, he was suspected of involvement in the death of the young journalist, Peter Sayers, surely his newspaper editor would be aware of that?" He paused for a moment, studying his listeners' faces before adding, "Don't you think so, Mr Foley?

Neither Foley nor Wells replied, giving Father Donne the opportunity to make a further point.

"And why did you think it was necessary to listen in to our phone conversations and to have us watched from outside?"

"Precisely because we didn't want the boy to take off, Father. He needs to be controlled, otherwise…"

"Otherwise, what, Mr Foley? Perhaps it would help if you were completely honest with us. At the moment we don't know which bits are truth and which is fiction. Perhaps you can enlighten me?"

* * *

The gentle knock on the door was enough to rouse Alec from his dreaming slumber. He stretched and yawned, uttering a half-choked "come in" as he propped himself up against the white, feathered pillow, and began to appraise his new surroundings in the light of a new day. The door opened to reveal the pretty, blond haired daughter of their host, holding a small tray charged with a cup of tea and a couple of chocolate covered digestive biscuits.

"Mum thought you might like to have this," she said, her lips broadening into an easy smile. Alec didn't say a word as the girl moved effortlessly into the room to lay the tray on the bed-side table. They had met the night before, of course, and had chatted a little over dinner. He had mostly listened, entranced by the girl, drawn inexorably to her femininity, as she told him about her school and her ambition to study law at university. When she asked him about his schooling, his mother intervened to say that Alec had been tutored at home because of the problems they were having with his estranged father.

"What was that like?" Sally had asked, "being taught at home I mean. Didn't you miss seeing your friends every day?" Again his mother spoke for him.

"We had his friends come to the house quite often," she lied, "so Alec didn't really miss them, did you son."

"No, not really Mother," the boy had responded, spontaneously picking up his cue. "And my tutor was very good," he added, embellishing the performance a little more.

"Did you sleep alright?" Sally asked, watching Alec take his first sip of tea. "I never sleep well if I'm in a strange bed."

"Yes, I slept very well, thank you," Alec replied, carefully reuniting the cup with its delicate china saucer. "I dreamt that we were going to be friends," he added candidly with a smile.

The girl blushed and felt a tightening of the muscles in her stomach. She didn't want to confess that she had also dreamt last night, of more than friendship. There was something about the boy that was beyond simple attraction; something inescapable that she knew would bring them together, sooner rather than later. She tried to relax her stomach muscles and to take a deep breath before replying.

"I think we will be, Alec," she said, sitting on the bed and taking the boy's hand in hers. "I'm sure we will be." She leant over to kiss him gently on the lips and felt no resistance from him. "I'd better go," she said, reluctantly pulling herself away from him. "Mum'll wonder what's up."

"We mustn't let your mother or mine know anything about this," said Alec, holding the girl gently by the arm, "at least, not for the moment."

She stood up and leant over to kiss him again, on the cheek, and agreed that whatever 'this' was, it would be their secret.

* * *

"Look, Father, I'm going to tell you the truth about this whole affair, but I'd like to do it in the confessional," said Foley, to the surprise and astonishment of the priest.

"But I thought you said you were a non-believer, Mr Foley. Surely the confession means nothing to you," replied Father Donne, trying to decipher the man's motive for such a suggestion.

"Quite right. But it means a lot to you, Father. So anything I tell you during confession will remain there, understood?"

From the corner of his eye, Father Donne could see the twisted little smile that had cracked across Marcia Well's face, as if she had realised that Foley had his man in his pocket. The priest had little choice but to agree that he, and the almighty God above, would be the only ones privy to these new revelations. Just for good measure and to secure the deal, Foley added:

"And you will, of course, be subject to the official secrets act."

Well's smile turned into a sardonic grin.

* * *

Foley followed Father Donne to the church, across the walled garden and in through the small door that led to the vestry and then into the body of the building.

They sat in the confessional box, separated by a wooden latticed grill that obscured the face of both confessor and confessee. The ritual 'bless me father for I have sinned' which usually signalled the start of these brief disclosures was replaced by Father Donne's anxious petition for the truth. Foley began, his voice quickly dropping to a whisper as he adjusted to the acoustic amplification of the wooden confessional.

"Most of what you already know is the truth, Father Donne. There is a government scientist, a geneticist as we said, who has been working with animals on genetic changes that might eventually be beneficial to mankind. However, some years ago, and in the belief that other, shall we say, less friendly governments were planning similar actions, it was decided that the incredible results that the scientist and his team had achieved should be the subject of some human experimentation. Knowing that this would be highly controversial and unlikely to be agreed in open parliament, a decision was taken, at the highest level I might add, to keep the project covert. At first, it was thought that a number of women might be persuaded to volunteer their services to the project; to be the mothers of any children born. But the risk of any one of them breaking rank would have destroyed the whole concept right from the beginning. So it was decided to choose a person and to artificially inseminate her." Foley paused for a moment, awaiting some response from the other side of the box.

"Go on, Mr Foley. I'm still listening," urged the priest, recalling Aldous Huxley's Brave New World and thinking that this modern version was as ugly as Huxley's original.

"Well, we began our search for the perfect subject, the woman who would be part of this experiment. With all the data at our disposal it wasn't difficult to find someone to fit the bill. That part of what we told you is perfectly true, Father. Frances was a perfect choice and so were you." Again he paused, perhaps expecting the priest to ask what he meant by that, but just another 'Go on,' followed.

"We would have taken the child away as soon as it was born, but the plan changed as you and your sister became involved and we later realised that the child was being reared in virtual seclusion. Perhaps given the boy's psychic powers, any direct intervention might have been difficult anyway, even at the very beginning."

Father Donne stopped the monologue to ask a question:

"So Samuels, how did he get to meet Frances?

"Ah, well, we arranged with Frances' boss that the scientist, whose covert name was Alec Samuels, should meet with her at some opportunity. We told Bryant, her boss at the time, that it was part of an undercover operation. He was shocked to hear that Frances might be involved in anything shady but didn't take much persuading. I had the impression that he didn't value the woman very much, in terms of his business, of course, and in any case he would have been instructed to dismiss her, if he hadn't already made up his mind to do it." At this, Father Donne could not prevent the escape of an indignant huff and crossed himself before adding a further encouragement for Foley to continue this damning but indemnified confession.

"What you were told about the growth rate and sexual maturity of the genetically altered chimpanzees is also true, but the growth rate continues, Father. All of the apes have aged considerably and some have already died. We believe that this will happen to the boy." Foley stopped again and this time he could hear the priest praying, beseeching his god to look after Frances and her son. The prayer stopped and he asked a second question:

"And the sexual proclivity of the animals, does Alec have this?

"We believe so, Father, and it's why we need to find the boy, before he impregnates every young woman he can find. What we didn't tell you was that, when they reached puberty, the male chimpanzees exuded some sort of chemical substance, a pheromone that the females found irresistible."

"And you think that might be so with Alec?"

"It's certainly a possibility that we cannot afford to ignore."

A meditative silence engulfed the box as Foley's words bounced around the wooden walls of the confessional, forcing their way into the priest's consciousness.

"And the female chimpanzees," he said at last, "the ones that were pregnant, what has happened to their offspring?"

"They have developed at a normal rate of growth but both male and female infants have retained the intellectual superiority of their fathers, as far as we can tell. They are as yet sexually immature, and it will be interesting to see whether the same degree of intelligence is inherited by a second generation of offspring."

The two men fell silent once more, each contemplating the likely consequences if Alec were to father a number of genetically altered children. Father Donne broke the silence.

"Is there any more you should be telling me, Mr Foley?"

"Only that it is imperative that we get the boy back as soon as possible, for his sake as well as ours. We have no real idea what these genetic changes might mean for us in the long run if Alec is allowed to procreate in an uncontrolled way." Foley stopped abruptly as his last words dripped inexorably from his lips, like drops of water from a leaky tap. He realised that he had said too much and was not surprised to hear the priest shuffle uncomfortably on the other side of the screen, then prompt with another question.

"So are you saying that you would allow Alec to father children in a controlled way? Is that what your testing facility is about, Mr Foley?"

"Look, Father, we know that there are other governments carrying out the same experiments, some of whom may be further advanced than we are. We cannot afford to be left behind in this particular race, just as we must ensure our military security. It is vital that Alec is brought back into a secure environment." He stopped again, taking in a deep breath to control the agitation that his voice betrayed. "Please, Father Donne, you must tell us where Frances has taken the boy," he continued in more measured and deliberate tone, hoping for a positive response from the priest.

"I'm sorry, Mr Foley. What I told you earlier was the utter

truth. I do not know where Frances has gone for which I am very grateful, as I would not know whether to tell you or not. I believe I now understand what your experiment is about and it seems that it is the narrow interests of a particular section of humanity that you seek to benefit and certainly not humanity as a whole. You and your scientists have chosen to meddle with God's finest creation in an attempt to do what, Mr Foley?"

Foley could find no answer that he was prepared to share with the priest. Instead, he whispered menacingly through the lattice grill.

"You and your sister will be charged with crimes against the national interest if the boy and his mother are not returned to us within two days, Father Donne. There will remain a watch on your house and the church and, incidentally, there is now a tap on the phone in the church. I believe this confession is at an end." He stood up and left the confessional, leaving the priest to reflect on his last, threatening words.

Chapter Thirteen

Frances followed Helen into the farmhouse kitchen, insisting that the least she could do was to help with the dishes after the copious lunch they had all enjoyed.

"Your lad and my Sally seem to be getting on like a house on fire," said Helen as she filled the washing-up bowl with hot, soapy water. "I'll wash if you don't mind wiping."

"No, of course," replied Frances, wondering whether the fire brigade might be needed at any moment. She absent-mindedly picked up the cotton tea-cloth that hung over the kitchen radiator, uneasy about the obvious attraction between Alec and the girl.

"Does Sally have a boy-friend?" she asked as casually as she could.

"She did have, but they split up about three months ago. Can't say I was sorry, as I reckon he was only after one thing, if you get my meaning." She handed Frances another freshly rinsed plate to be wiped, then added, "na, my Sally knows what's right and what's not. I don't have any worries there." She smiled happily before tackling the cutlery that lingered at the bottom of the bowl. "They grow up so quickly mind. Seems like only yesterday she was toddling about and playing with dolls."

The wet plate slipped from Frances' grasp, striking the hard stone floor before exploding into myriad pieces which hurled themselves in every direction.

"I'm so sorry!" said Frances, bending down immediately to start picking up the bits of porcelain which now decorated the kitchen floor. "I'm so clumsy at times," she added, embarrassment casting its red shadow across her face.

"Don't you worry none," replied her ever-indulgent host, lending her rubber-gloved hands to the job of picking up the larger pieces. "Here, let me do this. Less chance of me cutting my hand with these gloves on. I'll sweep up the little bits in a sec."

"What was that noise?" said a voice whose owner followed shortly after through the kitchen door.

"Hello Dad," replied Helen, "it's only a plate. Fell on the floor and smashed." Frances was grateful that she hadn't been singled out as the perpetrator of this little foible, especially as Stephen's warning about old George being a bit of a grumpy old sod was no exaggeration.

"You oughta be careful with your washing-up, my girl. Can't afford to keep losing plates like that. Money don't grow on trees you know."

Helen looked up at Frances, whose blush was now a shade or two deeper, and rolled her eyes skyward before turning the old man's attention away from the stricken crockery.

"Sally not in the living-room then? I'm surprised she didn't come in to see what was going on."

"Nope," replied her father, "no-one in the living room. And Sally hasn't come to sort out my washing-up neither," he added with a look that settled somewhere between disbelief and annoyance. The blush on Frances' face drained away as quickly as it had appeared, replaced by a bloodless blanket of white.

"Perhaps she's gone off for a walk with Alec, showing him the estate, eh Dad."

"I'll just see if I can find them," said Frances quickly, leaving the room and her bewildered hosts in her wake.

* * *

They must have driven down this lane on their way to the farm house, but now it was light and Alec could see the high hedgerows that shielded the fields on either side. There was no pavement, so they walked along the road. Sally held his hand and assured him that traffic rarely ventured this way, unless it was heading for their house; then it was usually the postman early in the morning in his red van. The weak winter sun had finally burned off the mist that had shrouded the earlier part of the day, but it was still cold. Sally put her arm around the boy's waste to feel his heat. They headed off the narrow lane and over a stile into a grassy field. The grass was still wet but not muddy as they walked silently on, neither questioning where they were going, or why they were going there. The barn stood to one side of the field, near another narrow lane that gave access to a neighbour's farm some way in the distance. As they approached the building Alec could see the high wooden doors that kept the weather out. He wondered how they would get in, but knew that Sally would have a way. At the side of the barn was a small window which at first glance appeared as tightly locked as the rest of the barn's openings. Sally approached it confidently and, taking a pen knife from the pocket of her jeans, she slid the blade beneath the frame to prise it open.

"This window's got a broken lock. You can always get in here," she said, smiling at the boy who watched her deftly climb in through the open frame. "Come on," she prompted, "it's much warmer in here."

Alec followed her and climbed down through the window onto the stacked bales of hay that filled half the space in the barn.

"Do you come here a lot, then?" he asked the girl as she chose one of the bales to sit down on.

"Mum doesn't know, but sometimes I need to get away, you know, just to be alone for a while. Don't worry, I don't bring boys here. Mum would kill me," she explained, then suddenly realised the absurdity of what she had just said. "You are the first," she added coyly, excusing herself before grabbing the lapels of Alec's coat and pulling him onto her.

* * *

Alice Donne picked up the ringing phone and waited for the now familiar click and buzz to clear before greeting the caller.

"Can I speak to Mr Williams?" said the thin and agitated voice of a woman.

"I'm sorry, dear, but you have the wrong number," replied Alice, her own voice betraying an inexorable anxiety at hearing the signal that would tell the Donnes that Frances was about to call the phone in the church, the one that she believed was not subject to the prying of Foley and his people. Alice passed the message on to her brother who went immediately to the church to await the call back. Two minutes later, he picked up the phone.

"Hello, Frances," he said as anxious as his sister had been, "are you and the boy alright?"

"Yes, Father," she replied, ignorant in her excitement of the alien noise on the line, "only..." she stopped herself from finishing the sentence and the priest could hear the snuffles that punctuated her heavy, laboured breathing.

"What's happened, Frances? Is it Alec, has something happened to him?" He heard her blow her nose before she replied:

"I'm not sure, Father, but I think it is possible that he has begun to…" again she was unable to complete the words, but the priest filled in the gaps for her.

"Do you mean he has had sex, Frances?" he said directly, cutting through the chaste inhibitions of the boy's mother.

"I don't know, but he has met a girl. She's the daughter of the person we are staying with. I didn't know there would be a girl here. This afternoon they went off for a walk together." Now the torrent was almost impossible to stop as Frances described how the girl, Sally, seemed to have become remarkably fond of Alec in the very little time they had known each other. They returned from their walk after about an hour, hand in hand, and … Well, she couldn't be certain but it was possible that they had already…

"I'm sure that is not the case," broke in Father Donne, trying to sound convincing whilst Foley's words of warning bounced around in his head.

"Look, tell me where you are, Frances. If it's not too far, I might be able to get away to see you and the boy, to talk to him about what he said, what he said he would do."

Frances gave the priest the details of their safe house, tucked away in the Welsh countryside. She hoped that he would be able to be with them soon as she was at a loss as to how to deal with the situation. The thought that Alec might be taken from her was unbearable, but so was the possibility that the daughter of her trusting host was already pregnant with his child.

"Okay, Frances, I'll see what I can do about getting to you soon. In the meantime try to keep the boy with you at all times. He must not be left alone with the girl."

"Yes, Father," she said meekly, then hung up.

Father Donne kept hold of the phone in his hand, knowing that other ears had listened to their conversation, that Foley now knew where Frances and the boy were hiding.

"God, I hope I have done the right thing," he beseeched, finally replacing the receiver on the hook. He prayed a little more at the altar in the nave of the church before returning to the rectory to confirm with Alice that he had complied with Foley's instructions.

"What else could I do, Alice?" he asked abjectly, slumping into a chair in the living room. His sister didn't offer an answer, but sat next to him on the arm of the chair, cradling his head in her arms as they both wept.

* * *

Frances put the phone down and sobbed quietly to herself until Helen knocked on the closed door of the lounge to ask if everything was alright.

"Sorry, Helen," she said through a sniffle, as she opened the door to her host. "Problems with my husband again. We might have to move on soon."

* * *

The distant hoot of a tawny owl punctuated the silence of the still and moonless night. Frances had lain awake listening to it, unable to sleep, unable to focus on anything but the thought that her son may have had sex with Helen's pretty, young daughter. She thought about Alec's words again, his stated purpose. To breed, he had said, with young women, plural. Sally was besotted with him, Frances could see that in the way she looked at him, in the way she held on to him as they at last came back from their walk. Alec, she considered with some pride, had grown into a handsome enough young man, but to entrance someone so quickly? Was it the mythical 'love at first sight' that she had never believed in, let alone known. It was more than that. There was something almost animal, feral in Sally's attraction to Alec. Almost as if she had taken a love potion. The owl hooted again, momentarily distracting her from this last thought. Nonsense, she said to herself as the hoot died away, but the thought did not. The silence lay with her, an empty canvas on which to paint her fears. But now a new noise impinged on her consciousness, faint and distant. She latched onto it, trying to decipher the sound. She tried to look at the small alarm clock on the bedside table, but couldn't make out the hands in the darkness. There was a lamp next to it, she remembered, and she reached out to find the cable and the switch. The light hurt her eyes as she blinked against it, eventually adjusting her focus to see that it was 5:30. Far too early for the postman in his van. The noise was a little louder now and had coalesced into a discernable hum. Seconds later she recognised the raucous purr of a car engine, possibly more than one, heading towards the farm house. Who could it be at this time of the morning? Surely not Father Donne. He would not drive so far in the middle of the night. She leapt out of bed, almost banging her head on the steeply angled ceiling that met the floor to her left.

"Oh my God!" she said out loud, realising that it could only be Foley or a posse of police sent to bring her and Alec back to London, to the control of their 'institution'. She struggled to understand how Foley could know where they were. 'The phone in the vestry,' her intuition told her, 'it must have been bugged too! But surely Father Donne would have known.' She stopped thinking and dressed herself as quickly and as quietly as she could, hoping not to wake Helen and her sleeping daughter. In stockinged feet she crept out, leaving her bedroom door ajar for the fragile yellow light that the lamp spilled onto the landing. She went into the boy's room, not bothering to knock on the door.

"Alec," she whispered in his ear as he lay sleeping, "Alec, wake up! We have to go, now!"

The boy stirred and raised himself on one elbow.

"What is it Mother? What's wrong?" he asked, feeling his mother's hand against his shoulder in the semi-darkness.

"Just get up and get dressed as quickly as you can. We have to leave. I think Mr Foley knows we are here. Listen," she urged, putting a finger to her closed lips, "can you hear cars approaching?"

Alec sat up and turned his head towards the window, then left his bed abruptly to find his clothes and shoes. Frances went back into her room to pick her hand-bag off the back of the chair it hung from, then joined her son. Soon they were on their way across the short landing and down the wooden staircase, treading shoeless and with as little noise as possible.

"What about Sally and her mother?" said Alec, "shouldn't we wake them?"

"No, Alec. It's better that they don't know we have left. They can't then say anything to the police about it."

They put their shoes on in the hall and took their coats off the hooks on the coat-stand. Frances opened the front door as quietly as she could, then stepped out into the cold of the night, wrapping her woollen coat around her. Alec quickly followed her out, closing the door silently behind him. The house's elevated position was enough to give them a clear view of the road down in the valley that would eventually lead to the narrow lane which the cars would take to reach them. Outside, the engine noise was much clearer and accompanied by the visible proof of their approach; a string of headlights piercing the low lying mist that covered the valley floor. Soon they would be there.

"Where should we go, Alec?" Frances asked as they set off carefully down the flint steps, with very little light to guide them. Alec took his mother's hand.

"Follow me," he said, leading them both along the hedgerows of the narrow lane. They reached the stile as the lights of the leading car illuminated the hedge opposite the field as it approached the long shallow bend. Alec and his mother ducked down behind the stile, obscured by it and the dark mantle of the night. The cars passed at speed in a flash of four sets of headlights.

"Quick," said Alec to his mother whose hand was ice cold in his. "There's a barn on the other side of this field, and another farm beyond that. We need to find some transport."

'Yes,' thought Frances, 'that would be more than useful, were it not for the fact that I can't drive'. The thought didn't develop into a concrete objection to the plan as she felt the tug of her son's hand towing her across the grassy meadow. They soon reached the barn which loomed large and sinister in front of them. Frances wanted to ask whether this is where he had come with Sally, but this was not the time to have this particular fear confirmed; there were plenty of other fears to worry about.

They walked on past the barn, along the narrow road that twisted a mile or more up the hillside. Eventually, the outhouses of a farm stood weakly against the early morning darkness. Frances tugged at Alec's coat sleeve with her free hand.

"What if there's a farm dog?" she asked fearfully, "there's always a dog."

"We'll just have to be very quiet, Mother," Alec replied calmly, "then maybe it won't hear us."

They came to an open barn with more bales of hay stacked to the ceiling, but so far no dog to shatter the silence. They went on, past a couple more buildings until the more substantial shape of a large house could be made out less than a hundred yards away. Parked about halfway between the fugitives and the house was a pick-up truck, of the kind that Alec had seen in certain American films.

"Come on, Mother," he whispered, keeping his head low to the ground as he crept towards the goal.

Frances had no idea what the boy intended to do and decided that now was the time to raise her previously suppressed objection to the plan.

"But Alec, wait a minute. I don't know how to drive. I've never even had lesson," she said breathlessly, as her son pulled her in his wake.

"Don't worry, Mother, it'll be alright," replied the boy laconically.

They reached the vehicle with still no barking dog to raise the alarm. Alec tried the handle of the passenger door which, to his surprise and relief, gave in to the gentle pressure that he had put on it.

"Get in, Mother," he commanded as the door was pulled open, creaking slightly on its hinges. Frances hesitated for a moment, looking at her son in the half-light, bewildered by this new turn of events. Eventually and with his persuasive hand at her back she climbed up into the passenger seat.

"Pull the handle on the driver's door, will you Mother," he said casually, as if stealing a car was an everyday occurrence. He climbed aboard, then pulled down the sun visor to check if the keys had been left there, whilst his mother watched in astonishment.

"How do you know all this?" she said, seeing the boy lean across her and rummage through the glove compartment in search of the elusive key.

"I watch films, Mother," he replied, as if this were all the explanation that was needed. "No keys, though," he added, "so I'll have to try the other way." He bent down beneath the dashboard and pulled out a couple of wires. "There's a torch in the glove compartment, Mother. Would you pass it to me, please."

She mechanically did as she was asked, reassuring herself that this current escapade was no more peculiar than much of her life during the past three years. Alec shone the torch on the bunch of wires that hung beneath the steering wheel. He isolated the two red wires then looked around again, this time for something to strip them with.

"Do you have a nail-file on you, Mother?"

"Wait a minute," she replied, opening her handbag and searching through its few contents. "Will this do?" she said, triumphantly holding up the pointed metal file.

"Perfect," said the boy, taking the implement and attacking the ends of the wires. "I just need to wind these together. Could you hold the torch for me and shine it down here, onto the wires." He passed the torch to his mother and noticed that her hand was shaking slightly as she took the light from him. But if he had asked, she would have told him that it was not the cold or fear that was making her tremble. Instead, she felt a strange and liberating excitement, as if nothing else mattered in the world except that she was here with her extraordinary son, alone in the dead of night, escaping the monstrous intentions of Foley and his like.

"Now, the brown wire," said Alec, wielding the nail-file to strip off a little of the plastic covering. He touched the bare copper against the entwined red-coated wires and the engine exploded into immediate and noisy life. The bark of the hypothetical dog suddenly materialised, adding to the cacophony that blew apart the still of the night. With no further prompting needed, Alec depressed the clutch and threw the car into gear. The truck lurched forward as he stepped on the accelerator, almost cutting out before he pressed down on the clutch again. Thankfully, the yard was wide enough to turn the large vehicle around in one movement. The truck sped towards the open farm yard gate, the engine complaining as the rev counter edged towards red. Alec managed to find another gear and to steer the vehicle unimpaired through the gate and out onto the road. Behind him the farmer and his two sons could do no more than watch in sleepy confusion as their property disappeared into the distance.

* * *

Less than five minutes after Alec and his mother had climbed over the stile into the grassy field, the first of the cars pulled into the small yard in front of the house. The full beam of the halogen lamps splashed their harsh yellow light onto the stone clad façade of the building. On the top floor a bedroom light competed weakly with the glare, then another illuminated a second window.

Soon all four cars crowded into the yard. The two lead vehicles disgorged seven burly policemen and a police woman, each quickly taking up position to surround the house. From the back of the third car emerged Landon Foley and the redoubtable Marcia Wells. They climbed the flint steps whose shiny surfaces glistened in the glow of the unaccustomed light. Foley reached the house and knocked hard on the front door.

"Who is it? What do you want at this time of the morning?" came a timid and anxious voice through the closed door.

"It's the local constabulary, Mrs Owen," replied the police sergeant standing at Foley's shoulder. "Open up please. We need to talk to you."

A brief, mumbled conversation from inside the house ended with the door being opened slightly and Helen's blanched features peering around the crack. She saw the uniform and decided that it was safe to let these people in. The police sergeant remained outside, guarding the entrance, while Foley and Wells followed Helen into the hall, closing the door behind them. Foley flashed his identity card in token introduction, nodding to his assistant to do the same. Sally stood at her mother's side, holding onto her arm, just as confused as her mother as to what this could possibly be about.

"We are looking for a woman and her son, Mrs Owen and we have reason to believe that they are here. The woman's name is O'Donnell, Frances O'Donnell, and her son is called Alec. Are they here now?" asked Foley, scrutinising the faces of the two frightened women before him.

"Why? What have they done?" asked Sally, before her mother could answer. Foley ignored the question and prompted the mother again.

"Are they here, Mrs Owen?" he said sternly, "yes or no?"

"They were here," Helen began, her upper lip trembling a little with the cold and the confused emotion which this sudden interruption had provoked, "but their beds are now empty. I've got no idea where they are now."

"Do you know when they left?" asked Foley, nodding a signal to Wells who opened the front door to let in another man and a woman, each in civilian clothes. They were not introduced as Helen answered:

"Not at all. I thought they were still asleep in bed. Won't you tell us what this is all about?" she pleaded, putting a comforting arm around her daughter who had begun to cry.

"The woman and her son are suspected of being involved in the supply of arms to the IRA, the Irish Republican Army, Madam," said Wells convincingly.

"I know what the IRA is," Helen replied, taking an instant dislike to the women's patronising tone, "and if you want my opinion, that's just ridiculous. Frances was here because of her husband," she affirmed, unwilling to believe what they were being told. Foley turned towards the man who had just entered the house.

"Would you like to introduce yourself, Inspector?" he said, inviting the man to step forward.

"I'm Inspector Neville Cheeseman from Special Branch. It's our job to keep track of Irish Republican sympathisers and the like. As Mr Foley has said, we believe that this woman is actively involved in dealings with the IRA. It is vital that she is apprehended as soon as possible. So if there is any more information you can give us, I strongly advise you to do it now."

Helen felt the strength escape from her legs and she grabbed onto her daughter to avoid collapsing completely.

"Mum!" Sally cried out, "you'd better come into the living room and sit down."

Foley, Wells and the other woman followed them into the room where Helen crumpled into the nearest chair, her head in her hands. Sally sat next to her with tears dripping down her ashen cheeks. From the hall they could hear the sound of heavy footsteps climbing the stairs, the performance reversed a few seconds later. The inspector came into the room and spoke quietly to Foley:

"The beds are still a little warm, so they can't have left long ago. They probably heard the cars and shot off just before we got here. I'll get the handlers onto it." Foley nodded his approval, then turned to the other woman before introducing her.

"This is Doctor Mallen. She would like to speak to your daughter, Mrs Owen. Sally, isn't it?" he said, directing a look and a smile at the girl.

"Why?" shouted the girl's mother, "why do you need to speak to my Sally? What has she done?"

"It's really nothing to worry about, Mrs Owen," said the doctor, "but we just need to check something out. It'll only take a couple of minutes. Would you mind? Is there somewhere we can go privately?" she asked, sugaring the request with the same reassuring smile that had played across Foley's lips.

"You're not speaking to her without me there, lady, doctor or no doctor!" Helen retorted, forgetting the weakness in her legs and pushing herself forcefully up from the chair.

"Look, Mrs Owen," Foley intervened, "I would hate to think that you might be charged with obstructing the police in their enquiries. I really do think you need to cooperate with the doctor's request."

"It's alright Mum, I don't mind," said Sally, before her

mother could find another argument. "We can go to my bedroom," she added, wiping the wet from under her eyes, and pointing the way for the doctor to follow as her mother collapsed once more into the chair.

"So," began Foley again, "did Miss O'Donnell, Frances, say where they might go once they had left here?"

Before Helen could answer the noise of a scuffle could be heard from outside.

"What the bloody hell is going on? Helen, Sally, are you alright?"

"It's my dad," said Helen to Foley, getting up again and heading towards the hall where her father was being held by two of the uniformed policemen.

"Found him sneaking around the back of one of the outhouses, Sir," said one of the men.

"He's my dad," Helen repeated, "and you can let go of him!"

"What's goin' on, Helen? Great load o' noise woke me up," said the old man who was still wearing a pair of aging slippers, despite the damp and cold of the early morning. His daughter took him by the arm and led him into the front room.

"I'll make us a drink, Dad. Then I'll try to explain what this is all about, not that I understand much of it," she said, looking accusingly at Foley and Wells who had followed her out into the hall.

The doctor descended the staircase followed by Sally, whose pretty features were spoiled by the worry lines cutting into her face. Her mother could see that she had been crying again.

"Sally, what is it?" she asked, taking her daughter by the hand and leading her back into the living room, the girl's confused grandfather shuffling his slippered feet behind them.

Outside, the noise of dogs barking could suddenly be heard, startling the three beleaguered members of the household. The police sergeant appeared at the living room door to announce that the two police dogs were responding to the frenzied barking of another dog that could be heard some distance away. He also reported that a car could be heard driving at speed from the same direction.

"It's them!" exclaimed Foley. "Sergeant, you and the police woman stay here with the doctor. Cheeseman, grab a couple of bits of clothing from the woman and the son's bedrooms and set the dogs after them. Marcia, you come with me." They all swept out of the house, leaving old George, his distraught daughter and granddaughter in the bewildering limbo that was once their cosy living room. They heard the doors of one of the cars slam shut, then the roar of its engine as it shot off into the murk of the pre-dawn day.

The doctor spoke to the sergeant, asking him to leave the room for a moment.

"Perhaps your father could be asked to step out with the sergeant, Mrs Owen," she added, taking a seat herself opposite Helen and her daughter.

"It's alright, Dad, go with the sergeant," said Helen, resigning herself to their fate. George reluctantly left the room leaving the four women alone together.

"This is policewoman Thomas, Mrs Owen, Sally. She is here to help, as I am," explained the doctor in sympathetic tones as Helen looked up at the police woman and Sally looked down at her hands. The doctor took a deep breath, then spoke again, candidly explaining that she had examined Mrs Owen's daughter for signs of rape. Helen blushed deep red, although, to the surprise of the doctor and the attendant police woman, Sally did not. It was Sally who responded to the doctor's blunt disclosure.

"It wasn't like that, it wasn't rape. I wanted him to!" she said, almost screaming at the doctor as her tears started again. Helen silently put an arm around her weeping daughter's shoulder, pulling her forward in a comforting embrace.

"We will need to check, over the next few weeks, if Sally is pregnant," continued the doctor, ignoring the young girl's interpretation.

"I don't understand," said Helen, releasing her embrace for a moment, "what has this got to do with IRA sympathisers? It doesn't make any sense."

"Believe me, Mrs Owen, there are many things that I come across in my line of work that make no sense. You'll just have to trust me when I say that it is important that we keep a check on young Sally here, to see if she has become pregnant."

"And if she is, what then?"

"Well, then we'll just have to see, won't we," said the doctor, getting up from her seat. "Now, we will be leaving soon, but woman constable Thomas here will be taking statements from you all. And there will be a guard placed on your property, until we know that the fugitives are in custody. For your safety, of course."

"I'm sorry, Mum," said Sally, sobbing on her mother's shoulder.

"Don't worry sweetheart. Couldn't be helped," replied her mother, once again surprising the other two women in the room with her curious indulgence.

* * *

The pick-up truck careered down the narrow lane, brushing the hedges on either side. Alec had not found the switch for the lights and he fought to steady the speeding vehicle, peering through the windscreen and the hesitant light of early dawn. The barking of the farm dog behind them was echoed by more dogs across the field to their right. 'They must be on our scent,' he thought, 'but they won't be able to track us in this.' His mother sat tense and rigid in the seat next to him. She held on to the arm rest of the passenger door and noticed that it was not fully closed, but there was no time to stop and close it now. They were approaching a bend, but Alec did not slow down, intent on putting as much distance between them and the chasing mob as he could. Suddenly, a blinding light ripped through the semi-darkness as Alec steered the speeding truck around the bend. Heading towards them was the first of the police cars, its headlights full on and travelling at speed. Alec slammed his foot hard down on the brake pedal, but the truck skidded on the damp surface of the road. The back of the vehicle struck the unyielding thicket and flipped over, throwing Frances out as the passenger door flew open. Beneath the truck the two cylinders of propane gas that had sat unnoticed in the open back of the truck scraped along the tarmac road. The driver of the police car saw the truck sliding towards him on its back and braked hard, but too late. The two vehicles collided head on, twisting metal and limbs in an instant. One of the gas cylinders ruptured on impact and a spark ignited the escaping gas sending a ball of flame into the air. Seconds later a further explosion intensified the inferno, setting fire to the hedgerows on either side of the blaze.

The second of the police cars reached the scene, its driver stopping fifty yards away, unable to approach further because of the intense heat and flames.

Chapter Fourteen

Peter and Alice Donne sat on either side of the London Hospital bed as they had done for most of the previous three weeks. They had been told by the specialist that talking to the patient might bring her out of the coma she had been in since the accident. They were also told that some people lived for years without ever recovering consciousness, so they should not expect too much too soon. They wondered whether Frances knew already that Alec was dead, killed instantly in the terrible accident which also took the lives of Foley and Marcia Wells and the two policemen who were in the car with them. There were no bodies to recover, just a gruesome pile of charred bones, so intense had been the fire. Frances had apparently been thrown from the truck before it collided with the police car, so it was doubtful that she was aware of the terrible consequences of the crash. She was found lying face down in the muddy stubble field next to the road. Her left leg had been broken and she had lacerations to both her arms, the doctor had told them. There was also a serious head injury causing swelling to the brain, which was the suspected reason for the coma. It would not be until the swelling had subsided that the medical team would be able to ascertain whether there was any permanent brain damage. 'Perhaps,' thought Alice in a moment of fear and weakness, 'it would be better if she did not survive to be told that her son was gone.' The thought was not shared with her brother who once more put his trust in God and prayed that they would all get through this terrible nightmare.

They had learnt of the tragedy from Bill Tyne, the editor of the Daily Reader. He had been sensitive enough to call on them personally when he had heard the news from Stephen Finnigan, who had himself been informed by his distraught cousin. Tyne had reported to the Donnes, third hand, all that he had been told about the tragedy and how odd it was, Stephen's cousin had told him, that neither the police nor the doctor had been back to take the statements that the terrifying explosions had so violently postponed or to check on Sally's condition. Tyne soon discovered other oddities surrounding the affair as his, and he presumed other newspapers, received the official and only permissible version of the demise of Landon Foley and Marcia Wells who were described in the press release from Whitehall as 'two of the leading figures in the fight against terrorism and subversion in the United Kingdom.' Their deaths were attributed to a tragic, but simple road accident. There was no mention of Alec or his mother. Accompanying the handout was a judicial order restraining the 'fourth estate' from carrying any further news or comment involving either of the deceased.

Father Donne had since spoken to Helen Owen, assuring her that Alec and his mother were not at all involved in any nefarious activities and that it had been a terrible case of mistaken identity. He thanked Mrs Owen for her kindness towards them during their short time together and hoped that she and her daughter would be able to come to London to attend the private memorial service that he had planned for the boy. Helen didn't at first respond to the invitation, wanting answers to a couple of nagging questions.

"Why did they run away like that, Father?" she asked, still struggling to make any sense of the events of that night. Father Donne thought for a moment about telling the truth, but fiction would be kinder, and perhaps easier to swallow.

"I'm sure Frances will be able to tell us herself when she wakes up, Helen. Until then, I believe she must have thought that it was her husband that was coming for her and Alec. That would certainly have frightened her," he replied, confident that this version of events was plausible but crossing himself as he spoke, seeking forgiveness and divine approbation at the same time.

"But …" Helen began, but was not able to finish her sentence.

"Yes, Helen, please go on," urged Father Donne, wondering whether Frances' fears for the daughter were about to be confirmed but secretly hoping that no more awkward questions would require a deceitful answer. His hope was rewarded as Helen could only manage a:

"Nothing, Father. Thank you for asking us and I'm sure Sally and me will be there."

She scribbled down the address of the church that the priest dictated and thanked him again for his call.

* * *

There were just six people in the church to commemorate the short life of Alec O'Donnell. Two of those present knew just how short a life it had been, an incredible dash to puberty, a flowering of youth extinguished in the blink of an eye. Three others, Helen and Sally Owen and Sally's Uncle Stephen, were surprised, perhaps even shocked to see so few mourners. Where were the school friends, maybe teachers, aunts and uncles that must have peopled the boy's life? Bill Tyne had asked himself the same question, but suspected that he knew the answer, as incredible as it might seem.

Frances was not there. She had lain in the hospital bed, comatose and lifeless for five weeks now. The doctors had said that the swelling around her brain had diminished, but the signs were not good. There was some evidence of brain damage which would be irreparable, even if she were, eventually, to come out of the coma. This, though, said the specialist, was looking more and more unlikely. So the service was brief, with special prayers said for the recovery of the boy's mother. Alice Donne played the church organ and the little group sang a sombre hymn to bring the sad occasion to a close.

They adjourned to the rectory living room to drink some tea and nibble at the sandwiches that Alice had prepared. Bill Tyne and Stephen Finnigan soon left, but were warmly thanked by the Donnes for making the effort to come.

Alone with Sally and her mother, Peter Donne was determined to ask the question that had been on his mind ever since that frantic phone call from Frances. He looked at the girl who was sitting on the sofa next to her mother, an uneaten sandwich redundant on the plate at her lap, her cup of tea hardly touched. He looked at her mother, equally lacking any appetite, and said apologetically:

"Please forgive the question I'm about to ask Sally, but it's very important that I do." Helen looked back at him and she reddened slightly as she quickly put down her full cup and saucer.

"I'm sure, Father, that if it is important, you should ask it," she replied to the priest's surprise. It was as if she knew, and more remarkably, was prepared to accept without indignation, the question which was to be put to her young daughter. He turned to Sally.

"I'm sorry Sally, but I do need to ask this," he began, stopping to see the girl look up at him with tears in her eyes.

"Are you pregnant? Are you carrying Alec's child?"

There was no righteous protest from either daughter or mother, just a silent consideration of what was to be said next. Softly and sadly, the girl replied.

"No, Father, I am not pregnant. I have a medical condition and can't have children," she said, wiping a growing flood of tears from her eyes.

"Oh, I see!" said Father Donne, derailed by this least expected of answers.

"No," said her mother, putting a comforting arm around her sobbing daughter, "Sally is not pregnant, Father Donne. I am!"

Epilogue

The old man put down the book and looked out at the gathering of people before him. They had heard the story before, but were still enthralled by its telling and by the teller who now celebrated his 100th year. The world had changed greatly during his lifetime, with vast swathes of land across the globe engulfed by rising seas whilst desert swallowed much of Africa and Australia. The species known as homo sapiens sapiens, the humans who had inhabited the planet for an estimated 200,000 years, had been culled by famine and drought, by flood and fire, by disease and chaos to a level not seen since the devastation of the black death during the darkest period of the Middle-Ages.

Many great cities had ceased to exist with those humans who did survive the flood disasters of most of the planet's coastal agglomerations seeking refuge inland and on higher ground. Many failed and were lost. The world's economy, like much of its infrastructure, lay in ruins and environmental migration threatened to overwhelm those areas still able to support human life.

Alec had spoken to the gathering of how, a century ago, his mother had introduced him to this world on the brink of chaos. She was *homo sapiens sapiens*, but her child, now a centenarian, was not. He had never known his father, and were it not for the old book that now lay at his feet, he and the growing community of *homo sapiens intellectus*, would know little of their origins. The book had been given to his mother by a priest, a Father Donne, shortly before he died. It told of human modification of the genetic code by a government intent on creating a super-human for its own narrow and selfish purposes. It spoke of Alec O'Donnell, the now legendary progenitor of their kind, after whom the old man was named, of how he chose to die rather than submit to control and misuse by an authority that had lost its way. The listening throng learned about the boy's mother and her struggles with self-belief in raising her extraordinary child and how she died along with her son.

Of the two hundred and more people at his feet, many were of the old kind, but had fathered or given birth to the new breed who sat amongst them. It had soon become clear that the modified gene was dominant in both males and females and was always passed on to the next generation, so their numbers had grown quickly.

"Wisdom without understanding is useless," cried out the old-man Alec, "we must learn to use our intelligence to live with the world and not against it, to put aside the self-interest and petty intolerances of the species that preceded us if the planet on which we live is to recover."

The gathering broke out into loud and sustained applause, standing to its feet in a cohesive expression of unity. The old man raised his hand to silence them once more. "We are *homo sapiens intellectus*. The seed of change has long been with us and I truly believe that it is here to stay."